the night, the day

a novel

Andrew Kane

BERWICK COURT PUBLISHING CO.
Chicago, IL

This is a work of fiction. Except for a few historical references, any resemblance to specific persons, living or dead, is purely coincidental.

Berwick Court Publishing Company
Chicago, Illinois
http://www.berwickcourt.com

Kane, Andrew W.
The night, the day : a novel / Andrew Kane.

pages ; cm

Issued also as an ebook.
ISBN: 978-0-9909515-2-0

1. Jewish psychotherapists--New York (State)--New York--Fiction. 2. World War, 1939-1945--Collaborationists--France--Fiction. 3. Nazi hunters--New York (State)--New York--Fiction. 4. Israel. Mosad le-modiʻin ṿe-tafḳidim meyuḥadim--Fiction. 5. Man-woman relationships--New York (State)--New York--Fiction. 6. Psychotherapist and patient--New York (State)--New York--Fiction. 7. Jewish fiction. I. Title.

PS3561.A465 N54 2015
813/.54 2015934077

acknowledgments

I AM FORTUNATE TO HAVE an abundance of blessings of which I am undeserving. To the usual cast of characters, family members and friends, you know who you are and how grateful I am. I will single out but a few.

Debbie, I keep repeating the same thing but it's true: nothing is possible without you. Max, few fathers get the opportunity to say to a son, you are my hero, a man among men, an unending source of inspiration. Jess, as you will see on the following page, this book is yours. Your literary talents far exceed my own and I am eager for the day when the world will hear from you.

To my publisher and editor at Berwick Court, Matt and Dave, what can I say? Beyond believing in me, your critical eyes, skilled touches, and demands for excellence have made me a better writer and this a better book. Dave, may the late nights go on forever!

For Jessica

Our budding author

When we neither punish nor reproach evildoers, we are not simply protecting their trivial old age, we are thereby ripping the foundations of justice from beneath new generations.

-Aleksandr Solzhenitsyn, *The Gulag Archipelago*

prologue

July 13, 1995
A small private island off the coast of Guatemala

SHE STOOD ON THE DECK of the boat, watching the sunset, wondering what the darkness would bring. She felt her heart pounding, the blood pulsing through her veins. It was always this way when the end was near.

Her eyes shifted from the sky to the shore of the approaching island less than a mile away. Only moments remained before the culmination of years of work and planning. There was nowhere he could run; no more disguises, deceits or lies. The chase would soon be over.

She pictured him standing in his bedroom window, watching for her boat, savoring his Montecristo Habana. She imagined the smirk on his face as he awaited their evening together, and her satisfaction lay only in the fact that, after tonight, he would never again know such pleasures.

Why did he always stand at that window? she wondered. Was it his paranoia, or did he simply enjoy watching her arrive? Had she truly gained his trust in the time they had known each other, or had he been anticipating her betrayal?

Her mind drifted back to their first meeting, the day the trap was set. He had been lured to the mainland for a business luncheon, and there she was, alone, a few tables away as he waited for his appointment. It had been the perfect setup: the business deal, the luncheon – all a ruse to capture him. And it had been so easy to get him to love her. Too easy, in fact. Perhaps he had known all along. Perhaps *he* had been using *her* these past months; one last fling for an aging man.

Suddenly, her thoughts disgusted her and she dismissed them, convincing herself that he was as rusty as he was old. Regaining her confidence that she had the advantage, she held fast to her belief that the worst punishment he would endure would be the knowledge of her betrayal.

The boat approached the dock. For security purposes, the grounds surrounding the house were illuminated at night. She was always ferried from the mainland on his boat, escorted by two of his guards, while three other guards stood watch around the house and the island. But on this night, her usual escorts lay dead on the cabin floor, their clothing now being worn by her two fellow agents, Kovi and Arik.

She was concerned about the risks. In her favor was the fact that the old man didn't see very well from distances, and that Kovi and Arik were similar in stature to the dead guards. Against her was the possibility that one of the island guards might be nearby. She had been careful, had studied the place meticulously, memorizing the guards' rotation schedules, planning every detail of the operation. She was confident nothing would go wrong. But then, she knew that many missions failed from the unexpected.

Kovi jumped on the dock, grabbed the rope from the bow and began securing the boat, while Arik took her hand and escorted her onto the dock.

"Seems clear," Kovi whispered as he surveyed the area.

They started toward the house, moving as naturally as possible. Kovi and Arik kept their Uzis draped over their shoulders, the same way the guards wore them. They seemed nervous, vulnerable out in the open without a weapon immediately in hand. The time it took to reach for one's gun could mean the difference between life and death.

They made it to the front door without incident. Now, no longer in view from the bedroom window, Kovi and Arik instinctively grabbed their weapons.

She reached into her handbag, pulled out a Beretta, and signaled for Kovi to stand watch by the door as she and Arik proceeded into the house. Everything, thus far, was according to plan.

She knew that Carlos would be waiting in the master bedroom. With him, it always began there. He had once explained that it was just too painful for him to sit through dinner without first being with her. "When you get to be my age," he had said, "you wait for nothing." She had humored him. It was all part of her master plan. *For the greater good*, she told herself. She had long ago abandoned the fantasy that she could remain pure while doing this work. She had developed an uncanny ability to control her emotions, to do whatever needed to be done. The mission was all that mattered.

She came to the bedroom door. Arik stood aside and readied himself against the wall. She reached slowly for the doorknob, the Beretta hidden behind her back. Arik remained still as she turned the knob. She looked at him, wishing him luck with her eyes as she slipped into the room.

Carlos rose from his seat to greet her. "My dear," he said as he approached her.

She knew immediately that something was wrong; the look in his eyes told her as much. *He knows.* Without hesitation, she presented her gun. "It's over," she said, pointing the Beretta at him.

"You disappoint me," he responded, with the arrogance of one who no longer experiences fear.

"No. It is *you* who has disappointed me, and the rest of the civilized world. Now, raise your hands and turn around!"

Suddenly, she was distracted by gunfire from the hallway, jolted just enough to give Carlos the opportunity to pull out his own weapon.

"It appears we have a stalemate," he remarked, glancing at the

Luger in his hand.

The shooting in the hallway continued, spurts of automatic fire. "Arik," she called, ignoring her own predicament. But there was no response.

"My guards, they were prepared. As was *I*."

She reminded herself how crucial it was to take him alive. "Arik," she yelled again, her eyes glued to her target. "Kovi!"

Still, only gunfire.

Stay calm, she told herself.

"It's too bad, really," Carlos said. "You thought you had me, thought that you would bring me in for a public trial or something. Tell the world things that it's already sick of hearing about. Sorry to spoil your little plan."

The door burst open. Startled, they each dove for cover as Arik charged in. Carlos began firing from behind the bed, but Arik's Uzi easily overpowered the Luger. Her cries of "nooooo" from the corner were muffled by the gunfire. Within seconds, it was over.

She got up and went over to Arik. "Kovi?" she asked.

"Fine," Arik answered. "There were three guards, all dead."

The two of them looked at the pool of blood oozing from the limp body on the rug. Arik bent down to feel for a pulse. "Nothing," he said.

Containing her rage, she stood silently over Carlos' body.

"We have to get out of here," Arik said.

She knew he was right, but she couldn't bring herself to leave like this, to admit defeat. She looked at Arik. There was no way he could understand her thoughts. For him, a fourth-generation Sabra, this was just another mission; for her, Galit Stein, daughter of two Dachau survivors, it was much more. As far back as she could remember, she had sworn to make the murderers pay, to keep alive the stories of evil that had been fixed in her consciousness from her earliest days. This had become her sole purpose for existing. And now, Carlos Zacapa, formerly Nazi SS Colonel Carl Hoffmann, had stolen it from her.

She turned to the body on the floor and spit on it. "Damn you, Hoffmann, damn you to hell!"

Arik moved toward the door. "Galit, we must go. Now!"

She quickly regained her composure and fell in line behind him.

Kovi was waiting as they came out. "Where is he?" he asked.

"Dead," was all she said.

Arik shrugged his shoulders.

Watching the island fade in the distance, Galit was enraged, but also baffled by how Hoffmann could possibly have known her plans. Now that he was dead, she figured she would probably never learn the answer.

For a moment, she was reminded of the debacle years ago involving the auto worker in Ohio. She had convinced herself and her superiors that *this* time things would be different; after all, the evidence against Hoffmann was unimpeachable. It had been an uphill battle; most of her compatriots had lost their enthusiasm for hunting Nazis. Now she would be returning empty-handed, only making things more difficult for the next time, if there would even be a next time.

She imagined how Ezra, her unit chief, would react. He had warned her of the consequences should she fail: "Galit, you must understand, the world is no longer interested in this, especially after the Demjanjuk thing. Even our own government sees little purpose in rounding up sick old men who no longer pose a threat to our survival. If you do not succeed, this will be the last of it. We have more than enough to deal with from our present enemies."

She knew she could never accede to such defeat and be able to face herself or her parents again. Even though her parents did not know what she was doing, she was still doing it for them. And for the aunts, uncles, and grandparents who had perished long before she became part of this world.

No, she wouldn't accept it. There were still a few more, at least one other who had become known to her recently. She would convince the others, do whatever it took to get another chance. One more, she would tell them. She would make them listen. This time, no mistakes.

One more.

August 20, 1996
Sands Point, New York

JACQUES BENOÎT COULD NO LONGER bear the images racing through his mind. He had thought he had successfully destroyed all traces of his past, but now it was returning to haunt him. His prayers were useless, as would be any attempt to flee. He was trapped, his fate in the hands of the men outside.

He was certain they were out there, watching and waiting. He had glimpsed them several times over the past few weeks. Usually two, sometimes three. On the street, in cars, wearing suits or casual clothing. No patterns, nothing that the average person might notice. But Jacques Benoît was not the average person.

He exited the church with his wife, Martha, an American lawyer he had married twenty-five years earlier. It was a second marriage for each of them. She was divorced, and his first wife had died from cancer. That was the only truth he had told her about his life before they had met.

"Good to see you, Martha," the minister said as he took her hand.

"Very nice service," she responded, smiling.

"Jacques." The minister offered his hand and the two men shook. "Everything okay?"

"Of course," Jacques answered in his enchanting French accent.

The minister appeared unconvinced, but it was not a good time to get into anything. He would call upon Jacques later that day to continue his inquiries. It was part of his job to meddle, especially when it concerned his wealthiest parishioner.

Jacques and Martha approached their car. "What was that all about?" she asked.

"What do you mean?"

"Reverend Sanders asking you if everything was all right?"

"I don't know," he said, feigning a smile. "I have never been better." He tried not to be obvious about looking around. He didn't see anyone, but he was sure they were there.

Outwardly, Martha pretended to accept her husband's answer, but in truth, she had been worried about him for some time. It wasn't hard to notice his uneasiness – a stark contrast from the man she had known all these years. But every time she had approached him about it, he was politely dismissive, insisting everything was as usual. She had even thought of suggesting he talk to a professional, but she knew he simply wouldn't. Now that the minister had noticed something, maybe Jacques would be more responsive.

The chauffeur held open the door of the Lincoln stretch limousine as Martha and Jacques climbed in. "Bill and Susan have invited us to join them at the club for brunch," Martha said, waiting for Jacques to instruct the chauffeur to proceed directly to the exclusive North Shore Hunt Club.

Jacques hesitated. "You know, dear, I have a few calls I must make this afternoon. Why don't you go by yourself?"

"But, Jacques…"

"Now, now, love. Why should you miss such a wonderful brunch simply because I have some business to attend to? I will see you afterward for dinner on the boat. You can even invite Bill and Susan to join us."

She neither agreed nor disagreed, which was always a sign that she would do as he asked. He told the chauffeur to drop him at home and then take Martha to the club. A few minutes later, the limo pulled into the entrance of their Sands Point estate. Jacques got out, kissed his wife on the cheek, and watched as she drove off. He then turned and scanned the vast woods surrounding the house, still certain he wasn't alone.

Their home was much too large for just the two of them, but a man of his standing could live in nothing less. Their children were grown, and seldom visited. She had two, a son and a daughter from her previous marriage, both of whom were married with children of their own and lived nearby. His son from his first marriage lived in the Ionian Islands, on Corfu, and managed one of his many international resorts. The young man was in his mid-40s, single, and – to the best of Jacques' knowledge – was enjoying the life of a playboy.

Jacques let himself in. On Sundays, the housekeeper was off. He locked the front door and walked to the kitchen. He peered out the kitchen window, looking for movement in the woods. Everything remained still, but he knew they were there. *Smart. Skillfully hidden. But there.*

He left the kitchen and made his way through the foyer toward the back of the house into his study. As he entered, he looked around at the burnished mahogany and oak furniture, the walls filled with expensive art, photographs and various humanitarian awards. His eyes stopped at the Picasso sketch, his most valued material possession. He would miss that more than the others. He looked at some of the photographs, seeing himself shaking hands with three American presidents, two British prime ministers, and two French presidents. What a scandal it would be if the truth came out! But he wouldn't allow that. He *couldn't* allow that.

He was compelled again to the window. *Bastards!* They were playing games with him.

He reached into his desk drawer for the pills he had obtained weeks ago from his doctor. Weeks ago, when he had started feeling their presence. He looked at the bottle in his hands. Xanax, a nice redress for anxiety and insomnia. It frightened him to hold his fate in his hands like this, but what choice did he have?

Of course, he could fight. Between the court delays and his money, he would probably be long dead before they would win. But then there was the disgrace. He truly loved Martha, her children and his son. He had lied to them all and would readily give his life to sustain that lie. The truth just was too ugly.

He looked at the picture on his desk of him and Martha standing on the beach in Antigua on their first trip together. *Where had the time gone?*

He remembered how they'd originally met, just a few months before the picture was taken. He was in New York conducting business with an American conglomerate, a joint venture to open two new resorts, one in Hawaii, the other in the Virgin Islands. Martha headed up the legal team representing the Americans.

He had been amazed at the time, seeing a woman in such a position. In his native France, of famed enlightenment, this would never have been. But it didn't take long for his amazement to fade into understanding; in fact, the moment he heard her speak, her talents became obvious. And beyond that, he had found himself enamored with the sound of her voice.

He had known instantly, at that very first encounter, that they would marry. He had simply never met anyone like her. Frenchman that he was, it didn't even dawn on him that a woman like her might belong to another. To the French, such problems were trivialities, especially for one as rich and influential as he.

In any event, it hadn't been an issue. She had been only a few months past a messy divorce, which had left her rather sour on men altogether. But Jacques Benoît wasn't just any man, and he had vowed to make her know it.

At first, she had been resistant, delicately thwarting his advances. But eventually, after countless lunches, dinners, and meetings – all presumably under the guise of business – she had weakened, at least enough to be convinced into taking a week at his resort in Antigua. It was to be quite innocent and platonic, so he assured her, a reward for her matchless dedication and skilled handling of their business. In the end, it was anything but.

That week, he realized just how inspiring she was, how desirous she made him feel. With her, and *only* her, he believed he could become different, perhaps even forget. In his love for her, he sought his redemption, and in the life they eventually shared together, he had found it. And now *they* were here to take it from him.

Jacques looked away from the photograph, went to the bar and poured himself a full glass of Maker's Mark. The best thing about America, he always said, was its bourbon. He looked again at the bottle of pills. There were thirty of them, a month's supply, more than ample for his purpose.

August 25, 1996
Chicago, Illinois

DR. MARTIN ROSEN WONDERED IF he was losing his mind. The woman had been perfect – tantalizing, smart, funny – and yet, all he felt was a pressing need to get as far away from her as possible.

He sauntered down Wacker Drive, along the Chicago River, heading toward the Hyatt Regency. It was a typical late-August morning in these parts, bright, humid, in the upper 70s, with a slight breeze from the lake. From across the river, the Wrigley Building's clock tower told him it was 10:15, just forty-five minutes until his presentation. He knew he should be reviewing his notes, but he couldn't take his mind off the woman.

He smiled for a moment, eyeing the Wrigley Building and the Tribune Tower, reminding himself that this had always been his lucky town. It was here that he had met Katherine, so many years before, as a freshman in college. It was here he had broken with his past and shed all remaining traces of his former life. It was here he had discovered fun and freedom. It was here he had discovered himself. Or so he had thought.

Yet, after all these years of being away, now that Katherine had disappeared from his life, he wondered if he had really discovered anything at all. He came to the entrance of the Hyatt Regency. He had hoped that the walk might grant him some clarity but it hadn't. Now he would have to give one of the most important lectures of his career, his mind muddled by other matters.

As a clinical psychologist, he berated himself for his lack of mental discipline, despite his understanding that doctors were no different from patients, and that advice was always more easily dispensed than followed.

He took the elevator to his room on the twenty-second floor, slipped the security card in, opened the door, and went to the dresser to retrieve his lecture notes. As he reached for them, he was halted by his reflection in the mirror. Looking more closely, particularly at his eyes, he searched for signs of disturbance. Not exactly a clinical assessment, he knew, but he had always believed that the eyes were telling.

In his case, he saw nothing but exhaustion, bright blue irises surrounded by red lines, attesting to the less than three hours sleep he'd had the night before. He backed away from the mirror to see more of himself. He had never dwelled much on his appearance, but meeting a beautiful woman changes things.

That daily five-mile run was paying off. Thirty-eight years old, a thirty-four waist, and a healthy head of dark hair were nothing to sneeze at. Of course, there were some strands of gray popping up, and a few creases above his cheekbones. But all in all, he couldn't complain.

Bothered by his sudden preoccupation, he picked up his notes, turned away from the mirror, and noticed that the light on the bedside phone was blinking. He had two messages. The first one, he was expecting: "Hi Daddy, good morning. It's Saturday, so I don't have school. Love you, and come home soon!"

He smiled. His daughter, Elizabeth, just 4 years old, was already sounding like a grown up. After another beep, the tape continued for a few seconds with the silent sound of someone about to say something. Then a click. His smile disappeared; he knew it was Nancy, and understood why she was compelled to call yet had nothing to say. His mind drifted back to the previous evening.

It had been raining hard. Sheets of water crashed against the windows of the hotel bar. He sat alone at a table, nursing his Glenlivet, studying the menu. He had flown in that morning, had attended several symposia and lectures throughout the day, and was planning a quick dinner and an early night. That was when he saw her.

She sat at the bar, looking like one of those women he used to see in Ivory Soap commercials: Auburn hair, short and layered; slightly freckled skin; large eyes; the kind of nose some would pay for; full lips; and long legs. Her figure was hidden beneath a conservative beige business suit, but he was still able to tell that she took good care of herself.

The place was crowded – most of the conventioneers were stranded in the hotel due to the weather – and he noticed that she wasn't with anyone. He figured that she must be waiting for someone. Women who look that good are seldom alone. He stared for a while, couldn't help himself, but soon became self-conscious and returned to his drink.

Nothing on the menu seemed to grab him, and the noise of the crowd was grating after half a day of airports and flying. He decided to finish his drink, go upstairs and order room service. He paid the check, gathered his papers and got up to leave. As he headed for the exit, he turned one last time in her direction and noticed that she was gone. He looked around for a moment, then saw her coming up behind him. He opened the door and held it for her.

"Thank you," she said with a slight smile.

He saw now that she had chestnut eyes, a perfect touch to an already flawless package. "You're welcome," he replied.

They walked awkwardly toward the elevators and he pressed the button. They waited in silence. He glanced at her name tag: *Dr. Nancy Hartledge, San Francisco, CA.*

"You're here for the APA convention?" he asked.

"Yes." She smiled again, this time showing her teeth. She eyed his tag. "You're Martin Rosen! I've heard of you."

"The one and only. I think."

She chuckled.

A bell sounded as the elevator door opened. "Here's our ride," Martin said.

She was about to step in, but hesitated. "Tell me, Dr. Rosen, do you have any idea where a person can get a real Chicago pizza?"

Martin stiffened at what he suspected was an invitation. At one time in his life, Chicago-style pizza had been his specialty, as had knowing how to handle a come-on from a strange, beautiful woman. "My friends call me Marty," he responded as the elevator door closed in their faces.

"There goes our ride," she said.

Martin smiled.

"About the pizza?"

"Well, there's a place on Superior Street that's pretty famous, Gino's East."

She looked directly into his eyes, and softly asked, "Care to join me?"

They caught a cab and, ten minutes later, found themselves sitting in Gino's East. Martin looked around the restaurant, noticing that its appearance hadn't changed in the years since he'd last been here. The interior was completely unfinished, something akin to a large camp bunk, with past patrons' names marking up the bare wood walls and ceilings. There was a healthy crowd despite the storm outside.

"I hope the food's better than the decor," Nancy said, looking around.

"I guarantee it. Best there is."

The waitress came for their orders.

"Medium deep dish, the works," he said to the waitress.

"The works?" Nancy asked.

"Trust me."

Nancy ordered a Diet Coke and Martin got a Sam Adams. He thought it wise to ease up on the Scotch for a little while.

The waitress left and a stilted moment came upon them, as if each had suddenly realized they were total strangers. Nancy looked at the ceiling. "How did they get their names up there?"

"A ladder, I guess. Standing on the table wouldn't do."

"Not unless you're eight feet tall." She looked at him again. "I saw in the schedule that you're giving a lecture tomorrow."

"I saw that too."

"Really though, the topic, confidentiality, it's a good one. There's a lot to say about it these days. That's what your book is about, isn't it?"

"You mean to say you haven't read it?"

"Sorry."

"I knew there was someone, somewhere."

"But I have heard of it at least."

The waitress returned with their drinks, a basket of bread and a tossed salad for them to share. Martin took a sip and began doling out the salad. He was surprised at the pleasure he was taking in her company.

He skillfully shifted the conversation to her, and discovered that she was a child psychologist who split her time between hospital work and private practice. She seemed comfortable and enthusiastic discussing her work, a trait that Martin envied. He was tempted to mention the nightmares his daughter, Elizabeth, had been having but stopped himself. That was a can of worms. And he already knew what was causing the nightmares anyway.

The pizza arrived, oozing cheese, pepperoni and anchovies, and was quickly devoured. To top things off, they each had a cappuccino and shared a tiramisu. The intimacy of sharing aroused Martin. He wanted her, all right, about as much as he wanted her to disappear. He made a mental note to contact his own shrink as soon as he got home.

As they left the restaurant, another brief moment of awkwardness struck. The sky had cleared and they walked north on Rush Street, where jazz and pop music clubs had opened up to the sidewalks. From a block away, an old Sinatra tune emanated from Jilly's, one of the city's more historied nightspots. Martin felt his heart drop; the sights and sounds stirred painful memories.

"Sounds like a fun place," Nancy said.

"It is if you like Sinatra, Bennett, and Sammy Davis."

"You mean that's Jilly's?"

"'Tis. The 'chairman of the board' himself used to hang out there."

"So I've heard."

"Sounds like you're a fan."

"Of Sinatra, who wouldn't be? Sexiest man ever."

"Sexier than Elvis?" he asked.

"No contest!"

"Come," he said, gesturing toward the club. "Let's see if we can get near the place."

"Sounds like a plan to me." She took his hand as they crossed the street.

Lucky for them, the downpour had kept a lot of people at home, and they were able to gain entry without a reservation. They worked their way through the crowd and managed to find a table in the back next to the keyboard player, a heavyset black man with a goatee and a raspy voice. A waitress descended upon them immediately. For Martin, it was Glenlivet time again; for Nancy, the house champagne.

"So, come here often?" Nancy said, smiling.

"Oh, I'd say every fifteen years or so."

"That long, huh?"

He nodded.

She looked at him. And as if she could read the anguish inside him, she put her hand on his. "You okay?"

He hesitated. "Sure."

She left it alone. The keyboard player was singing "Under My Skin," and she started humming along.

"Sounds like he's gonna do Sinatra all night," Martin said.

"Doesn't bother me."

"Let's see if he takes requests." Martin turned around and said something to the keyboard player.

"Does he?" Nancy asked.

"If I told you, it would spoil all the fun."

A few seconds later, the keyboard player started singing: *If I don't see her, each day I miss her. Gee, what a thrill, each time I kiss her...*

Nancy blushed. It couldn't have been a more perfect choice.

Martin smiled, his first truly comfortable smile of the evening.

Believe me I've got a case, of Nancy, with the laughing face...

"You're a romantic, Dr. Martin Rosen. No one would ever know it, but I do now."

"Our little secret?"

"Cross my heart, but only if we dance."

Martin looked around. "There's no one dancing."

"So what?" She stood up, led him by the hand, and began moving to the music.

The moment seemed to grab him, to restore in him something he hadn't felt in a long time. They held each other tightly as other couples followed their lead and also started dancing.

"And a trendsetter to boot," Nancy said.

Martin had no response. He was lost.

They danced till the keyboard player took his break, then returned to their table.

"So, what's a guy like you doing unattached? You *are* unattached, I assume?" Nancy asked uneasily.

"Completely."

She lightened up. "And the answer to my first question is?"

"A very long story," he answered soberly.

She looked into his eyes. "A sad story?"

"Yes."

She reached out and touched his cheek. "I'll stop asking questions."

"It's okay."

"I know, but I'll stop anyway."

He looked back into her eyes. "You do have a laughing face."

She smiled. "Thank you."

They stayed until the club closed, then caught a cab back to the hotel. They sat in the back seat, the alcohol and music wearing off, and the reality that they lived on opposite sides of the country settling in. Tomorrow, after his lecture, Martin would be on a plane to New York, and later that week, Nancy would return to San Francisco. When – and if – they would ever see each other again was an issue neither wished to broach.

They exited the cab and entered the hotel. It was after four in the morning and the lobby was empty.

"Well, I guess this is it," Nancy said.

Martin responded with a somber look.

The elevator came, and they stepped in. Martin pressed his floor and was about to press Nancy's, when she grabbed his hand. "I don't think either of us wants to say goodnight just yet."

He looked at her and realized that he no longer had any choice in this thing. For more than two years, he had been numb to women. And now, standing next to him, Nancy Hartledge of San Francisco, whom he had just met, was causing all that to change. From the moment he had laid eyes on her, he knew he was in trouble.

They went into his room and fell into each other's arms before the door closed. Their mouths connected in a deep, long kiss, their hands grasping at each other's clothing. Martin felt himself rise. He had forgotten such a wanting; it had been much too long.

Nancy pressed up against him, pulling him closer, unbuttoning his shirt. Her blouse was a pullover, necessitating a momentary, painful break in contact as he peeled it off. It wasn't until she started at his belt buckle that he suddenly retreated.

"What, Marty, what is it?" she asked, reaching for him as he stepped back.

"I can't, I'm sorry. I just can't do this." He took her hands in his and looked into her eyes. "I'm sorry," he repeated tenderly, trying to pull himself together.

His sadness somehow infected her. "It's okay," she said, squeezing his hands.

He reached down, picked up her blouse, and handed it to her. Looking at her, he took a deep breath and said, "I think you'd better go."

With that, her sympathy transformed into anger. "Yes, I suppose I should." She threw her blouse on, picked up her bag and walked past him to the door. "I hope you figure your life out, Marty," she said. "I can see that you're confused and in pain." Her eyes were watering. "I hope you fix that one day."

And she was gone.

Now he felt he was unraveling, wondering if she would actually attend his lecture, knowing her presence would only distract him. He sat down and tried concentrating on his notes, then got up and walked to the window. From here, he could see across the river and much of Michigan Avenue. Once again, he was reminded of Katherine, of the endless strolls they used to take along Michigan Avenue, their times at the beach, their evenings on Rush Street. He wasn't sure if it was Nancy Hartledge or the view; either way, this town was getting to him.

He realized that any normal man would have relished a night with Nancy, would have extended his stay just to have more time with her. But he wasn't normal, hadn't been for the past two years, and wasn't going to be anytime soon.

He thought of calling his daughter, Elizabeth, but decided to wait till after the lecture when his mind would be clearer. He felt guilty for leaving her alone with the nanny; it was the first time he had done that since her mother had died. But she was in good hands, he assured himself.

He still had time, so he picked up the phone, dialed his office, and grabbed a pen and pad to write down messages. The first three messages were from patients, two current, one prospective. Nothing urgent. He scribbled the names and numbers on the pad, he would return those calls on Monday morning. Then came the fourth message: "Hi Marty, it's Ashok Reddy. I know you're still away, but I'm sure you will call in for messages. Anyway, I have a case that has your name written all over it. A real mystery of sorts; nobody here can make heads or tails of it. And wait till you hear who the patient is. Give me a ring."

It was typical of Reddy to whet his appetite like that, he thought, looking at his watch. As enticed as he was to call Reddy on the spot, he had run out of time. His audience awaited him.

Martin scanned the crowd as the chairperson approached the podium. It was five minutes after the hour, and these things usually began on time. He didn't see Nancy Hartledge and, strangely enough, that bothered him.

"Ladies and gentlemen," the chairperson, Dr. Leonard Johnson, began. "As president of the American Psychological Association's Clinical Psychology division, I am honored to introduce our speaker this morning. When the division leadership discussed whom we would invite to address us at this 102nd APA convention, prominent among them was Dr. Martin Rosen."

The room was quiet and attentive, but Martin barely heard Johnson's flattery. His eyes were on the door at the rear, watching the latecomers wander in.

"Today's lecture is on *Confidentiality in the Modern Age*, and there are few as qualified to speak about this crucial subject as Dr. Rosen. He is a clinical psychologist in private practice in Great Neck, New York, and an associate professor in the department of psychiatry at North Shore University Hospital. Having authored several articles and, most recently, the critically acclaimed book, *Are Patients Protected?* he has made the TV and radio talk show circuits and even the *New York Times* best sellers list."

Admiration and envy flowed from the audience. It was the dream of most psychologists to come as far as Martin had. Though Martin's only dream, at the moment, was to get this done with and flee.

"So, without further ado," Johnson continued, "I would like to present to you Dr. Martin Rosen."

Martin stepped to the podium while the audience applauded. He placed his notes on the lectern and waited for the crowd to settle. There seemed to be nearly 300 attendees, an impressive assembly considering that there were about fifteen other convention events being held simultaneously. He glanced around the room; still no sign of Nancy.

"Good morning," he began. "I am here to talk about a very ticklish subject that touches all of our professional and personal lives, and also significantly influences public policy.

"Years ago, confidentiality between doctor and patient, especially between therapist and patient, seemed a given. But today, things are different. In fact, I dare say, *quite* different. With the advent of HMOs and stricter guidelines instituted by all insurance companies; new laws about potential suicide or homicide, abuse of children, spouses and the elderly; and, above all, the burgeoning information age in which we live, the confidentiality between psychologist and patient has been dealt some serious blows. And what's really frightening is that most patients, and even some practitioners, are completely unaware that their conversations with one another are not necessarily protected…"

His presentation lasted just short of thirty minutes, followed by the usual applause, a few questions and answers, and then formal compliments from some APA bigwigs. It had come off much better than he had anticipated.

A few colleagues gathered around him to offer congratulations. Handshakes, smiles, jokes. He labored through the motions as long as he could stand it, and eventually managed to slip away back to his hotel room.

He glanced at his watch as he entered his room. It was shortly after noon, and he wondered if Elizabeth would be home. The nanny, her Guyanese accent more noticeable on the telephone than in person, answered.

"Hello, Jamilla," he said.

"Ah, Dr. Rosen, hello. How are things in Chicago?"

"Good. How are things over there?"

"Very good. Elizabeth misses you, but she's having fun at camp and I'm taking her to TGI Fridays for dinner tonight."

Martin felt a lump in his throat. Fridays' cheeseburgers were Elizabeth's favorite, and a steady date for Martin and his daughter every Saturday night, their special time together. "That's great, Jamilla. I really appreciate it," he said. "Is she there?"

"Of course. She's been waiting for your call. Hold on."

Elizabeth came on the line. "Hi Daddy."

"Hi princess, how are you?"

"I'm good, Daddy. When are you coming home?"

"Late tonight, princess. You'll probably be sleeping."

"Why not early? You can come out to dinner with us."

"Because I couldn't get an earlier flight. But I promise we'll do something special tomorrow, maybe go to the park, out for dinner."

Through the phone, he heard her tell Jamilla, "Daddy's taking me to the park and out to dinner tomorrow."

"Princess?"

"Yes, Daddy?"

"I love you."

"I love you too."

"See you tomorrow. Okay?"

"Okay daddy. Bye."

"Bye."

He reviewed his arrival plans with the nanny, hung up, stared out the window and thought about how much he missed Elizabeth. He kicked himself for having come back to Chicago. When he'd first planned to attend the convention, he imagined that some time in this town, the place where his relationship with Katherine had begun, might do him good, perhaps give him the chance to figure a few things out. Now he was even more confused. He just couldn't see himself getting involved with another woman, especially one he met *here.*

He picked up the phone and dialed Ashok Reddy's home number. He could have waited until Monday to return the call, but he was intrigued by Reddy's message.

Martin recognized his old friend's Indian accent. "Hello, Ashok. It's Marty."

"Marty! How the hell are you?"

"Okay. I'm still in Chicago."

"Yes, I remember. You are coming back tonight."

Martin smiled. Reddy had an impeccable memory for details. "So, what's the story with this case?"

"Things that dull in Chicago?"

"*Dull* would be good." Martin hesitated for a moment, surprised by his own candor. "I was just curious."

"Well, are you sitting down?"

"Yes," Martin lied. He was still standing, watching the street below.

"Jacques Benoît."

Stunned, Martin turned from the window and found the chair. "The Hotel King?" he asked.

"Bingo."

"What happened?"

"That's the problem, nobody really knows. He was brought into the ER at the beginning of the week. Apparently OD'd on Xanax. Swallowed a bottle of the stuff with some bourbon, thirty tablets."

"Where'd he get it?"

"His internist. Seems he complained of sleep problems a few weeks prior to the OD, even though he didn't take any of the pills till that day."

"What's to figure out, the guy tried to off himself," Martin said. "What does *he* say?"

"He admits he was trying to commit suicide. He claims it was impulsive, that he was under a lot of stress from all the expansion and changes in his corporation. His company's stock has been doing very well. New management and renovations of three of his hotels in the Middle East, and two more resorts he is opening in the Caribbean. Success isn't always a good thing, so he says."

"So he tries to kill himself?"

"With pills he had gotten a few weeks ago and hadn't used."

"Sounds a bit strange."

"If you ask me," Reddy reflected, "I think his whole story is bullshit, that's why I called you."

"Why me?"

"He needs therapy, and you know I only do pharmacology these days. He also needs someone who isn't intimidated by him, someone who knows how to look for things."

Martin was flattered but also wary. It was nice hearing such accolades from his close friend, who also happened to be chief of psychiatry at New York's esteemed North Shore University Hospital, but Martin was convinced that Reddy had an exaggerated sense of his abilities. "If he's bullshitting, who says he'll comply?" he asked.

"His wife."

"You mean one of the richest men in the world is pushed around by his wife?"

"Not exactly. She is an exceptionally intelligent woman, and quite distraught, much more so than the patient, I might add. He appears to really care for her, seems remorseful and eager to put the whole thing behind them. She also suspects there is more to this than meets the eye, says if he goes for therapy, it will make her feel better. He says he will do it. When I told him who I would send him to, he even seemed pleased."

"How does he know me?"

"Maybe he caught one of your countless talk show appearances or saw your name on the best-sellers list. You're not the most inconspicuous man in America, Marty."

"How long was he in the hospital?"

"Four days. Got out yesterday."

"Only four days for a suicide attempt? What kind of treatment is that?"

"HMO special," Reddy responded, chuckling.

"Come on, Ashok, get serious." Martin knew that a man like Benoît would have nothing but the best medical insurance and would have paid out of pocket for any expenses having to do with something like this.

Reddy stopped laughing. "Boy, Marty, you sound a bit uptight over there. Everything all right?"

Martin had long ago realized that there wasn't much he could get past Reddy. "Everything's okay, I suppose."

Reddy was silent. He had been concerned about Martin's return to Chicago since he'd first heard of the invitation to speak at the convention. Being a good friend, he had held his tongue then and would do so now.

"Anyway," Martin continued, "let's get back to Benoît."

"Okay," Reddy agreed. "We kept him for four days because he was behaving fairly normally and insisted he was perfectly fine. He didn't appear to need any medication, and was genuinely contrite about his act. Promised not to do it again, to go for therapy and all that. There wasn't much more we could do for him and, as you know, there are patients in worse shape waiting for beds."

"Business must be good for you to so quickly discharge a cash-paying patient," Martin said snidely.

"Just great. Anyway, will you take the case?"

"Sure. I'll uncover the deep mysteries of the man's mind."

"Good, then I will give him the go-ahead to call you. I told him I wanted to speak with you first to see if you were taking on any new patients."

"Never too busy for you, Ashok."

"That is good to hear. When you get back, you will come for dinner. Savitri has a friend she thinks you might be interested in."

Martin was used to Reddy's efforts at matchmaking. "Sure. Okay."

"Talk to you soon then."

"Yes. And thanks for the referral."

"Anytime."

Martin hung up the phone, then picked it up again and dialed for the hotel operator.

"Can you connect me with Dr. Nancy Hartledge's room?" he asked.

"Please hold."

He held the phone for a moment, but hung up before he even heard a ring. He didn't know why he hung up, nor why he placed the call to begin with.

He got up and started packing. He would grab an early dinner, then head out to the airport. Soon he would be back with his daughter, the only thing in his world that made any sense.

chapter 3

November 10, 1994
Brooklyn, New York

MARTIN STOOD ON THE STREET, immune to the evening chill, staring at the house. The pavement, wet from an earlier rain, reflected the streetlights above. It was close to 10, quiet and serene.

He had come not knowing what to expect. Whether he would actually cross the street and ring the bell, or keep his distance and simply watch, he couldn't choose.

It had been the worst day of his life. Desperately in need of connecting to something, he had returned here, to the place where his life had begun and where, one day years ago, a part of that life had ended.

He had been standing in the same spot for close to an hour. Paralyzed, almost inert, he found himself beyond tears, beyond grief.

The living room and dining room were dark, but through a street-level window, he could see light emanating from the kitchen in the back and the figure of a familiar woman moving about. Upstairs, another light burned in the room that used to be – and probably still was – his father's study.

Martin's mind traveled back five years to the night he had given his parents the news of his engagement to Katherine, the very last time he had talked with either of them. He would never forget his mother's silence, the anguish in her eyes as his father lashed into him. He remembered having waited for her to intercede, to make peace between them as she always had. But this time things were different.

"So, this is what you do to us. This is how you finally kill us!" his father harangued.

"No, Papa, this is how I find love and happiness for myself."

"Love and happiness?" Abraham Rosen looked at his wife. "Our son is unable to find love and happiness from a Jewish girl." He threw up his hands.

Leah Rosen couldn't respond.

"I'm sorry, Papa. I'm sorry my life didn't turn out the way you wanted it to. I'm sorry I didn't become a rabbi like you, that I didn't devote my life to my religion and my people."

"Your religion! Your people! You have no religion. You have no people. All you have is that foolish psychology, and now you will have a *shiksa* wife and *goyish* children. A fine return for all the work your mother and I have done!"

Martin was silent. There was nothing to be gained with words. From his earliest days in yeshiva, when his rebelliousness and skepticism took root, he had always known that some day it might come to this.

Abraham addressed his wife again. "I told you this was going to happen. From the day you convinced me to let him go to University of Chicago, I knew he would be lost to us." Abraham's face turned crimson. He pointed at Martin. "And for this, my parents and my brother walked into the gas chambers." He was trembling.

Leah Rosen finally broke her silence. "Enough!" Tears rushed from her eyes.

Martin moved to embrace her, but she held out her hand to stop him.

"Mama," he pleaded.

"No, Martin, I can't. I'm sorry, I just can't."

There had been two other times when Martin had stood in this spot, watching the house as he was now. The first had been a year after his marriage to Katherine, the day she gave birth to their son, Ethan; the second was two years later, after the birth of Elizabeth. On both occasions, he had lacked the temerity to cross the street, and now he once again wondered if he could bring himself to do it.

He wasn't afraid of being turned away; he was confident they would never do that. The rift between them had not been a "disowning," it had been an estrangement that probably could have been repaired over time with a little nurturing. But Martin, in his own way, was as stubborn as his father.

Katherine, ironically, had encouraged him to mend things. She felt strongly about the children having a relationship with their grandparents, and her own parents lived far away in Illinois. Martin agreed, and frequently promised to "eventually" do something about it. But now it was too late, at least as far as Katherine and Ethan were concerned. A few hours earlier, he had buried them both.

He had met Katherine during his first week at college, almost twenty years earlier, at a bar called Jarod's. It was his first Saturday night in Chicago, and his roommate, a Jewish kid from Springfield, Massachusetts, had invited him to come along with some other guys. "Just lose the yarmulke," his roommate said. Martin, who had never gone anywhere without his head covered, was drawn to the idea, wondering what it might feel like. He soon learned that this mere change in appearance would engender a sense of liberation he had never known.

So, when the young woman sitting at the next table smiled at him, he had no hesitation in simply saying "hello." His new friends were awestruck at the ease with which he did this. He was neither afraid nor imbued with the arrogance that normally obviates such fear. He was simply innocent.

And Martin had found Katherine irresistible. She was his height, with soft, unblemished skin, flaming red hair, green eyes, a dancer's figure, and a smile that lit up the room. They left Jarod's together and walked around the campus talking for hours – finding they had absolutely nothing in common. Next thing they knew, they were inseparable.

It took quite some time for Martin to muster the nerve to marry her. She had always understood and never pushed. But he knew he wanted a complete life with her. After eight years together, through college and graduate school, they became engaged and decided to relocate to New York. Martin hoped that the proximity to his parents might facilitate their eventual acceptance of Katherine, but it was not to be.

At first, they lived in Forest Hills and Martin opened a private practice in the affluent town of Great Neck on the north shore of Long Island. Katherine worked as a nurse at the North Shore University Hospital and, over time, befriended several doctors, all of whom were happy to refer patients to Martin. Martin's reputation and practice grew, and he eventually earned the position of associate professor in the hospital's department of psychiatry. Shortly after Elizabeth's birth, they bought a house in Lake Success, just minutes from the hospital and Martin's office.

Now Katherine was gone, and Ethan along with her, taken needlessly by a drunk driver who flew over an embankment on the Long Island Expressway and came head-on into their car at 60 miles an hour. Their bodies had been charred. The medical examiner said they had died instantly. There had been no suffering. It was little consolation.

Martin, feeling nothing but the crisp air against his face, wondered once again what to do. He was tired and empty, having spent much of the day cursing a God he probably never believed in, hating the world and everything in it, save his little girl. The grief had already graduated to numbness. Soon, he knew, it would turn to guilt. He would somehow manage to blame himself. Perhaps because he had married her in the first place; because he had scorned his parents, his God, and his people; because he had renounced who he was, abandoned those who had perished for revering that which he had so freely discarded. The guilt would never leave him. In that respect, he would always be the boy who grew up in that house across the street.

The light in the kitchen went off and he could no longer see his mother walking about. He knew she was heading upstairs with a cup of tea for his father; that she would quietly place it on the desk in his study without distracting the rabbi from whatever religious text he was pondering. This was the ritual Martin remembered, every evening like clockwork. In that, he found some repose.

He glanced at his watch. It was getting late. He had waited for Elizabeth to fall asleep before leaving home and had instructed the nanny to beep him if she should awaken. He wanted to be next to her as she slept, to make sure she was safe and protected. He wanted her to know he would always be there. But tonight, he just had this thing he needed to do.

He contemplated once more whether to take those steps to cross the street. What would he even say to them? How would they receive him? He looked at his watch again, wondering why the hell time always moved so quickly, and with a final gaze at the house, he turned on his heel and went back to his car.

September 4, 1996
Great Neck, New York

THE GREAT NECK PENINSULA IS located on the New York City border, adjacent to Queens County, in the northwest corner of Long Island. Several small towns and villages inhabit its borders, populated mostly by upper-middle-class Jews and Asians amid a smattering of other religious, ethnic and socioeconomic groups. The Asian presence is relatively recent, while the most apparent demographic change of the past decades has been a sizeable influx of Iranian Jews, or "Persians" as they prefer to be called.

Martin's office was on the ground floor of a four-story condominium on Middle Neck Road, in what was known as "The Old Village," just north of one of Long Island's busiest commercial districts. Middle Neck was the "Main Street" of the peninsula, lined mostly with small prewar buildings, broad sidewalks, and a plethora of highbrow shops and restaurants. The street was usually crowded enough to render the comings and goings of the therapist's office virtually unnoticed, something both Martin and his patients appreciated.

Martin walked into the waiting room and extended his hand. "Mr. Benoît, I'm Martin Rosen."

Benoît rose, smiled, and shook the psychologist's hand. "Nice to meet you, doctor," he said.

Martin noted the body language, the unstated confidence. Benoît stood equal to his height, at least twenty pounds heavier, but carried himself in a manner that projected strength rather than heaviness. He had a full head of shiny gray hair, his eyes were brown and intense, his cheekbones high, and his chin was so tight that smiling, somehow, seemed to strain him.

Martin led him into the office and gestured to a comfortable black leather couch.

"Ah, the proverbial couch," Benoît remarked. "Shall I lie down?"

"No need, sitting is fine," Martin responded.

Martin didn't practice classical psychoanalysis, a technique in which patients lie down and freely associate while the therapist sits behind and is minimally interactive. Martin's sessions were face-to-face, with plenty of feedback and even confrontation when necessary.

The office decor was more contemporary than Martin would have chosen on his own. It had been Katherine's creation. In the end, he had been surprised at how comfortable he felt with it. His desk was a tinted glass slab, resting on two black lacquered platforms. Behind the imposing black leather executive chair were Formica bookcases, well-stocked, the books neatly arranged. Another bookcase ran the length of a second wall, a third wall was devoted to diplomas and awards, and the fourth was adorned with three matching pastel collages.

Beneath the diplomas was the patient's couch – Martin wanted them looking at him, not his credentials. Along the adjacent wall, beneath the collages, was Martin's therapy chair, a black leather recliner in which he never reclined, at least not in the presence of patients. He purchased the recliner while in graduate school and had grown attached to it over the years. For the amount of sitting he had to do in the course of a day, which could sometimes add up to twelve hours, it was perfect.

The two men settled in. Martin placed a clipboard on his lap and uncapped the fountain pen that Katherine had given him for his 35th birthday. Martin was too practical a man to indulge himself with a $200 Montblanc. Katherine firmly believed that occasional extravagance made life more fun.

"Well, so here we are," Benoît said.

Beneath the charm, Martin read the man's discomfort, a common reaction for first-timers, but compounded for someone of Benoît's stature. Martin was accustomed to this; one didn't practice in Great Neck without encountering the rich and powerful. He smiled responsively. "May I call you Jacques?" he asked.

"Oh yes, of course. Everybody does."

Martin guessed that this probably wasn't true, though he appreciated the graciousness nonetheless. After gathering standard information from Benoît, Martin got down to business. "So, you've been out of the hospital for a few days, how have things been going?"

"Perfectly well. I am back at work, full time, feeling good, with no complaints. Everything is exactly as it was before this *unfortunate* incident."

"So, how can I help?" Translation: *Let's get past all the reasons why you may feel you don't need any more treatment. You're here. What do you intend to get out of it?*

"Well, I suppose I should discuss what happened. They tell me that if I can understand it better, it is less likely to happen again."

"*They* being?"

"Dr. Reddy and all the kind people at the hospital."

"Your wife as well," Martin added, revealing a bit of his initial conversation with Reddy.

"Yes, I cannot forget my darling wife. She has been so worried, coming to you is the least I can do to appease her."

Martin was pensive for a moment; they were off to an adequate, though formal, start. Normally, he would go slowly, chat some and build rapport. But there was something about this guy that tempted him to rattle the cage just a bit. "Good, so you're here to learn more about yourself and also to make your wife feel better. I can at least help you with the first part."

Benoît smiled.

"Let's talk about the afternoon you took the pills," Martin continued.

Benoît nodded.

"Do you know why you felt so despondent?"

Benoît sighed as if in deep thought. "I can only tell you what I told them in the hospital. I am in the hotel business, as you probably know. I own about thirty resorts all over the world. In the past year alone, we have made eleven new acquisitions. Things have been, as they say, taking off. I travel the world constantly. There is more pressure than you can imagine. Shareholders, hungry vice presidents, corporate customers. I am not growing any younger, and perhaps I felt it all somehow slipping away. Does that sound strange?"

Martin considered the question. It did sound strange, at least as a reason for suicide. "I'm not sure," he said.

"Yes, I suppose I expected that answer. Dr. Reddy was also, how should I put it… skeptical."

"Does that upset you?"

"To be honest, I am used to people accepting what I say."

"But you *can* understand our concern, considering the circumstances."

"Well, I'm here." A forced smile.

Martin considered the historical information Benoît had provided. As he had anticipated, it was clinically unremarkable. Benoît claimed he did not have any relatives who suffered from depression, and denied having had any previous bouts himself. This was it, a single, isolated incident, leading to an impulsive, irrational act. Martin had thought of asking about the Xanax, the fact that Benoît had complained to his doctor about not sleeping, but hadn't taken any of the pills until the overdose, almost a month later. But he decided to hold back. Benoît seemed discomfited enough for one session.

The visit passed quickly and another appointment was set for the following week. Since Benoît was a busy man, past his immediate crisis, and seemingly no longer a danger to himself, Martin felt that weekly sessions would be sufficient. Benoît affirmed his availability, at least for a while; he had delegated many of his business responsibilities to some of those "hungry" vice presidents. If he had learned anything from all this, he told Martin, it was that he needed to slow down.

As Benoît was leaving, he turned to Martin. "By the way, would it be all right for my wife to speak with you?" he asked.

Martin was curious. *An interesting proposition*, he mused. Sometimes such an arrangement could get tricky, but Martin still wondered if it might help. "That depends on how you feel about it," he responded.

"Oh, it's perfectly fine with me. I have no secrets from Martha. Anything you can do to help her through this will be greatly appreciated."

Speculating as to what sort of trap he was getting into – it was Martin's belief that patients frequently set traps for their therapists – he said, "Fine then, have her give me a call."

MARTIN ROSEN HAD FINISHED WITH his last patient of the day, but his mind was still on Jacques Benoît. He had to admit, the man was a mystery. As a therapist, Martin naturally assumed that his patients kept things from him. This was often unintentional, though generated by a sense of embarrassment or guilt over whatever wasn't being disclosed. With Jacques Benoît, however, things felt different, somehow more deliberate and calculated. Martin couldn't put his finger on it, but something wasn't right.

He gathered his things, closed his briefcase and decided to stop for a bite on the way home. Every Wednesday evening, like clockwork, he took himself out for dinner and a nightcap, yet he still regarded it as a decision rather than a ritual. Perhaps it was because he didn't like rituals, or perhaps he didn't like to feel that he "needed" the night out. Either way, after long days like this, he certainly could use it.

He dialed home to remind Jamilla that he would be late. He usually informed the nanny of his whereabouts when he wasn't in the office, even though he carried a beeper. He liked to cover all bases.

He came out of the building and turned south on Middle Neck Road. His car was in a lot around the block, but his usual nightspot, Millie's Place, was only a mile or so down the street and he felt he could use the walk. Most of the stores were closing and the walkway was fairly quiet. He appreciated the town this time of night.

He came into Millie's Place and took a seat at the bar. The regular Wednesday night crowd was there, as well as a few newcomers. Millie's Place always attracted newcomers. It was that type of restaurant, a Long Island hotspot with an upscale crowd, top-shelf booze, gourmet eats and nostalgic tunes. It wasn't the scene that drew Martin, it was that Millie's had been Katherine's favorite restaurant. They had frequented it together and he felt comfortable there.

The bartender, Steve, gave him a welcome smile, placed a double Glenlivet rocks on the bar without being asked, and said, "How goes it, Marty?"

"It goes," Martin responded as he took his first sip.

Steve brought up a bowl of peanuts.

"You shouldn't have," Martin said.

"A guy's gotta eat."

Martin toasted and downed another sip.

"So, what's it gonna be tonight?" Steve asked.

"Don't know. What's good?"

"The chateaubriand's always good."

"Too pricey."

"Okay, how about the veal Marsala? Gary's got a brand-new recipe he's trying out. Been a real hit tonight."

Martin turned around and scanned some of the tables. Of the few diners remaining at this hour, not one appeared to be eating veal Marsala. He smiled at Steve. "I guess I'll just have to take your word for it."

"Now, there's a trusting soul."

Steve handed Martin's order to a waiter and went back to work. Martin concentrated on his Scotch and exchanged smiles with some of the regulars, though they knew he wasn't one for chitchat. This was his time to himself.

Suddenly, he felt a tap on his shoulder. He turned to see a woman he didn't recognize.

"I'm sorry," the woman said. "I just saw you from the other side of the bar and thought I might come over and introduce myself."

Her accent was British, her looks somewhat Sharon Stonesque: shoulder-length straight blond hair, hazel eyes, seductive smile, thin but shapely figure.

"I hope I'm not being too forward," she said.

"Well, uh, no." Martin wore his uneasiness.

"I'm sorry, I just thought that maybe… it doesn't matter." She turned away and started back to the other end of the bar.

"No, really, it's okay," he said as he reached out and took her arm.

She stopped and smiled. "Sure?"

"Yeah, sure."

A moment of silence.

"Can I get you a drink?" Martin asked.

"Only if you insist."

"I do," he said, trying to make up for his initial reaction. "What'll it be?"

"A glass of Merlot."

He gestured for the bartender. Steve came over, an astonished look on his face. He had never seen Martin talk with a stranger. On rare occasions, maybe one of the regulars who knew the deal, but never a stranger. "A glass of Merlot," Martin said.

Steve glanced at the woman, then looked at Martin approvingly as he poured the wine.

"My name is Cheryl, Cheryl Manning," she said, holding out her hand.

"Marty Rosen." He took her hand, feeling it as both delicate and strong, confirming his sense that there was something dichotomous about her, the way she had come up to him so boldly, yet cowered at the first sign of resistance. He didn't want to play "shrink," but it was in his blood. It also made him feel safe if he understood things, or at least thought he did.

"Looks like you're a regular here," she said.

"How can you tell?"

" I noticed when you walked in, how the bartender brought your drink without your asking. Then I watched the two of you chatting and all."

Martin had to admit he loved the way Brits spoke, especially the women. He was also flattered. "You saw all that?"

"I watched you quite carefully," she said.

Martin took a rather large sip of his drink.

"Oh, I'm sorry," she said. "There I go again, making you uncomfortable."

He looked her over. She was a real stunner, and her accent was just something else. *That*, and the bit of alcohol he'd consumed on an empty stomach, made him say, "I suppose I can get used to it."

Steve came back, and placed some utensils and a napkin on the bar. "Food'll be right out, Marty," he said as he took Martin's glass to replenish it.

"You're eating?" Cheryl asked.

"Yes, dinner. Care for some?"

"No thank you, I've had mine."

Steve brought Martin's drink over with his meal. "Looks like that guy wants to get me drunk," Martin said to her.

"He seems to like you."

Martin considered the comment. "We've known each other for a long time." He took a bite of his veal.

"So," she said, "what kind of work do you do?"

Martin didn't welcome the question; he knew his answer would change things and, he had to admit, he was starting to enjoy himself. He couldn't help remembering Nancy Hartledge, the psychologist he'd met in Chicago, wondering if this was going to be a repeat performance. Of course, if he were advising one of his patients, he would say it was entirely up to him. But Martin was always lousy about taking his own advice.

"I'm a clinical psychologist," he said.

"As in, head shrink?"

"Some people use that term."

"Have you been analyzing me?"

"You want the truth?"

"Absolutely."

"I never work unless I'm paid."

"Oh come now, that's as much bull as I've ever heard," she said playfully.

"Distrustful, aren't we?"

"I thought you weren't analyzing!"

"Touché. Caught me." He saw that her drink was low. "How about another?" he asked.

"I'd love one."

At that moment, Steve just happened to appear with a fresh glass of Merlot.

"He's a regular mind reader," Cheryl observed.

They shared some laughter.

"Now it's your turn," Martin said. "What do you do?"

"Me? Oh, nothing so interesting as being a shrink, I assure you."

"And what, pray tell, might that be?"

"Public relations. A firm in the city, you probably haven't even heard of it."

"Try me."

"Okay, Lipton Associates."

"You mean Jacob Lipton Associates?"

"So you *have* heard of us."

"Anyone who reads the financial section of the newspaper knows who Jacob Lipton is. Holocaust survivor. Came to this country with nothing. Built up his own company from scratch. Made most of his fortune in the past few years doing PR for mergers and acquisitions, placating the worried, so to speak."

"That's my boss."

"How did you come to work for him?"

"It's a long story, but I'll give you the short version. I studied at Oxford, came to the U.S. in search of fortune and fame, answered a few ads in the *New York Times*, one thing led to another, and here I am." She held up her hands, indicating that was that.

He noticed she didn't reveal much.

"You do seem to know an awful lot about the financial world for a psychologist," she added.

"I follow a bit here and there, mainly to keep up with my patients."

"That makes sense. Working in Great Neck, you must deal with a lot of wealthy people."

"I didn't say I worked in Great Neck."

"I'm sorry," she said, "I assumed you did, coming here often, knowing the barkeep and all."

They sipped their drinks and shared a glance or two. Martin looked at his watch. "It's getting late," he said. "Can I drop you someplace?"

"That would be nice. My flat is just up the street. I moved out of the city two weeks ago."

"Why's that?"

"I couldn't take it anymore. Needed some peace and quiet. Everyone said Great Neck's the place to go. Long Island Railroad is close by, only a thirty-minute commute to work – quicker than the subway from the Upper West Side – and there are lots of young people, fancy places to spend money. No feelers, rapists or pickpockets."

"Sounds like you're enjoying yourself."

"I am now."

She held his arm as they walked. It was only three and a half blocks to her building, a ritzy three-story condo on Middle Neck Road, somewhere between the restaurant and the old village where Martin's office was. He led her up the walkway of the circular driveway and noticed a doorman emerge.

"Nice place," Martin said.

"You should see where I lived in the city. A real dive, and for the same money."

"Ah, the advantages of suburbia."

"Would you like to come in for a drink?"

"Thank you, but it *is* late." He sounded like he was trying to convince himself more than her.

"Okay, well maybe another time."

"Yes, another time sounds nice."

They exchanged phone numbers, said good night, and ended

with a customary yet tender handshake. Martin watched as she greeted the doorman, entered the building, and waved goodbye one last time before disappearing from sight. He stood there for a moment, wondering. Chicago had been a disaster, and now this. He knew he wasn't ready for anything, that the smartest thing would be to discard the number and pretend the evening hadn't happened. But somehow, he couldn't. There was something about her that wouldn't allow for that. And something about him that wanted to give it a try.

Cheryl Manning entered her apartment, turned on the light, went directly to the phone in her living room and dialed a Manhattan number. "It's me," she told the man at the other end.

"Everything okay?"

"All is proceeding according to plan."

"You've made contact?"

"Yes, he's actually… rather charming."

"What?"

"No need to worry. I have it under control. He doesn't suspect a thing."

"Just be careful. And *don't* get involved."

"I never do."

"This time things are different."

"This time is no different than any other time," she said. "I'll do the job the way I always do."

There was a brief hesitation, then the other voice said, "Good then, keep us posted about developments. We'll see you in a few days."

"Okay. Take care."

"Yes, will do. You too."

MARTIN ROSEN SUPPRESSED A YAWN. He was finding it difficult to concentrate on his first patient of the day. The past few nights had been fraught with tossing, turning, and ruminating over just about everything: Katherine, Elizabeth, Nancy Hartledge of San Francisco, and the newest member of the cast, Cheryl Manning. It had already been a few days since he'd met her, but she was still fresh in his mind.

"You okay, Doc?" the man on the couch across from him asked.

"Pardon?"

"I asked if you're all right."

Embarrassed, Martin snapped back to reality. "Yes, I'm fine," he said, sounding a bit tentative. He looked at the clock. Five minutes remaining to the session. He'd spent close to an hour with this man and hadn't offered a thing.

"You sure? 'Cause you don't seem yourself today."

Martin realized that he should have known better than to try to fool this particular patient. "I'm sorry, Dan. I've been having a few long nights, not much sleep."

"I know the feeling, Doc, believe me."

Martin looked at his patient and smiled. Dan Gifford had been seeing him for just over a year. Their relationship was good, perhaps one of the best doctor-patient relationships Martin had ever had. Martin even occasionally speculated on how they might have wound up great friends, had they met under other circumstances.

Dan Gifford felt a similar connection, which was what kept him coming back. He'd been to two other therapists before Martin, and neither had lasted beyond three sessions. He was about to give up the search, when a friend from AA gave him Martin's card.

When he first started seeing Martin, Dan Gifford had six months of sobriety under his belt. At 46, he was the Chief Assistant District Attorney of the organized crime bureau of the Queens County DA's office, where he'd worked for the past twenty years. His daily existence was a deluge of stress and, while he had been thriving professionally, his personal life was in shambles. His drinking problem, the last vestige of a serious mixed substance-abuse habit that he'd picked up during the Vietnam War, had lingered long beyond the opiates, which he had managed to kick as soon as he returned home. He discovered later, in his treatment with Martin, that the alcohol had really been a deeper problem, one that had started long before the war, during his teenage years and maybe even earlier. His father and grandfather had also been alcoholics.

The actual reason Dan had sought therapy went beyond the alcohol. His wife had gotten involved in Al-Anon while he was still drinking, and had left with their 6-year-old son about a month before he started going to AA meetings. Dan wanted them back and knew he had a lot more to work on than just giving up booze. Enter Martin Rosen.

Dan appreciated Martin's perspective on things, the shrink's wry sense of humor, and that Martin knew what it was like to lose a wife and child. In the time that they had known each other, Dan had learned that Martin enjoyed golf, fine food, action movies, and an "occasional" drink. It was generally *verboten* for therapists to divulge personal information, but Martin saw the rules of "the old school" as too clinical for his liking. He preferred relaxing with patients and relating to them as humanly as possible.

Martin found Dan fascinating. First, there was Dan's service in Vietnam as a naval intelligence officer. Dan never actually spoke of details – most of it was highly classified and not necessarily relevant to the treatment – but Martin knew that naval intelligence officers were regarded as the cream of the crop.

Dan's current job, prosecuting organized crime figures, also captivated Martin. The commonality of their vocations, both being immersed in probing and analyzing the proclivities of the psyche, was often striking. Dan had some ideas of his own regarding human behavior, and Martin had always found them edifying.

"So, you were telling me about your meeting with Stephanie," Martin said, referring to a dinner date Dan had with his wife the night before. Dan often scheduled his get-togethers with Stephanie the evening prior to his therapy session so the details would be fresh in his mind when reporting them.

"Yeah, well, it didn't go as I'd hoped. This case I'm on is just eating me alive. I can't break free from it, not even for a second."

Dan was referring to the trial of one of the city's most notorious Colombian drug lords, Miguel Domingo. Dan was the lead prosecutor and had spent the past year preparing for the trial, which had begun three weeks earlier. He had personally managed to turn a key witness, Domingo's former lieutenant, Roberto Alvarez, to testify for the state. At present, Alvarez was in protective custody, and only Dan, four hand-chosen NYPD officers guarding Alvarez, and the DA himself knew the location of the safehouse.

"I probably should have canceled with her," Dan continued. "It's not a good time for me to be thinking about anything."

"When is a good time?" Martin asked.

"When I'm not sitting on a major case." *Defensive, testy.*

"Oh," Martin responded, unruffled. "And when is that?"

Dan sat back. "Good point," he said in a soft, contemplative voice.

Martin looked at the clock. "It seems we're out of time, Dan, but I do feel bad that my mind wasn't on full speed today. How about we make this one a freebie and we'll get together tomorrow again for a real session?"

"Don't be ridiculous, Doc. The session was great, worth every penny. Look at it this way: when I was drinking, I was still better at my job than most guys. Same's for you, you're better in la-la-land than any shrink I know. And I don't have time tomorrow anyway."

Dan handed Martin the check. "Take the money, Doc, and buy some nice lady a real fine dinner. You've earned it!" He turned toward the door, and added, "I'll see you next week."

Dan Gifford walked through the waiting room, glancing at the older gentleman who was seated and obviously waiting for Dr. Rosen. The man lifted his eyes from a magazine and smiled politely. Gifford responded with an obligatory nod as he hastened from the office.

Gifford stepped into the street, cognizant of a nagging feeling about the man he had just seen, the very same feeling he'd had exactly a week ago, when he'd last left Rosen's office. It was the same man, the same smile, and the same sense of something familiar. Gifford still couldn't place it, but he was certain he'd seen that face before. Perfectionist that he was, he knew he would chastise himself the moment he connected the face with a name. But for now, all he could do was excuse himself for slipping. He simply had too much on his mind.

It was only 8 a.m. and already Gifford could tell it was going to be one of those gloomy, late-September days. The forecasters had called for rain, and the sky looked like it was about to make them prophets. He had forty-five minutes to get to the Queens Criminal Court House through rush-hour traffic on the Grand Central Parkway. No problem for a chief assistant DA. He would take an alternate route, Union Turnpike all the way – it was less trafficky because it had lots of lights, but he could speed through them. No cop in his right mind would give him a ticket.

He walked toward his car, which was parked half a block down on Middle Neck Road, when he saw something that sparked his curiosity – a black, late-model Mercedes E-Class sedan parked across the street, with two men in the front seat. He slowed his pace a bit, watching from the corner of his eye. One of the men lit a cigarette, the other just sat there. The engine was off and the windows were halfway open. The car itself fit in perfectly with the neighborhood, and probably no one else would have paid it any attention. But Dan wondered about it, the kind of wondering that had made him an excellent intelligence officer and now a top prosecutor. It just didn't feel right.

Perhaps I'm being paranoid, he mused, but these days paranoia is a healthy instinct. There were dangerous people looking for Roberto Alvarez, and he was one of very few who knew the witness' whereabouts. He considered that the car might be NYPD protection; he wouldn't put it past his office to secretly place him under surveillance for his own good. But using a Mercedes for such purposes was unlikely; only the Narcs used foreign cars.

He took note of the license plate as he got in his car, though he figured that if his suspicions were warranted it would probably wind up a dead end. It couldn't hurt to check, but he wouldn't be surprised if it was a rental with a bogus credit card.

As he pulled away, he noticed that the Mercedes didn't follow. Another person might have been relieved by that, but not Gifford. He realized there could be more than one car out there, very carefully, professionally on his tail. He was among the best at playing cat and mouse; good enough to know that there were experts who could fool even him.

His mind was running wild, wondering if they knew what he was doing in that building. And what about Martin Rosen? Gifford entertained the possibility that the Colombians could be targeting Rosen, whether to simply kidnap and trade for Roberto Alvarez or because they believed that he might tell Rosen where Alvarez was. Either scenario seemed far-fetched, he realized, but when playing with these guys, one couldn't be too careful. The Colombian mob rivaled only the Russians in their depravity. They would go after a man's wife, children, friends; whatever it took for them to get what they wanted. He kicked himself for not having canceled his sessions during the trial; the last thing he wanted was to bring Rosen in on this. Everyone he came in contact with was in danger.

Suddenly, Stephanie and Dan Jr. came to mind. If he had any vulnerability, they were truly it. He knew it was also stupid to see them during all this, instead of telling Stephanie to take the kid and visit her mother for a few weeks. But he also knew that every case was fraught with danger, and that Stephanie was finished with uprooting her life. She wasn't about to go anywhere. As for what he should do, he simply had to choose whether to have a normal existence or not. In the past, the booze had kept him from facing such conflicts. Now the things he wanted, and Martin Rosen, would no longer grant him that refuge.

7

JACQUES BENOÎT FELT CONFIDENT. HIS second session with Dr. Rosen was over, and he had successfully continued his pretense that everything was copacetic. Satisfied with his performance, he toyed with the idea of speeding things up a bit on his next visit. Then again, he reminded himself of the benefits of patience. *Everything in due time.*

He stepped out of the building and into his limo. "Where to, sir?" his chauffeur asked.

"I don't know," he said, lost in thought, "just drive around."

The limo proceeded down Middle Neck Road, and Benoît peered out the window at the pedestrians. It was a pleasant morning, and the walkways were getting busy. Benoît thought about what he was doing here, driving through this "Jewish" town, coming from his Jewish shrink.

He also thought about his own home in Sands Point, which was only about a ten-minute drive from here. When he had first moved there forty years ago, it had been a secluded enclave for upper-crust WASPS, allegedly exclusive of Jews, an ideal place for him to fit in. An even more perfect place to hide.

Over time, however, some wealthy Jews had discovered the dazzling cliffs and scenic shores of this Long Island Sound community and began buying some of its abundant properties. Benoît had found the change unsettling, but by the time it was happening, it was his fear, rather than hatred, that had plagued him. He was now long past his anti-Semitic, racist days. He had become a successful businessman, and had refused to join the "brotherhoods" or to associate in any way with his wartime cohorts who had also escaped. He was finished with the reckless, puerile ways of his youth. He wanted to be left alone, to be as anonymous as possible, free to go about his new life unencumbered.

As a man who coveted his privacy, he skillfully avoided the paparazzi and never granted interviews. So far, he had been successful, but the fear of being recognized never waned. He knew there were people out there who could expose and indict him, that at any moment his facade could be shattered. He no longer had any desire to harm them; in fact, he had grown weary of trying to understand how he had ever behaved so monstrously. But in his mind, he wished they would just go away.

He had tried to change things, had started going to church, giving more money to charities than most men make in an entire lifetime. Still, he knew his ultimate debt remained unpaid.

He thought about that debt, the crimes he had committed. He had managed to forge a new existence, but now *they* had reawakened the memories. Now he could no longer erase the evil by which he had long ago defined himself. Now he could see it all once again, and with a clarity that time would never dull.

August 11, 1943
Lyon, Vichy France

He looks at the house. He knows the people who live there. It is the home of a banker his parents have occasionally borrowed from. His father had once described the man as "decent, for a Jew." On several occasions, the banker's wife, a belle in every sense, was subjected to his attempts at flirtation. It is the French way for men to fraternize with beautiful women, and vice versa, be they married or not. But this woman dismissed his every advance; these Jews were so different.

The Gestapo chief turns to him. "Is this it?"

He believes it is but consults the list to be sure. The Germans admire efficiency and have no tolerance for errors. So far, he has impressed them, but one meager mistake could change all that.

The list confirms it. This is the home of Philip Saifer and family, which includes the lovely wife and two young children, a 10-year-old daughter and a 7-year-old son. The list contains hundreds of such families, addresses, names, and the exact number of members in each. Several pages in length, it has taken him and his men months to compile, and holds the destiny of well over a thousand lives.

"Most definitely," he responds to the chief.

It is a late summer afternoon. The men are overworked and overheated in their uniforms. This is the fifth home in what, so far, has been a long day. They have been gathering these families throughout the city for several days now, starting with the wealthy and prominent, like the Saifers.

He, too, is hot in his uniform. For years, all through his childhood, he wanted nothing more than to don the garb of a police officer. His parents own an inn on the outskirts of the city. They had always hoped he would follow in their footsteps, but his childhood had been fraught with fantasies of a different life. Catering to loud-mouthed fools, many of them Jews – cleaning their beds and bathrooms, serving their meals – it had never been for him. He needed more excitement, and he craved the deference, even fear, from others that he now enjoyed.

His hard work had gained him the rank of Captain two years earlier, just after the Germans invaded and occupied the north of France, and the Vichy regime was established to "rule" in the south. Now, having retained that position despite increasing Nazi influence over Vichy, he has what he always wanted: respect. Not only do his fellow officers and civilians revere him, even the Gestapo treats him with dignity, though he knows that is ephemeral. In his heart, he actually hates the Germans, as any self-respecting Frenchman must, but he also realizes that doing their bidding is the only way to maintain his life as it is. He must demonstrate his cooperation.

What does it matter to him, rounding up a bunch of slimy Jews for a bunch of equally slimy Germans? At least this way, France will finally be rid of one of its oldest scourges. Then, when the liberation comes – his country is always, sooner or later, liberated – all of France will belong once again to the French.

He looks at his men, expecting weariness in their eyes, yet they appear eager, waiting for his command. He wonders if this is because they know this is the last house of the day, or if they are beginning to enjoy themselves.

Including him, there are ten Frenchmen, four Gestapo police and their chief. The Nazis are spread too thinly throughout Europe; this is all they could spare for a city the size of Lyon. But he knows reinforcements are on their way.

"Proceed!" he orders.

At once, the Vichy and Gestapo policemen approach the house. They are not storming, this is not a military operation, nor do they anticipate any resistance. *The Jews acquiesce so pitifully*, he muses, though he knows they have no other options. He wonders how the banker's wife will look when she sees he is in charge of all this.

He and the Gestapo chief remain in the street, watching. One of the men pounds on the door, yelling, "Open up, this is the police."

He observes the banker open the door and the men force their way in. He hears the wife scream, "What is this?" And he no longer wonders what her screams would sound like. His men scamper throughout the house, as two Gestapo officers escort the banker and the wife out to the street.

The Gestapo chief steps up to the couple, looks each of them in the eye, and asks, "Where are your children?"

He watches carefully. This part he chooses to leave to the Germans; they are so adept at being cruel.

"They are visiting their cousins in Switzerland for the summer," the banker responds.

"Liar!" the Gestapo chief yells as he whips the butt of his pistol across the man's face.

The man falls to the ground.

He looks at the banker's wife, wondering if she even recognizes him. She is absorbed in her fear and gives no indication. "I am the policeman you refused to sleep with," he wants to say. Instead, he appears indifferent.

The Gestapo chief turns to her, "Where are your children?"

She remains silent. The banker is on his knees, spitting blood, but manages the words: "I told you, they are not here."

He knows the banker is lying, as does the Gestapo chief. The children cannot be in Switzerland for the summer because that would have required transit papers, and there is no record of any such papers.

"I will ask one more time," the Gestapo chief says.

"They are in Switzerland," the wife finally says, tears flowing from her eyes. "We got them travel papers, illegal ones, forged. We paid heavily for them, there is no record."

He ponders this. He knows there has been an underground market in travel papers for Jews. Now, perhaps, he has an opportunity to crack the ring and find the perpetrators. How will the Germans regard him after that? He will be a hero. He steps forward, stands beside the Gestapo chief, and says to the woman, "That is most interesting."

He puts his face an inch from hers. Still no sign of recognition. "Tell me, who sold you these papers?"

She is silent.

The Gestapo chief turns to the husband.

"Wait!" she says. "A Frenchman. I do not know his name, but I can describe him. He is short, stocky, wears glasses and works for the Foreign Ministry."

He contemplates her response. Now he knows she is lying. The Ministry is heavily policed, with impeccable security; there is no way the papers could have come from there. Illegal papers are, however, being manufactured by the partisans. Of that much he is aware. But is she lying about the source of the papers, or about their existence altogether? Illegal papers are hard to come by, and most are so poorly done that they are of little use. The banker's house, on the other hand, is quite large. There are many nooks and crannies in which the children could be hiding.

He looks at the Gestapo chief. "She is lying," he declares.

"No! I am telling the truth," she yells as the Gestapo chief turns to the two German officers.

"Take them away."

One of the Germans lifts the limp banker off the ground and drags the man to the truck, while the other grabs the wife. She is crying and has lost her resistance; she is fearful for her husband. The other Gestapo and Vichy officers exit the house.

"Well?" he asks.

"Nothing," one of his men answers.

The Nazis look at their chief and nod in agreement.

"What do you suggest?" the Gestapo chief asks him.

He knows this is a test of his resolve, one he will not fail. He addresses his men: "Search it again! Tear it apart if you must!"

The men scurry back into the house. The chief turns to him with a smile of approval. "I will return to headquarters with the parents. You and the others can join me there when you find the little runts." The German is careful not to phrase his words as orders per se, but that is exactly what they are.

He nods. He is loath to be commanded by a German but realizes he has little choice. He wants to spit on this German, but for now he will do as he believes he must.

He joins the men in their search. Two hours pass. Rooms, furniture and walls are torn apart, and still nothing. He knows they are somewhere, he senses it. He also knows they are not going to be found. He calls off the search. The Gestapo will be displeased, but he will surprise them yet.

He gets into his car alone and follows behind the officers in their truck. He drives for three minutes, then pulls over to the side of the road. He knows they will wonder where he's gone, but when he finally reappears, they will understand and praise his ingenuity.

He gets out of the car and starts backtracking by foot. It is dark, and he is able to stay in the shadows. He catches sight of the house, hides himself in a wooded area, and waits. Close to an hour passes. He could use a cigarette but is afraid the flame might reveal his presence. He is growing restless, but he will stay all night if need be.

Suddenly, after another hour, he thinks he sees movement in

the house. His eyes have adjusted to the darkness and he is certain, yes, he is sure... there it is, the girl emerges from a basement window. He watches her help her little brother and wonders where they could have been hiding down there, but that is unimportant now. All that matters is that he has them.

Gun in hand, he sneaks up as the girl pulls her brother from the window. He knows he will not need the gun, they are children after all, but he will use it to scare them, to prevent them from running.

"Very good," he says, revealing his presence.

The children turn to face him.

He sees the fear in their eyes. The girl has a small suitcase in her hand. He figures the suitcase has money, jewelry, or both, something to purchase safety and transit.

"What do you want?" the girl asks. Her tone is strikingly similar to her mother's.

"What do I want?" he ponders aloud. "Well, it looks like I want you and your brother. Two little Jews who thought they could escape." He grins. "And while I'm at it, I think I'll take a peek in that suitcase."

He grabs the case and slowly opens it with one hand, while his other hand steadies the gun. "Well, well, what do we have here?" He examines what looks like a fortune in cash and jewelry, then closes the bag. He knows exactly what he is going to do with it.

He is certain these children were not simply abandoned by their parents without strict instructions of where to go. The Jews have all kinds of connections and plans. He searches them and finds in the girl's pocket a map of the southern hills. A trail is drawn in red on the map, and an "X" marks a destination. He assumes that this is some sort of place of refuge, a Jewish hideout or perhaps even a partisan base. Whatever it is, he is certain his German "friends" will make good use of it.

He leads the children to his car, places them in the back seat and the suitcase in the trunk. He has no plans to share the contents of the suitcase with anyone. They will be added to the already sizable nest egg he has accumulated over the past few days. *The roundup is bound to continue for months*, he surmises. *Who knows how much of a fortune I will amass by the time it is over?*

He arrives at one of the city's gymnasiums where the Jews are being held, and escorts the children inside. He has not been in this building since the roundup began. The scene strikes him. Hundreds of Jews, many of whom have been there for close to a week, lacking baths and adequate toilet facilities. The stench of feces and urine is nauseating. He had planned to find the parents and personally bring the children to them, to teach them and the others a lesson in Vichy ingenuity, to see if the mother would at last acknowledge him. But he finds he can no longer stay in this place, the foulness is too overwhelming. He deposits the children with a guard and leaves.

He sucks in the fresh air as he hurries to his car. He is fighting an urge to vomit. There are Vichy police and guards outside the building; he must not show weakness in front of them. He gets into the car, pulls out his handkerchief and retches. Afterward, he looks around, taking comfort in his certainty that no one had seen.

He passes the train station on his way home, noting that it is from here the Jews will be sent to Drancy, an internment camp on the outskirts of Paris, before they are transported to their final destination. He is impressed with German efficiency, the choice of freight cars rather than passenger trains because they can hold more people. He only wishes they would hurry up and finish this ugly business. The next transfer from Lyon is in two days; he assumes the banker's family will be included. He is aware of their ultimate fate. He has heard stories of the camps in Germany and Poland. He chooses not to dwell on that. He cares only about purifying his country, not where these "wanderers" are headed. That, he leaves to the Germans.

He continues on his way. In the morning, the Gestapo chief will learn of his having found the children, greet him warmly and praise him for a job well done. He will react with the obligatory grace. The map he confiscated will simply be icing on the cake. For that, the Gestapo will be in debt to him.

He arrives home. His parents, who he lives with, are still awake, cleaning up after their guests.

His father sees him. "A late night for you," he says. "You look tired."

"I've been chasing after criminals."

"Criminals," his father says skeptically. "What kind of criminals?"

For some reason, he cannot bring himself to tell the truth. He wonders why he feels this way; after all, his father is neither a friend of the Jews nor ignorant of his role in the roundup. Yet, somehow, he has a sense of shame – at least in front of this man – over hunting down children.

"Partisans," he responds.

"What's in the bag?" his father asks, pointing to the suitcase.

"Oh, this," he says defensively. "Just some papers from work."

His father gives him a disdainful look and walks away. Until this point, he had no clue how his father felt about the Vichy government's collaboration with the Germans; the subject had never been discussed. He'd wondered if he would have been better off with the truth. Now he knows better.

He goes upstairs to his room, removes his uniform, and examines the contents of the suitcase. There are many fine pieces of jewelry, mostly diamonds and gold, and enough cash for an ordinary man to live on for a year. He inspects the jewelry carefully and recognizes one of the brooches, a pink cameo the wife had worn the day he had attempted to seduce her. It is a simple piece, probably late nineteenth century Italian, a design of a wavy-haired woman walking through the wind, carrying a vine, framed in gold. Rather pretty, he tells himself as he notices an engraving on the back: *To Leila, all my love, Philip.*

He stares at the brooch, admiring its workmanship. His father and many other hardworking Frenchmen could barely afford the types of ornaments frequently adorned by the Jews. And now all this belongs to him. He knows he will sell the jewelry when the time is right – but this piece he will keep, as a memento of sorts.

He pulls a panel from the floor and retrieves a large wooden box that is hidden underneath. He deposits the cash and jewelry in the box, puts it back in its hiding place and replaces the floorboard. He lies down on the bed and closes his eyes. It has been an arduous day, and tomorrow will be much the same.

Jacques Benoît knew that he could never erase these images. These, and others. He thought about the brooch, why he had kept it all these years. Perhaps because it was his only link to the past, a reminder of what he must always hide if he was to survive. And perhaps it was also a symbol of his guilt, an irrational need to keep something of this woman and her family alive. Whatever it was, he could never bring himself to discard it.

He had often imagined what would happen if he were captured, how the world would know only his depravity, the man he had once been; how they would embrace but a piece of the truth and ignore the rest. Who would care about his accomplishments over the past forty years? Who would give weight to his benevolence and philanthropy? No one, not even his wife and family.

That was why his visits with the Jewish psychologist were now so crucial. Initially, he had agreed to see Martin Rosen, not to comfort his wife nor to satisfy Dr. Reddy, but as a ruse, a way of confusing his hunters into thinking that maybe he wasn't their man to begin with. After all, how could the person they suspected him to be *ever* seek help from a Jew? It had been a clever move and must have assuredly infused doubt in their minds, especially after that fiasco over the identity of the auto worker in Ohio, the trial, the publicity, the eventual embarrassment.

But now, after having met Rosen, Jacques Benoît had a new and even better plan, one that strengthened his resolve and convinced him that, so long as he played his part carefully, he could finally gain what he needed to be free.

He recalled the information he had gathered on Martin Rosen's personal life. It was surprising even to him what a man of resources could learn about another man. His people had scoured Rosen's background down to the nitty-gritty details, and with all he now knew, he was certain he had made the right choice. In every way, Martin Rosen was ideal for what he had in mind.

Jacques Benoît contemplated all this as his limo continued down Middle Neck Road through the busiest section of town. He turned around for a moment and looked out the rear window, wondering if he was being followed.

JACQUES BENOÎT SAT ACROSS THE table from his wife in silence, waiting for the inevitable question about his therapy session. He couldn't blame her, really; in a single act, he had shattered her nearly perfect existence. Now, still skeptical of his explanations, she sought answers.

Martha Benoît had the things most women yearned for: a loving and successful husband, devoted children, position and respect in the community, more money than she could possibly spend in a lifetime, and health. At 63, she still had the figure of a high-priced model, which she owed to genetics, a daily two-hour exercise grind and a strict organic diet. Her tennis player's tan obviated the need for heavy makeup, while her wavy auburn hair and hazel eyes made her appear more free-spirited than she actually was.

"So, how did it go with Dr. Rosen?" she asked, caressing the rim of her wine glass with her forefinger.

Jacques hesitated for a moment, sipped his bourbon, and answered, "Fine. The doctor is a real gentleman."

"Oh please, Jacques," she snapped back. "It doesn't concern me how the doctor is. I want to know how *you're* doing!"

"How do I appear?" he asked.

"Why, *wonderful*, of course. A few weeks ago, you tried to kill yourself, and you've been just wonderful since. Doesn't that strike you as odd?"

He paused. "I suppose it should."

A welcome interruption ensued as the maid entered the dining room with dinner.

"That's all right, Consuelo," Martha said as the maid was about to serve the Cornish hens. "You can just leave the tray on the table. We'll help ourselves tonight."

Consuelo quickly complied. Jacques looked at his wife with amazement. She was truly annoyed, a side of her he'd rarely seen.

"I am sorry for what I did, Martha. You know that you are the last person on earth I would ever hurt."

"But I'm the person you *did* hurt, Jacques, and so far, the reasons you've given me are wholly insufficient."

"I feel as though you are cross-examining me."

"I have to tell you how I feel."

"I do not know what more you expect of me. I am seeing that psychologist, I am trying to find out if there is some, as you say, *underlying* reason for what happened."

"Are you?"

"Why else would I start seeing that fellow every week? I *do* have other things to do with my time."

"Perhaps to placate me."

"Please, my dear, I know you are not stupid."

She was silent for a moment. "Sometimes I wonder."

"I have always regarded you as the smartest person I've ever met, you know that."

Something inside her told her that she had pushed as far as she could, at least for now. He was in good hands with Dr. Rosen, so she'd heard from several sources, and she would just have to trust in that. She looked at him, regarding the warmth in his eyes. He was a good man, she believed, loving and selfless in every respect. He was right, he could never do anything to hurt her. Yet, what had happened to him, as impulsive, irrational and uncharacteristic as it may have been, left her uncertain about the future.

Jacques continued. "I spoke with the doctor about your talking with him. He says it's fine and that you should call."

She forced a smile.

He stood up from his chair, walked over to her and ran his hands through her hair. "Everything is going to be all right, my dear, I promise," he said softly.

It amazed her how easily he could make her feel the same way she had the first time he ever touched her. This was the man she had fallen in love with, the man who had always been able to arouse her lust, the man who had inspired cravings she'd never imagined herself capable of. And even now, years later, he affected her so.

She grasped his hand and rose to meet him face-to-face. They hadn't stood this close to each other for some time, several weeks before his suicide attempt by her count. It felt good, as if he were finally returning to her. She brought her hand slowly to his face, gently touching his cheek as she leaned into him and kissed his lips. It was a tender kiss, but one which vibrated through her entire body.

"I love you," she whispered, tears forming in her eyes.

"And I love *you*," he responded as he drew her into another kiss, deeper and harder.

Enveloped in his hold, she wanted nothing more than to have all of him. Releasing herself, she took his hand. "Let's go upstairs."

"But what of dinner?" he asked, grinning mischievously.

"It will have to wait."

THE VILLAGE OF LAKE SUCCESS was aptly named, in light of its grand homes and winding, impeccably groomed streets. It was not a place Martin and Katherine could have afforded, were it not for the financial assistance of Katherine's parents. Martin had initially been opposed to the idea – there were plenty of fine neighborhoods within their price range – but Katherine's father, a prominent Peoria surgeon with whom Martin had developed a most amicable relationship, had convinced his new son-in-law to at least take the money as a "non-interest loan." Katherine fell in love with the neighborhood, saw it as a wonderful place for children, and Martin couldn't bear to disappoint her. He promised himself, and Katherine, that he would pay her father back in full, though the man had never expected or even desired to see the money. Martin's first two royalty checks on his book took care of the first and last installments, and his only regret was that Katherine hadn't lived to see the house become *theirs.* He believed, however, that somehow she knew.

The house was a four-bedroom, center-hall colonial on Bridle

Path Lane, a street that had once, years before the development of the area, served the very function for which it was named. Set back nicely from the road, on about half an acre of property, it boasted all white hand-split cedar shakes, with old-world crystalline windows and traditional drapery adding as much to its exterior as to the rooms within. Its simplicity, which lent it a storybook complexion one might find somewhere in Middle America rather than here among its more imposing neighbors, had clinched it for Katherine. It had reminded her of home.

For Martin, it had all been a big surprise. He had never imagined himself taking pride in something so mundane as a house. But as Katherine slowly added her touch, the more he came to appreciate it, and her. It became, in every sense, a reflection of their lives: pure and warm. And within its confines, he would always feel her presence.

"Daddy's home!" Martin heard as he entered the house.

Elizabeth came running from the den and jumped into his arms, yelling, "Daddy!"

He hoisted her up and held her tight, relishing every squeeze and kiss, though his bones and muscles were telling him that she was getting too heavy, and he too old. A wave of sadness passed through him. "How's my girl?" he asked.

"Good, Daddy, really good."

He put her down, trying to conceal the strain.

"Come see what we were doing!" she commanded as she led him back to the den.

Jamilla was sitting on the den floor, pondering the pieces of an almost completed puzzle. As usual, she was dressed simply: fitted blue jeans and a black T-shirt bearing a faded image of Celine Dion. She was a small-framed woman in her early 20s, with long, straight black hair, dark skin, brown eyes, and what Martin had always regarded as sweet facial features. She looked up at him with the same smile that had so impressed him the first time he'd met her, the smile that had told him that she would be the perfect caregiver for his daughter. "Ah, Dr. Rosen, how are you tonight?"

Martin had grown accustomed to her accent though, when he hired her two years earlier, he was worried that it might hinder Elizabeth's language skills. He had since learned quite the opposite, that nothing could impede his daughter. He looked down at the progress Elizabeth had made on the "7 years and older" dinosaur puzzle, confirming his sense, once again, that the girl had inherited her mother's brains.

"Pretty well," Martin answered, dismissing the fact that he was actually spent. He never wanted Elizabeth to see him as anything less than enthusiastic after an entire day of being away from her. "A bit hungry though."

The nanny jumped up. "Of course. Dinner will be ready in a jiffy."

Martin smiled. "A jiffy works for me."

Jamilla chuckled as she went to the kitchen.

"See what I did, Daddy? I almost finished the whole puzzle by myself. Jamilla helped, but I did most of it. *Right, Jamilla?*"

"Right!" the nanny yelled from the kitchen.

Elizabeth got on her knees and pointed to one of the completed dinosaurs. "This one's a stegosaurus."

"That's correct," Martin said, beaming.

"And this one's a triceratops."

"That's right also."

Elizabeth got up and stood beside her father, admiring her work. "Isn't it cool, Daddy?"

"Very cool, princess." He looked into her bright blue eyes. "As cool as it gets."

"Dinner's ready!" Jamilla called.

"Come, let's eat," Martin said. He took Elizabeth's hand and started toward the kitchen.

"Daddy, do you think Aunt Esther will come to my birthday party?"

Martin smiled sadly; Elizabeth's birthday was a good six months away, and was probably the next time he would see his older sister, Esther. Through all his choices, and the estrangement from his parents, his relationship with Esther had always endured. She was his only sibling and, while she maintained the traditional lifestyle of their parents, married a staunchly Orthodox man and had five children, neither she nor he could ever disavow themselves of the closeness they had shared as children. She remained, in effect, his only link to his past.

"Of course she will. Doesn't she always?" he said.

"What about Michali and Devorah?" Elizabeth asked, referring to her cousins whom she had barely met two years earlier, when Esther had visited a few days after the funeral of Katherine and Ethan. It was the only time Esther had brought any of her children, and she had chosen the girls, who were also her youngest, so they could play with Elizabeth while she spent time with Martin.

Martin was always dumbfounded when Elizabeth brought this up, wondering if she truly remembered her cousins, or if simply knowing of their existence made her mention them from time to time. "We'll see," he answered, hoping she'd drop the subject.

"Yeah, we'll see," she responded, squeezing his hand.

He wasn't sure whether she was parroting him, or if she was truly wise in ways he didn't comprehend. He opted for the latter because it warmed his heart, which was exactly what he needed at the moment.

"Daddy?"

"Yes, princess?"

"How come I only have one grandma and one grandpa? Cindy and Andrea both have two grandmas and two grandpas."

Another bombshell. Boy, she's on a roll tonight, he thought.

In truth, this was the second time Elizabeth had drawn this comparison with her two best friends, the first having been a few weeks earlier. What went on in a 4-year-old's head amazed Martin, and he was certain she would repeat the question until he provided a sufficient answer. He turned to her, squatted down to her level, and said, "Honey, remember I told you that you also have four grandparents, just like Cindy and Andrea?"

She nodded. "But how come I don't see your mommy and daddy?"

"That's a good question," he uttered, more to himself than to her, realizing that this wouldn't get him anywhere.

"Because they're far away?" she probed, recalling the explanation he'd given her in the past.

Martin cringed. When he'd said that, it had been the first and only time he'd lied to her. He hadn't known what to say and realized that it had been a dumb lie to begin with, considering that Katherine's parents, who lived a thousand miles away in Illinois, spoke with their granddaughter weekly and visited several times a year. He should have guessed this wouldn't silence her.

"Well honey," he said, "being 'far away' can mean many things. It can mean that they actually live far away, like Grandpa Joe and Grandma Evelyn, or it can mean that we're just not close with them, that we don't talk to them or see them because we're not…" he searched his mind for the right term, and all he could muster was, "friends."

"Why not?"

"That, my love, is a very long story."

"Is it a sad story?"

"Yes, I'd say it is."

"Will you tell it to me?"

"One day, when you're older."

She looked into his eyes, and somehow understood that it was time to leave this alone. She took his hand, and said, "Boy, I'm really hungry!"

He stood up, looked down at her, and marveled. He couldn't get over the way she was growing up. It was one of those rare moments that he entertained the thought that maybe there was a God after all.

DAN GIFFORD GRABBED THE PHONE after barely half a ring. He knew who it was; no one else would figure him to be in the office at 11 in the evening. "Gifford," he answered anxiously.

"It's Marcus, getting back to you on that license plate." Bobby Marcus was one of two NYPD detectives assigned to Gifford's bureau, and a close friend and confidant of the chief assistant DA. "Sorry it took so long, Dan, the computers downtown were on the fritz all day."

"Sounds just like the DA's office," Gifford gibed. "What do you have?"

"Something *really* strange."

Gifford perked up. "Yeah?"

"As you suspected, it ended up being a dead end. The license plate came up a blank."

"A blank?"

"As in classified. Computer won't give us a name and address without a special request from the captain, and even he would have to go through channels. If I take this any further, a lot of people are gonna know. You want me to?"

"Not quite yet."

"You got a plan?"

"Yeah," Gifford responded pensively. "At least my suspicions are confirmed. Something funny's going on."

"Sure, but *what*?"

Gifford had no answer.

"Sorry I couldn't be of more help."

"No, you did fine. In any case, it doesn't sound like it has anything to do with the Colombians," Gifford said.

"Maybe. You never know. You say there were two men in the car. Are you sure they were watching you?" Marcus asked with hesitation.

"All I can say is that they gave me a bad feeling. They were definitely watching someone. I assumed it was me because of Alvarez."

"Maybe you're getting paranoid in your old age. Better see that shrink of yours more often."

"Very funny." Gifford wasn't embarrassed about his relationship with Martin Rosen, not among friends, all of whom knew about his drinking problem.

"You want me to stay on this thing, look deeper?"

"How?"

"I don't know, maybe tell some friends to keep a lookout for that car. Spread the word informally that if anyone sees it to get in touch."

"Might as well. Can't hurt."

"We've already got someone watching your wife and Dan Jr. You want me to post someone on the shrink too?"

"The department's going to holler."

"Hey, you suddenly workin' for the budget office? Don't worry, a couple of guys owe me. They're giving it their own time."

Gifford contemplated for a moment. If it was anyone else, he would have said thanks, but it wasn't that way between him and Marcus. They just did things for each other; "thanks" never entered into the equation. "Yeah, okay, might as well put someone on the shrink. But discretely, I don't want to spook him."

"Just like with Stephanie, the shrink won't have a clue. Anything else?"

"No, that's about it," Gifford said.

"Feel like you could use a stiff drink about now?"

"Exactly. But I'll just have to settle for a hot bath and a bed."

"Sounds good to me."

"It'll do."

"Later then."

"Later."

Dan Gifford hung up the phone, swiveled around in his chair, and looked out the window at the night. The advantage of working in Queens was that there weren't many tall buildings, and his window gave him an unobstructed view of the downtown Manhattan skyline. On a clear night like this, it was something to see.

He took in the view, wondering. At least he hadn't been imagining things, hadn't lost his touch. He thought about Dr. Rosen and about Stephanie, asking himself if he should share any of this with them. He figured Stephanie, accustomed as she was to the pitfalls of his work, would sooner or later notice that she was being watched. It would upset her, but he would deal with that. Rosen was smart too, but not particularly schooled in these matters.

He considered the consequences of keeping this from Rosen. He hadn't held anything back yet from the shrink, regardless how embarrassing or scary. While he understood that therapy required complete, unadulterated disclosure, his honesty was more motivated by the person of Martin Rosen. There was simply something about Rosen that made Gifford comfortable. It was that very something that had helped him this past year, that very something that he feared he might jeopardize if he started keeping secrets.

As he stared out the window, Gifford also thought about the man he'd seen in Rosen's waiting room. He wasn't sure why that came to mind at this time. Most likely because it was just another thing gnawing at his psyche.

Tired, baffled and ready to call it a day, Gifford was acutely certain of only one thing: all this was definitely making him thirsty. He swiveled around to his desk, gathered his stuff, and focused his mind on the hot bath and bed that awaited. The rest he would deal with tomorrow.

chapter 11

MARTIN ROSEN SAT ON HIS bed and looked at the phone on the night table. The clock beside the phone told him it was 10:30, but he felt like it was much later. He reached for his wallet and removed the card with Cheryl Manning's phone number, picked up the receiver, dialed, listened to five rings, then hung up.

He eyed the phone again for a few seconds, lifted the receiver, and dialed a different number. There were two rings, and a woman's voice answered, "Hello."

"Hi, Esther," he said.

"Marty!" she responded. "*How are you*?"

He heard the clanging of dishes in the background and assumed she was in the kitchen, putting things away. Usually at this time of night the kids were asleep, her husband, Zev, was out at the local yeshiva, studying Talmud with his buddies, and she was tidying up. "Good," he answered, trying to sound upbeat. "What about you and yours?"

"We're all fine. Is everything okay?"

The question brought a smile to his face; his sister was always able to see through him. "Everything's all right."

"And what's with my favorite niece?"

"Your *only* niece is, what can I say, wonderful. She asks about you guys all the time."

"The girls ask for her too."

A silent moment; a reminder of how seldom they saw each other.

"So, how was Chicago?" she asked.

He knew she would do this. That's why he had avoided calling her since he'd returned. "It was okay, I suppose."

"It was hard," she said, more as a question than a statement.

"I survived." Translation: *Let's not get into it.*

"So, what's up?"

"Same old, same old. Practice is busy, book's been keeping me busy."

"Having any fun?" Translation: *Any women?*

Martin hesitated. This was the one person in the world from whom he rarely kept anything. "Some," he answered tentatively.

"Some? There's a noncommittal response."

"Okay, so I met someone. It's really nothing. We haven't even gone out yet."

"Did this happen in Chicago?"

"Well, I met someone there too, but that was… I don't even know what that was."

"So, tell me about the other one."

"I'm not sure I know what that's about either," he said.

"I have to tell you, little brother, you're confusing me. Sounds like you're avoiding the topic."

"I always thought you'd make a terrific therapist."

"Thanks for the endorsement, but I'd really like to hear about the woman."

Martin smiled. He loved the way his sister cut to the quick. "I met her briefly the other night while I was having dinner. We talked, I walked her home, that was it."

"That was it?"

"I'm not sure." Hesitation. "There was something about her…"

"You know, Marty, it has been a while," she said.

Silence.

"I just want you and Elizabeth to be happy," she added.

"I know you do."

"Maybe we can get together one Sunday? The girls really do want to get to know their cousin better."

Since Katherine's death, Esther had said this numerous times and Martin had consistently shied away. It wasn't that he doubted her sincerity, only that he didn't want to cause problems between her and her husband. Now, however, after his last conversation with Elizabeth, he wondered.

"How would Zev feel about it?" he asked.

"I know you're worried about that, but you don't have to be. Zev's mellowed some. I think he's even in favor of the idea, probably believes the exposure might bring you to do *t'shuva*."

"*T'shuva?*"

"You know, 'repent,' become Orthodox again, convert Elizabeth, the whole nine yards."

"Do *you* think that?"

"Who, *me*?" Laughter. "Come on, Marty, I know you better. But I would like to see you."

"It would be nice."

"So, let's make a date."

"Good idea. I'll call you next week."

"I look forward to it," she said.

"By the way, how are Mom and Dad?"

"The same."

"Healthy?"

"As ever. They'll probably outlive both of us."

"No doubt."

A moment of silence. There was nothing more to discuss on that front.

"Look, Marty, about this woman, it would be nice if you could give someone a chance."

"I don't think she's Jewish, Esther," he said matter-of-factly, though he'd been anxiously waiting for the right moment to inject that into the conversation. The truth was, he had no idea what religion Cheryl was, nor did it matter. He was only trying to prepare his sister and, if he looked even more deeply into his motivation, perhaps he was fishing for her approval.

"Marty," she said earnestly, "all I want is for you to be happy. I hope you believe me."

"I do."

"Good, so we'll talk soon and make plans."

"Yes, we will."

"Okay then, little brother. Take care of yourself."

"You take care too."

"Will do. And call that girl!"

"Okay. Have a good night."

"You too. Bye."

"Bye."

He hung up and, before he could catch his breath, the phone rang. He lifted the receiver, thinking it was Esther calling back. "Forget something?"

"Excuse me?" a different female voice said.

"I'm sorry, I thought you were someone else," Martin said, not knowing to whom he was speaking.

"Oh you did?" the stranger asked.

"Yes… um… who is this?"

"Someone you called earlier," she answered.

"Someone *I* called?"

"Well, whoever *you* are, your number's right here on my caller ID."

Martin suddenly figured out what was happening. "Cheryl?"

"Yes, that's me. Now, who are you?" she asked.

Martin wondered for a moment why his name didn't also appear on her caller ID, but then realized that it was probably because his home phone number was unlisted. "Marty Rosen, from the other night. Remember me?"

"Oh, the head-shrinker! Hi!"

"Hi."

"How are you?"

"Right now, a little flustered. Your call took me by surprise."

"And you probably don't like to be caught by surprise."

Martin couldn't argue with that, but he hated being figured out this early on. "Well, in this case, it was a pleasant surprise."

"I'm glad you think so."

"I had called to see if you might want to get together," Martin said.

"You mean a date?"

"I suppose that's what I had in mind."

"You haven't done this in a long time, have you?"

"How can you tell?"

"Lucky guess." She hesitated. "I'd love to," she finally said.

They made plans to meet for dinner the following evening, said their goodbyes and hung up.

Sitting on his bed, Martin stared into space, wondering what he was getting into and why he felt compelled to see this woman again. He searched his psyche for the feelings that had restrained him these past two years, the sacred images of Katherine that had marred all contenders for what he had believed would be an eternity. And in the absence of those images came the realization that there was something about this Cheryl Manning, and a voice down deep in his gut telling him it was time.

chapter 12

MARTIN ROSEN NOTICED THAT THE woman sitting in his waiting room appeared a great deal younger than he'd expected. Having the advantage of knowing her exact age, he wondered if her countenance was the result of some cosmetic surgeon's wizardry or a gift of nature. Either way, it surprised him.

"I'm Martin Rosen," he said, extending his hand.

She stood and took his hand firmly, as if meeting him was the most important thing she could possibly be doing at that moment. She was tall, and had a languid smile that betrayed some underlying distress. Her hair, auburn and wavy, was cropped a touch above shoulders, and her makeup and perfume were just subtle enough to do their job. She was quite attractive, he noted, and exquisitely attired in a navy suit that he guessed was a custom Versace or the work of some such guru.

"Martha Benoît," she responded.

Martin escorted her into his office and invited her to take a seat on the couch while he took his place in his chair.

"I want to thank you for agreeing to see me," Martha said. "I know it's unusual to meet with the spouse of a patient."

"There really is no problem. It's done fairly often these days. The strict analysts believe that meeting with a patient's family members can somehow contaminate the process, but I don't ascribe to that. So long as I have the patient's permission, I find it can sometimes be helpful."

"I'm glad you feel that way. The last thing I want is to intrude upon Jacques' privacy."

Martin detected anxiety in her tone, but didn't yet assume what it was about. There was, of course, the usual nervousness that everyone had upon meeting someone in his profession, but he suspected something more. He also sensed that Martha Benoît was a woman who didn't typically get nervous.

"Well," Martin said, "I can assure you that Jacques was wholeheartedly in agreement with our meeting. If I suspected he was feeling coerced by you, I would have declined."

Martha attempted a smile, this time more naturally.

Martin saw she was having difficulty opening up. "I understand you're an attorney," he said.

"I used to be, before I met Jacques, that is. It's been a while since I've practiced."

Martin noted that she wasn't defensive about the fact that she had stopped being a professional; on the contrary, she appeared at ease with the subject. "How long?"

She started counting in her mind, then answered, "Oh, it must be at least twenty years." There was resolution in her voice, an awareness that she couldn't defy her age in every aspect of her life.

"And how did you and Jacques meet?"

"You mean he hasn't gotten around to that?"

"We've only had two sessions. It takes a while to get to the important things," he said.

"Yes, I understand." Reflective. "Well, I was his lawyer, at least one of his lawyers. I was heading up a team working on a deal he was making with Ameresort, a U.S. company that manages vacation resorts in the Virgin Islands, Bahamas and Hawaii. Jacques was in New York, arranging some joint ventures with them, and apparently with me as well." Her eyes became watery.

"This has all been quite difficult for you," Martin said sympathetically.

She reached for the tissue box on the end table. Whenever a patient did this, Martin recalled one of Katherine's unforgettable statements about his vocation: *All you really need is a room, two chairs, and a box of tissues.* His heart sank for an instant.

"I'm sorry," she said. "I don't usually do this."

"Sorry for what? This has been a crisis for you. If it didn't bring tears, *then* I would worry."

"You're very kind. I can see why Jacques likes you."

Martin was skeptical of that last remark. He was usually able to get a quick read on a patient's feelings about him, but with Jacques Benoît, it was different. Notwithstanding the billionaire's geniality, and despite whatever impression the man may have given his wife, Martin still wasn't convinced. "I'm glad he feels that way. It certainly makes the work easier."

"Perhaps that's so, with other people. But with Jacques, I can assure you, doctor, *nothing* is easy."

"So I gather."

She reflected a moment. "He told me that he gave you permission to discuss his case freely."

Martin nodded. In most cases, he would have felt uncomfortable with so broad a release, but in this situation, there was no need to be concerned. So far, Jacques Benoît had revealed nothing.

"Well then, can you tell me how you think he's doing?" she asked.

"I could if I knew. To be honest, I'm not really sure at this point. I believe it would be more useful for you to tell me how *you* think he's doing."

"That's just it, I'm not sure either."

"I suppose that's why you wanted to see me," Martin said.

"And why you agreed," she responded.

They looked at each other in silence. "Tell me," Martin said, "is he being his usual self?"

"He's trying to be."

"So you sense something unnatural about his behavior?"

"I think so," she said. "He tries to hide things from me, but when you know a person for so many years, you begin to see him more clearly than he sees himself."

"It doesn't necessarily take years."

"So, you see it too?"

"I suspect so."

"What do you think it is?"

"I was hoping you might shed some light on that," he responded.

"I'm absolutely clueless," she said. "I have no idea what was bothering him then, and I have no idea now."

"But you did know that something *was* bothering him?"

"I suspected. I believe that our minister also noticed it. He was going to stop in on Jacques the day..." She appeared unable to finish her thought.

"The day he tried to kill himself."

She nodded, dabbing her eyes.

"What do you think of his explanation?" Martin asked.

"You mean about the business getting away from him?"

Martin nodded.

"I'm sure it's true, partly, but that's been happening for a few years and he's handled it. There has to be something else that drove him over the edge."

"I agree. It must be very difficult living with someone in such a predicament, feeling closed out and helpless."

"That's putting it mildly."

"You're angry."

"I'm... frustrated."

"Yes you are, and you're also angry."

She torpedoed him with her eyes. "Okay, so I'm angry. How does admitting that enable me to help Jacques?"

"I don't know that it does, but I do know that it's unhealthy to hide your feelings."

"Believe me, Dr. Rosen, I'm not one to hide anything. I just don't see the purpose in walking around in a huff all the time."

"Fair enough," Martin said.

She eased up a bit. "Word is, you're good at what you do."

"Well," Martin said, reflecting, "even if what you've heard is true, it may not make a difference with someone like Jacques."

"You mean, you may not be able to help him?"

"I don't know. I'm a psychologist, not a dentist."

"Pardon?"

"I don't pull teeth."

Her face offered some appreciation of the levity. "So, what do we do?"

"We keep trying."

She appeared pensive. She had known from the start that she was going to have to help bring Jacques around to face whatever it was that plagued him, only she had felt more confident that therapy would help matters along. And now, realizing she had been naive in her expectations, she felt like a fool.

"You're disappointed in my response," Martin said.

"I suppose. But it's the truth."

"You know, if I may, there's an old joke that we psychologists like to tell."

She looked at him with interest.

"It goes like this," he said. "How many shrinks does it take to change a light bulb?"

She managed a smile, waiting for his answer.

"One," he answered. "But the light bulb has to really want it."

Her smile widened a touch, but only briefly. "And you don't think Jacques wants it?"

"I'm not sure at this point what Jacques wants."

"Neither am I." She paused a moment. "Tell me, do you think he'll try to kill himself again?"

"I honestly can't say."

"So my husband is an enigma to you?"

"At this point. And it seems he's a bit of one to you as well."

"Maybe even to himself," she muttered.

"That, I don't completely buy. People don't try to kill themselves without a reason."

She kept silent.

Martin shrugged.

"Well, doctor, I thank you for your time. *And* your honesty."

Although the meeting had been short, Martin felt no reason to prolong it. "You're quite welcome. I only wish I had more to offer."

"Perhaps you will, in time." She rose from her seat.

"I do hope so," Martin said as he stood to shake her hand.

Noting the elegance with which she carried herself, he watched her depart and wondered about what she had said.

There has to be something else that drove him over the edge...

Not only were her suspicions regarding her husband's motives consistent with his own, they also told him something about the relationship the Benoîts shared.

He tries to hide things from me...

Martin walked behind his desk, sat down in his chair, leaned back and stared at the ceiling. He had never doubted that there was more going on here than Jacques Benoît had been presenting. And now, having met Martha, it was apparent that the deception was indeed deliberate.

He closed his eyes, trying to clear his mind for a few minutes before his next patient.

MARTIN ROSEN LOOKED INTO HIS daughter's eyes and found not even a hint of weariness. It was well past her bedtime, and still she appeared ready for a full day's play. It hurt him to put her to sleep at moments like this. He never seemed to have enough time with her. But it was late, and he had somewhere to be.

"Will you be home soon?" she asked, touching his face.

"Not too late, but hopefully you'll be fast asleep by then." He took her hand and kissed it. "Jamilla's downstairs. She'll be up in a few minutes to check on you."

She looked at him in silence.

"Okay, princess?" he asked.

"Okay, Daddy."

He kissed her lips, her cheek, and her forehead. Kissing her was addictive. He then tucked in her blanket. "Snug enough?"

"Yes," she answered, turning over on her side, a final sign of surrender to the inevitability of sleep.

It amazed him each time he saw the way she could transform

herself so suddenly from fully charged to absolute fatigue. It was a common behavior in children, he knew, but watching it happen was something else. He smiled widely, leaned over and kissed her again. "Goodnight."

"Goodnight, Daddy," she said, already half-unconscious.

Martin Rosen watched Cheryl Manning come through the door of the restaurant, and was hit with a sudden moment of clarity. He had been waiting at the bar about five minutes, nursing his Glenlivet, contemplating what he was getting into. And now he understood that he was exactly where he wanted to be. Their eyes connected, and he watched her move through the crowd, his jitters intensifying as she drew nearer.

"Hi," she said, offering her hand.

"Hello," he reacted, reaching out. It felt good to make contact. "I'm glad you called."

"So am I."

The room was noisy, another typical night at Millie's Place, but somehow their voices managed to resonate above the fanfare.

Dutiful bartender, Steve, appeared. "What'll it be for the lady?" he asked.

Martin looked at her. "Merlot?" he asked.

She nodded.

Martin gave the order to Steve, who seemed unable to hide his amusement.

"Good of you to remember," Cheryl said, while Steve shuffled off to prepare the drink.

Martin smiled.

"What?" she asked.

"Nothing, really."

"Oh, come now. That little smirk of yours surely means something."

"It's nothing, I assure you."

"So we're going to keep secrets?" she asked.

"I hope not."

"Then what were you thinking?"

"Okay," he said, seeming a bit embarrassed. "It's the way you speak."

Her eyes asked for clarification.

"The British thing."

"What about the *British thing*?"

He sensed himself ambushed. Her breath smelled delicious, as did whatever fragrance she was wearing, and her smile was about as dangerous as they come. "When you say certain things, like, 'Good of you to remember,' it sounds sort of… nice."

"Nice? You mean you like the *British thing*?"

"Yes, I like it." Hesitation. "I like it a lot."

"See now, that wasn't so hard, was it?" she asked.

"No."

"It was a first."

He looked at her, not quite getting her point.

"Your first compliment," she explained.

"I suppose it was."

"I hope there will be more."

"I'm sure there will be."

Steve brought her drink and the hostess came to show them to their table. Martin had requested the back room, the most private section of the restaurant. The hostess seated them, handed them menus and offered the usual salutations, though neither of them paid much attention. Their minds were fixated on each other.

"You really like this place," Cheryl said, looking around.

"I'm used to it."

"You like things that you're used to?"

"Familiarity has its benefits."

"And its disadvantages."

"Those too."

The busboy placed a basket of goodies on the table – flatbreads, mini corn, bran muffins, pumpernickel, onion rolls – and filled their glasses with ice water. Martin noticed that the fellow couldn't stop looking at Cheryl, but it didn't bother him. He figured that most of the men in the place were probably doing the same.

He opened his menu, feeling a bit anxious about the flow of things. "So, what will it be?"

"What do you suggest?" she asked, her menu still closed.

"The night we met, I had the veal Marsala, it was quite good."

"Then veal Marsala it is," she said.

"Are you usually this easy?" His better sense had already told him that she probably wasn't.

"That depends on what it is we're talking about."

"I'll bet it does."

The waiter approached, rambled through a list of specials, and took their orders.

"He didn't know you," Cheryl said, regarding the waiter.

"Not everybody does."

"But this is your place."

"He must be new."

"I'll bet, aside from this place, that a lot of people know you."

"What makes you think so?"

She pondered before answering. "I have a confession to make."

His eyes suggested she continue.

"I checked up on you."

He'd expected something like this. She knew what he did, where he worked and lived. "And what did you learn?"

"A lot, actually. It was easy. As I said, you're pretty well known. I should have recognized your name right away. I do read the *New York Times* Book Review."

"So, if you didn't recognize my name, how exactly did you find all this out?"

"A phone call."

"To whom?" He had to admit, he enjoyed the way she made him probe, and he knew she liked it too.

"Well, I used a little trickery, but I suppose it's okay."

"Trickery?"

"The state psychological society. I phoned them and told some very nice, chatty old lady that I was looking for a psychologist and had received your name from my doctor. I was calling to make sure you were legit. Without even looking you up, she just started laughing and said, 'Oh, Dr. Rosen is quite renowned,' and all that. I thanked her. She wished me well in therapy."

Martin was impressed and somewhat uneasy.

"You're upset?" she asked.

"I wouldn't go as far to say that I'm *upset*, but you could have asked *me*."

"You're right, I should have. It was a violation of your privacy, I'm sorry."

"It's okay," he said, his tone softening. "It's public information anyway, and I suppose a single woman in New York these days has to take every precaution."

"It's no excuse, but thanks for understanding."

Silence.

"So, how does it feel to be a best-selling author?" she asked.

"That would take an entire night and then some to describe."

"I'm not going anywhere, are you?"

I suppose not, he mused, sipping what remained of his Scotch.

She listened attentively as he complained about the grind, the speaking engagements, signings, et cetera. With the exception of his recent gig in Chicago, he had managed to keep it all local so he could be home with Elizabeth. And of course, there was his practice, his concern that the time and energy demanded by his celebrity was detracting from the quality of his work with patients.

"You're very dedicated," she observed.

"I try to do a decent job."

"Do you enjoy it?"

"Sometimes. Now, what about you?"

"What about me?"

"Do you like working in PR?"

"Sometimes."

He smiled.

"It's very competitive," she said. "Stressful, and hard for a woman to get ahead. I guess it's like everything else."

"I'll bet you do okay for yourself."

"I work hard."

"Any interesting accounts?"

"Not really. A few household appliance companies, charitable organizations and things like that."

"I've read that your firm does a lot of work for the Israeli government."

"Yes," she responded. "Jacob Lipton, as you know, is a Holocaust survivor, and quite committed to helping Israel. They do seem to need good PR these days, but I'm not involved in any of that."

He detected a slight tension in her voice. "Everything okay?"

"Yes," she said. "I just get a little uptight when I think about work. It really is a pressure cooker, you know?"

"Household appliances and charitable organizations?"

"You would be surprised. In PR, everything is high stress."

Martin left it alone. The last thing he wanted was to make her uncomfortable.

The waiter brought their entrees.

Dan Gifford sipped his decaf, marveling at how the world was changing. Sitting in Starbucks on Austin Street in the heart of Queens, adjacent to the new Barnes & Noble superstore, watching the people, he appreciated the recent innovation of cafes in bookstores and wondered what was coming next. He also wondered where Bobby Marcus was. The cop was already twenty minutes late for their meeting.

A young woman smiled at him from another table. She was definitely cute, and in his previous life, he would have managed all the right moves. But these were sober days, demanding what Dr. Rosen had coined "sober behavior." This girl would be easy, like a drink. Getting his wife and kid back was another story. He smiled politely and turned toward the door as Bobby Marcus entered.

Marcus approached him. "Sorry I'm late. Got caught in an argument with the captain about spending too much time chasing ghosts for what he thinks is your paranoia."

Gifford ignored the gibe. Tension between the cops and the DA was an old story. "Got anything yet?"

"Still nothing."

"Yeah, well, you can stop chasing down the car, make the captain happy. I have another idea, a little dangerous, but a shortcut to what we need."

"I'm listening."

"Know anyone in the Nassau County PD?"

"Maybe."

Cheryl took Martin's arm as they left the restaurant and began strolling down Middle Neck Road. It was another balmy September night.

As they approached her building, she turned to him and touched his cheek. "Thank you for a wonderful evening."

"Thank *you*," he responded.

He wasn't disappointed about not being invited up to her place; he was quite content leaving the evening exactly where it was. He was pretty sure that his desire for her was mutual, but he guessed that she too would just as soon save it for another time. "I hope we do this again," he said.

"So do I," she replied.

Realizing how badly he wanted to kiss her, he inched his head closer, his movements ordained by a force beyond his control. He softly touched his lips to hers and felt her bring her arms around him. And as his mouth opened, allowing their tongues to meet, he found himself being drawn to a place from which he knew there was no turning back.

It lasted less than a minute, though it seemed much longer, and in the end, he had to force himself to call it a night. Again, he watched her walk away into the building before he turned and went on his way. But this time, he left with neither wonderment nor confusion. He was at last certain in one thing: he could live again.

chapter 14

MARTIN ROSEN HELD HIS HANDS comfortably around the grip, bringing the golf club back with a slow, smooth motion, then swung forward, releasing his strength as he struck through the ball, twisted around, and carried the club up toward the heavens. He lifted his head at just the right moment to observe the trajectory of his shot, and smiled at what he saw.

"She's coming back," Ashok Reddy said, standing behind him.

"Sure is," Martin said, seeing how the ball, which initially appeared to be going too far to the right, was turning back in toward the middle of the fairway before landing. It was what golfers called a "draw," a very delicate shot requiring a precise amount of spin applied at the moment of impact by a slight shift in one's wrist motion. Too much spin and the ball would have drifted further left into a "hook." Too little spin and the ball would have continued on a straight path to the right, probably into the rough, the woods or another fairway. Many a golfer could spend a lifetime developing a consistent draw, but Martin was a natural. From the first time he had stood on the tee box, about four years back, he had been hitting his drives this way. And still, no matter how often he succeeded, it never ceased to amaze him.

"Feels good?" Reddy asked.

"Always."

"Looks about 260," Reddy said, referring to the distance in yards.

"I'll take it."

"Who wouldn't?"

They were on the first hole, playing with two other golfers in their regular Wednesday morning game. The four of them were all friends, and they always played for money to make things more challenging. One of the men, Thomas Ahn, a Korean who lived next door to Martin, was an orthopedic surgeon at the hospital. The other, Vic Stern, was a stogie-smoking lawyer who specialized in suing doctors for malpractice. Stern always took a bit of a verbal beating from his buddies, but he was able to handle himself. His golf game, he thanked God, in no way reflected his performance in court; in court, he usually won.

Stern took a draw on his Dominican, placed it on the ground and stepped up to the tee.

"You know, it's dangerous to do that," Thomas Ahn said.

"To do what?" Stern snapped. He was always a bit on edge before his first shot of the day.

"To put your cigar on the ground that way," Ahn answered. "You can get E. coli."

"*E. coli?*" Stern responded.

Reddy joined in. "Yeah, from the goose shit in the grass."

Stern: "What goose shit?"

Ahn: "The goose shit from the geese."

Stern: "I don't see any goose shit! All I see is grass."

Reddy: "And how do you think the grass grows?"

Stern: "What about you, Marty? You think I'm gonna get E. coli?"

Martin smiled, enjoying the banter. "Anything's possible," he said. "But look on the bright side, it's a quicker death than cancer."

Stern: "Now it's *cancer*?"

The others laughed. It had been Stern's contention that cigars didn't cause cancer, and he was able to make his arguments sound halfway credible. Right now, however, that was the last thing on his mind. "Okay guys," he said, "if you can keep your traps shut for a few seconds, I'm gonna show Marty how to hit a ball."

He bent down, teed up his ball and looked out at the fairway. Then he took his stance, swung, and let loose with a terrible slice, sending the ball so far to the right, he'd be lucky to find it.

The other two took their shots, both decent and playable, but nothing within thirty yards of Martin. He was still beaming as he got in the cart with Reddy. The psychiatrist patted him on the back and said, "This might be your day if you keep it up."

"That's a big if," Martin responded.

He ended up taking the hole with a par, one better than Reddy and Ahn, both of whom bogeyed with a five. Stern double-bogeyed after a penalty for his lost drive.

"Not a bad start, $6 richer," Reddy said as they rode to the second tee.

"Profitable game," Martin replied.

"You seem different today," Reddy said.

"How so?"

"I'm not sure, and I hope you don't take this the wrong way, but you seem… happy."

Martin appreciated the observation. Reddy was an insightful man, not just because he was a psychiatrist, but because he was a sensitive human being, something Martin had appreciated from the first time they'd met four years earlier. Their bond was strengthened by the fact that Katherine and Reddy's wife, Savitri, had become best friends during the brief two years they had known each other.

"Do I?" Martin asked, trying to give his friend a hard time.

"Yes, you do."

Martin smiled.

"Is there something I should know about?" Reddy asked.

"Possibly."

"And what might that be?"

"A lady."

Reddy was stunned, it was the last thing he'd expected to hear.

"How long have you been keeping this?"

"Haven't been keeping it. Just met her a week ago. I've seen her twice, the night we met, and last night for dinner."

"Twice in one week," Reddy said. "That sounds like a record for you."

Martin hit his friend in the arm.

"I'm just saying that you have been…"

"I know, Ashok, I know how I've been."

Reddy reflected a moment. "Do you like her?"

"I think so."

"What is her name?"

"Cheryl, Cheryl Manning. And before you ask your next question, she's English, lives in town, and works in public relations for Jacob Lipton."

"*The* Jacob Lipton?"

"Yep."

"So when do Savitri and I get to meet her?"

"You know, you sound like you're my father."

"Well, I've been meaning to tell you, Marty, I think of you like a son."

Martin responded with another hit in the arm.

"If you keep doing that, it will ruin my golf game," Reddy said.

"Trust me, Ashok, it's already ruined."

They shared a laugh. There was a short wait at the second tee, as the foursome in front of them was moving slowly. They stayed in the cart. Martin put his head back and closed his eyes, trying to catch a moment of sun. It was a resplendent day, blue sky, mid-70s, but it was September, and how many more such days were in store before the winter was anyone's guess.

"You will bring her by though?" Reddy asked.

"When the time is right."

"Good then, I will tell Savitri to expect you next…"

"I'll let you know!"

Reddy took the hint and changed the subject. "By the way, how is our patient, Benoît, doing?"

The question posed a conflict for Martin. True, Reddy was the referring psychiatrist, but that did not necessarily entitle him to information. The ethical and legal requirements for exchange of information about patients to *anyone* required consent, preferably written. In this case, however, there wasn't anything to tell beyond what Reddy had known when he'd made the referral. "The same," Martin said.

"I would have guessed as much," Reddy responded. "He is going to be a tough one to figure out."

Martin nodded.

"That's why I sent him your way, Marty. You are the miracle worker, and if you cannot untangle this, nobody can."

Martin chuckled, though Reddy's flattery left him uneasy. He hadn't been feeling great about his therapeutic skills these past few days. On the contrary, he believed his patients were being shortchanged, neglected for his own preoccupations. He had committed himself to change that, and was planning to discuss the issue with Reddy. This wasn't the best time but, considering their schedules, it was as good as any. "You know, I've been meaning to talk to you about the 'miracle worker' thing," he said.

Reddy appeared curious.

"It's just," Martin continued, faltering, "I don't feel like I've been into it recently."

"You mean you have been distracted?"

"I guess you could put it that way."

"This woman?"

"And other things."

"What other things?"

"Life, I suppose."

Reddy looked empathic.

"There was another woman recently," Martin continued, "in Chicago." He searched for Reddy's reaction, but the man was not surprised. "It was, how should I put it, confusing. My head was a mess."

"Women can do that."

"Not like this. I swear, Ashok, I was ready to check myself in someplace."

"Hey *guys,*" Vic Stern interrupted. "Cut the yapping, it's time to hit."

Reddy looked at Martin. "To be continued."

The four men hit their drives. This time, Martin pushed his ball too far to the right, landing in a fairway bunker. It would be hard for him to recover. Reddy clocked one straight down the middle of the fairway, a good 250 yards. Stern and Ahn also hit respectable shots, though not as far as Reddy's.

Back in the cart, Reddy resumed the conversation. "It seems this woman may be getting to your golf game."

Martin smirked. "Nothing gets to my golf game, Ashok."

"If you could say the same about your professional life, everything would be all right."

Martin felt chastised but not angry. He deserved the comment, he could even have predicted it, and he wondered if it was perhaps what he needed. "You're probably right," he replied.

"I am right."

They approached Martin's ball, but the foursome in front of them was once again too close to hit.

"Look, Marty," Reddy continued, "I know it is difficult listening to people's problems all day, especially when you have a few of your own. I don't have any words of wisdom for you, except to say that you carry a lot of guilt and anguish in your heart. I am not one to judge whether that is right or wrong, and God knows how I would be in your situation. All I know is that you are a talented psychologist. If you are slipping, it's no tragedy, so long as you know it and do something about it."

"And what am I supposed to do about it?"

"*That* I do not have the answer to, but somehow *you* have to figure it out. Who knows, maybe your psyche is telling you that it is tired of all the pain it has endured, that it wants to move forward, while another part of you refuses to do so? Maybe it is time to allow yourself to heal?" Reddy stopped himself, seeming unsure whether he was overstepping his boundaries.

Martin looked at his friend warmly. The words, neither eye-popping nor disturbing, were the truth, pure and simple. He had known all this, but hearing it from someone he respected seemed to put it into perspective. And perhaps, he admitted to himself, he had just needed someone to talk to. "It's okay, Ashok. I appreciate it," he said, squeezing Reddy's shoulder.

"Good, now hit the ball."

Martin got out of the cart. "What's the distance to the hole?"

"At least 230. Ever hit a three-wood out of a sand trap?"

"A wood in a trap?" Martin asked.

"I have seen pros do it."

"Then I guess I'll have to be a pro."

"You can always play it safe and hit an iron, but then you will be out of the hole," Reddy said with a grin.

"No, I'll go with the wood."

Reddy chuckled. It was a risky play at best.

Martin stepped into the sand and dug his shoes in a little for stability. The lie of the ball wasn't all that bad, he told himself, the right swing, and he could do it. He took a deep breath, took the club back and smacked the ball with all he had. He saw that he had hit it "clean," just as he'd intended. But out of the sand, it was anyone's guess where it might fly. He lifted his head and watched with glee as it landed right on the edge of the green.

Reddy applauded, as did Ahn and Stern from the other side of the fairway. "It often amazes me what a person can do," Reddy said, "if he puts his mind to it."

chapter 15

DAN GIFFORD FELT UNEASY ABOUT having canceled his appointment with Martin Rosen. Despite the demands of his job, he had always kept his therapy sacrosanct. Now, with his suspicions about the men in the Mercedes growing, he was determined to get some answers, and the only way to do so required he be somewhere other than the doctor's office at that particular time.

Bobby Marcus had reported to him that police surveillance of Rosen had been uneventful. For the past week, there were no cars seen outside Rosen's office, nor anyone following the psychologist. This only compounded Gifford's resolve. Although it was unlikely that a pair of Colombian hit men would be driving around in a vehicle with classified license plates, Gifford couldn't afford to dismiss the possibility altogether. There was little, if anything, that couldn't be arranged by paying the proper people. And if the men in the car were Colombians, they might have allowed themselves to be seen as a warning, to scare him into botching the case. On the other hand, they could have just been watching and waiting for the right time to take him out, and had gotten a bit sloppy with their camouflage. Whoever they were and whatever they wanted, Gifford intended to find out now.

It was Monday morning, 8 a.m., the time he usually left Rosen's office. It was a reach, he knew, but he figured that this was just about the best opportunity for them to get at him, since it was a steady appointment and the bad guys knew he would be alone. The rest of his schedule was not nearly as predictable.

He and Bobby Marcus sat in his car. He looked over at Marcus and smiled as the black Mercedes pulled into the exact same spot it had been in a week ago. "Well, well, what do we have here?" he said.

"Looks like you were right," Marcus responded.

Gifford looked at his watch for the umpteenth time. "That Nassau County guy is late."

"Hey, it's a favor."

Just then, someone walked up beside Marcus' window and stuck his head in. "Anthony Marcus, it's been a while," the stranger said.

"Sure has," Marcus said, reaching to shake the man's hand. "Mike Calderone, meet Assistant DA Dan Gifford."

Gifford shook hands with the Nassau County detective, noting the firm grip. Calderone was tall, dark-haired, green-eyed, had a soft looking face and was impeccably attired, looking more like a lawyer than a cop.

"So, what's up?" Calderone asked.

"It's like I told you on the phone, Mike. Suspects are sitting across the street now, as we anticipated, in a black Benz, twelve cars up. We just want to roust them a little, find out what they're up to. It's your turf, so I figured…"

"Yeah, you figured I got nothin' to do with my time out here in the burbs, so I might as well volunteer for some part-time interdepartmental liaison duty."

"Sort of," Marcus replied.

"Look, detective," Gifford jumped in, trying to sound official even though this whole operation was anything but, "it was our hope that *you* would do the rousting, this being your beat."

"Don't sweat it, counselor. Anthony and I go back some. He

got me out of a little jam in your wonderful county a few years ago, said he might come calling, and here he is. So let's just do it and get it done with."

Marcus looked at Gifford. Gifford nodded and Marcus got out of the car. "Be back in a few," Marcus said.

"Careful," Gifford said.

"Always am."

The two cops crossed the street and slowly approached the Mercedes from behind.

"Good day, gentleman," Calderone said as he looked in the driver's side window of the Mercedes.

Marcus made his presence known on the other side of the car, watching both men, his hand glued to his gun, still holstered under his jacket.

The men in the car looked at each other but made no move to resist.

Calderone flashed his badge. "Could you please step out of the car?"

"What's this about, officer?" the man in the driver's seat asked.

Marcus immediately recognized the accent as Middle Eastern. His curiosity swelled.

"Just step out of the car, please," Calderone said.

The driver looked at his partner again, nodded, and the two slowly exited the car. Marcus noticed immediately that both of them were packing guns under their jackets.

The driver stood nose to nose with Calderone. "I demand to know what this is about!"

"May I see some ID?" Calderone asked.

"I think you ought to tell us what this is for," the man who had been in the passenger seat said, sounding somewhat calmer than his partner.

"Look, buddy," Calderone snapped, "I don't know where you're from, don't much care either, but in *this* country, when a police officer asks you for something, you cooperate." He knew what he was saying wasn't completely true but figured a bunch of foreigners wouldn't know any better.

The men looked at each other silently, neither reaching for his wallet.

"ID please," Calderone repeated.

"I want to know what this is about," the driver repeated, his tone suggesting that he wasn't going to be intimidated.

"Okay, that's it," Calderone said, putting his hands on the driver, turning him around, placing him up against the car and spreading his legs.

Marcus didn't like where this was going, but he followed Calderone's lead and did the same thing with the passenger. It seemed to him that, while these strangers were submissive for the moment, they were more than capable of resisting had they been so inclined.

"What do we have here?" Calderone asked, lifting a Beretta from under the driver's jacket.

Marcus found a similar weapon on his man.

"We have permits for those," the driver said.

"I'll bet you do," Calderone said. "Let's see 'em." He smiled at Marcus, they were about to find out who these guys were.

The passenger glanced at his partner, then reluctantly reached in his pocket for his wallet, pulled out his permit and handed it to Marcus. The driver did the same with Calderone.

Marcus and Calderone examined the permits. "These are diplomatic, Israeli Consulate, interesting," Calderone said. "And what brings the Israeli Consulate out to this neck of the woods?"

Marcus was growing uneasy with Calderone's approach. These guys were obviously professionals, probably a lot more dangerous than Calderone was assuming.

"I demand to know why you are harassing us," the driver said. He turned around to face Calderone and Marcus. "What you are doing here is illegal, and a violation of our diplomatic immunity."

"Well I'm more concerned with what *you're* doing here," Calderone said.

"I appreciate that," the passenger said, again sounding more measured than his partner. "But as my colleague stated, we are protected under diplomatic immunity from answering your questions. Surely you don't want to start an international incident."

"That is correct," Marcus interjected. "The last thing any of us needs is an incident. I'm sure you gentlemen have a perfectly reasonable explanation for your presence here, one that will satisfy us so that we don't have to take this further."

"Yes, officer, we do," the passenger responded. "But I believe that we should have an explanation as to the reason for this treatment."

Marcus looked at Calderone, who held up his hands as if to say, *it's your call.* "Okay," he said, "we've received some complaints of loitering from people who live in these buildings. The description of the vehicle and suspects fits the two of you." It was pretty lame, he knew, but it was the best he could do. He looked at the passenger. It was quid pro quo time.

"Well, you see," the passenger said, appearing embarrassed, "it is rather awkward, and we hope you will be discrete."

Marcus nodded. Calderone remained stone-faced.

"We are attached," the man said, "to a certain senior Israeli diplomat who is presently enjoying the company of a young lady who lives in that building. We accompany him wherever he goes, and he comes here a few times a week. He is a very important man in our country, married, with several children, so you can understand our difficulty."

Marcus understood that he was getting just about as good as he gave. He would learn nothing else from these two. He handed back the permit and gun, and Calderone followed suit.

"We are sorry if we were, what you call, loitering. We will try to be more inconspicuous," the passenger said.

"Yeah, I'm sure you will," Calderone said.

"Is that all, officers?" the driver asked.

Marcus looked at Calderone, indicating that they'd stalemated. It was time to go. "Okay, gentlemen," he said, "sorry for the trouble."

When the two cops were far enough away, the driver turned to the passenger. "What the hell was that about?"

"Good question. I'm not sure."

"Well, we are going to have to find out."

In the distance, through the rearview mirror, the driver watched Marcus shake hands with Calderone, then get into a car in which a third man was waiting, while Calderone got into another car. It all appeared very curious. The car with Marcus and the third man pulled out and started down the street, and as it passed, the driver committed the license plate to memory. "Yes, that we will do."

Gifford was completely bewildered. "What are two Israelis with guns and diplomatic status doing hanging around outside of Rosen's building?"

"You don't buy the bit about a diplomat banging some broad?" Marcus asked.

"Not much, what about you?"

"Ditto. And I bet they didn't buy our explanation any more than we bought theirs."

"What did Calderone think?"

"Who knows, he's hard to read. He seemed to enjoy himself a bit too much, but in the end, he was simply repaying a favor, did his part and went home. Probably doesn't want me to call anytime soon."

"What's his story?"

"Referring to what?"

"The favor he owed," Gifford said.

"Just got him out of a jam once, that's it," Marcus responded curtly.

"What kind of jam?"

"You really want to know?"

"Sure. The lives of cops interest me."

Marcus appeared lost in thought for a moment.

Gifford knew that Calderone's problem had no relevance to anything concerning him, but what Marcus had once done for Calderone was another matter. Cops usually helped each other, it was part of the job, even when that help stretched the bounds of the law, and Gifford was curious to see just how far Bobby Marcus would go.

"It was about five years ago," Marcus began. "Remember when our esteemed mayor wanted to improve the quality of life in this great city by ridding the streets of drugs and prostitution?"

"Last I heard, he's still working on that." Gifford's voice was neutral. His opinions on the mayor were mixed, but he knew that the rank and file of the police department despised the guy.

"Yeah, well, he and the PC came up with this terrific idea: raid the brothels, massage parlors, juice bars; arrest everyone, johns, pros, pimps, you name it; sort it all out later."

"Sounds like a plan."

"Anyway, one night I'm in the 109th on graveyard and two wagons are on their way in with a bunch of pros and johns from a local rub joint. Word's out, one of the perps is a Nassau County dick. Remember, the order was to arrest *everyone*, no exceptions. And a sergeant and a lieutenant are present on the scene to make sure it all goes according to Hoyle."

Gifford already knew where this was heading.

"So I hear what went down," Marcus continued. "The guys inside are burned up that a cop's being brought in on a rap like this. I'm the ranking officer inside, so they come to me. Frankly, I thought it stunk too. I go downstairs and catch the wagon as it pulls in, see what I can do before the guy goes through the system. The lieutenant, who will remain unnamed, is a poker buddy of mine. The Nassau dick is trying to be cool, but underneath I could tell he's scared shitless. He's got a wife, three kids, ten years in, and he's about to lose it all for a hand job. Long and short of it is, I get him lost before the fingerprinting. I'm saving the details for my book."

"Proud of yourself?"

"I did what I had to do."

"What about the other johns?"

"Hey, it sucked for them too, but I can't help everybody."

Gifford sort of understood, it was the thin blue line. He let it drop. "So, what do we do about these Israelis?"

Marcus shrugged. "It's your call," he said.

Gifford realized that to anyone else, Marcus would have recommended leaving it alone. It was unlikely that the Israelis had anything to do with the Colombians or Gifford's trial, and nobody, as far as *they* were concerned, was in danger. So basically, it was none of their business. But Gifford was a bulldog. Once he had his teeth into something, he had trouble letting go. "I just can't help wondering what they're up to."

"I was afraid you'd say that."

chapter 16

MARTIN ROSEN SAT IN HIS chair and made himself comfortable. "So, how are you doing today?" he asked.

"Quite all right, I must say," Benoît replied, his face once again full of cheer.

Martin was growing accustomed to Benoît's exhilarated starts. "That's good," he said. "It's always nice to see a patient feeling well." Translation: *Nice, but a waste of my time.*

"Yes, I am so far removed from the way I was, it is hard to believe I could ever have acted that way."

"I can see that. I find it hard to imagine as well. That's what makes me so curious about it."

"Curious?"

"It sounds like you're feeling that there is a part of yourself that confuses you."

"Yes," Benoît said, appearing contemplative. "That is true, to a point. The more I think about it, though, the closer I come to understanding it."

"And what have you figured out?"

"Well, I believe it has something to do with my past," Benoît said. He hesitated for a moment, as if gauging Martin's reaction.

Martin perked up but remained silent.

"Have I told you yet what I did during the war?" Benoît asked.

"No. In fact, you really haven't divulged much about your past."

"Yes, I suppose I haven't."

"Well, what *did* you do in the war?" It was unlike Martin to press like this. Usually, he allowed his patients as much leeway as they needed in broaching delicate material. But with Benoît, he was growing impatient, eager for something to sink his teeth into.

"I was a partisan, fighting underground against the Nazis and their puppets in the Vichy government. I was a captain. Most of the men in my command were people I had grown up with in Lyon. Several were friends. And most of them died.

"I was an only child. My parents were innkeepers, who also died during the war. When France was finally liberated, after years of being underground, I decided to leave for the Caribbean. I had some money that my parents had left me, so I built a small inn on Guadeloupe. I was alone with nothing. Everything and everyone was gone, but *I* survived. It took some time but eventually I prospered. After a while, I married, had a son, and began investing my money in other hotels throughout the Caribbean. I eventually returned to France, but never for more than a few weeks. The memories were just too painful.

"I suppose it was my intention to become so strong and powerful that no one could ever take anything away from me again. I expanded to the south of France, Hawaii, the Fiji Islands, the Greek Islands, and in time I became the proprietor of the world's largest resort conglomerate. Then I brought the company public, thinking it was a good idea at the time, which it was, financially speaking. What I hadn't anticipated were the stockholders, officers and boards. Instead of feeling safe and in control of what was *mine*, I began to worry about my ability to hold on to it. I became poisoned by the fear of losing control. I don't know if you understand how this feels."

"I don't," Martin admitted.

"I thought I was handling the situation, but as time went on, the illusion faded. I was growing old and circumstances were forcing me to let go of it all. You see, it was never about the money, it was about the *control.* If I lose that, I lose everything. And I swore years ago that I would never let that happen again."

Martin found this interesting. Details about the billionaire's life had always been scant in the media, the obvious result of Benoît's staunch avoidance of publicity. The connections Benoît was drawing to his past losses also seemed a nice start, though Martin felt they were a bit too cut-and-dried. There had to be more to explain a suicide attempt. He wasn't sure exactly what. Perhaps an event from Benoît's childhood made the blow of losing his family even more disastrous, or maybe something else, occurring later in life made the issue of control so crucial to Benoît's existence. Whatever, Martin knew it had to be there.

"It seems you have been thinking a great deal about all this," Martin said.

"Yes, I have." Somber.

"Tell me about your first wife."

"What is there to tell?" He shrugged his shoulders as if the subject was uninteresting.

"I'd like to know about the relationship, how it began, how long it lasted, how it ended, those sort of things."

Benoît complied and proceeded with the story. The woman's name was Janette, and they had met about a year after the war while she and her family were visiting Guadeloupe. She was originally from Paris and had been staying at his inn. Her father was a successful furrier. In fact, he became one of Jacques' first investors. They fell in love instantly, a different love than he had with Martha, more "juvenile, even fanciful," as he now put it, "but no deeper." They married within three months, had their son a year later, and got along "fabulously." They had "many wonderful years together." Everything was "perfect," until the cancer.

Martin listened attentively. Benoît went on for close to twenty minutes describing yet another loss.

"How did you feel when she died?" Martin asked.

"Relieved," Benoît answered in a snap. He looked at Martin. "She suffered a great deal, for a very long time. Her pain was unbearable, for her, myself and our son. In the end, she wanted to die." He stopped himself as soon as his voice became tremulous.

"It is an upsetting topic for you."

"Yes, quite."

Martin waited for more.

"I do not know what else to say about it."

"Do you still think about her?"

"From time to time. She was… very special."

Benoît's words struck a chord for Martin, as an image of Katherine flashed through his mind. "I'm sure she was," he said.

Benoît was silent, his expression mournful.

"Where is your son?"

"In Corfu, running one of my resorts, when he's not chasing women."

"Do I detect a note of disappointment?"

"No, not really. It would just be nice if he settled down, I suppose."

"Would you prefer to see more of him?"

"Well, I do see him quite often. I travel frequently."

A moment of silence.

"Well, have I got your mind spinning?" Benoît asked.

"Not exactly spinning, but… working."

"Good then, I like a man who earns his keep."

Martin smiled and noted that there were only a few minutes remaining to the session.

Benoît removed a pre-written check from his wallet and handed it to Martin. "By the way," he said, his mood seeming to lift, "do you trade on the stock market?"

Martin reacted impassively. He wasn't sure what was coming. He stood up and walked toward his desk. "Why do you ask?"

"I was just wondering."

Martin knew there was more to this but didn't see the harm in responding. "I dabble," he said.

"Do you know anything about technology companies?"

"Some."

Benoît offered an awkward smile. "I do not know if this is… inappropriate, as you Americans like to say, but if you are interested, I have a promising tip."

"A tip?"

"I am sure you have heard those nasty rumors about how the wealthy get all the information, access to initial public offerings and all that."

Martin nodded. He was beginning to feel uneasy.

"Well, they are not just rumors," Benoît said.

Martin realized what Benoît was about to do, but still didn't understand what it signified. "I imagine they're not," he responded.

"Anyway, I know there must be another patient waiting. I just wanted to thank you for the help you are providing me. It is really first-rate and this meager check, well, it just does not seem quite enough."

"Would you like me to raise my fee?" Martin joked.

Benoît smiled. "No, of course not. But I do enjoy helping friends out now and then."

"And how do you do that?"

"Gamatron."

"Pardon?" Martin said.

"Gamatron Technologies. It is a small software company based in North Carolina, outside the Raleigh-Durham area. Have you heard of it?"

"No."

"Neither have most people. It is a small company that trades on the NASDAQ for about a dollar and a half, and has not moved much during the past year. The big secret is that Gamatron has recently created a group of business- and home-software applications that are more user-friendly than Microsoft's products, and because of this, they are about to be taken over by LMI. The news is going to be released in two days and the stock should probably soar."

Martin had certainly heard of LMI, Lamark Media International, one of the largest communications companies in the world. He had no doubt as to the veracity of Benoît's information nor the accuracy of the man's calculations. "Jacques, I appreciate your intentions in this, but it would be highly unprofessional, maybe even illegal, for me to act on this information in any way..."

"And you would prefer I leave these tidbits of information outside of this room," Benoît added.

"No, you should feel free to say whatever you like in this room. I just need to tell you that my fee is all I expect. No favors, no bonuses, no gifts." Martin tried not to sound admonishing. He didn't want Benoît to feel rejected, but the ground rules were essential, even if it meant passing up an opportunity to make some quick money.

"Yes, you are absolutely right. It was silly of me to even mention such a thing. It is just that, well, someone *could* make a lot of money with such information, and…"

"I'm sure someone could. But under the circumstances, that someone can't be me."

"I understand. I am sorry if I made you uncomfortable."

"No problem. It comes with the territory." Martin glanced at his watch, signaling that their time was up. "We can discuss it further next session," he added.

"It will not be necessary. I am sure we can find something more pleasant to talk about."

Martin was struck by the implication of the word "pleasant," fearing that his patient had found this little interlude anything but. He made a mental note to revisit this issue in the future, clear the air, so to speak. The two men said their goodbyes and scheduled to meet again next week.

After Benoît left, Martin sat for a short while before ushering in his next patient. He usually left time between sessions to think, catch his breath, take a bathroom break, whatever. This time, he stared out the window, reviewing the revelations from his visit with Benoît, contemplating the amount of loss the man had endured, wondering what other vulnerabilities lay beneath the billionaire's veneer. And imagining just how much money he could have made.

Jacques Benoît came out of the building and noticed that the two men in the black Mercedes were no longer in sight. He had spotted them his previous time leaving Dr. Rosen's office and had been surprised that he had missed them on his first visit, though he had no doubt they'd been there. They were always somewhere.

He entered his limousine. Last week, they didn't even follow, though he guessed that someone else had been assigned that task.

These two had been sitting on the doctor's office. Who knew, maybe they were even wiretapping the place, trying to get a sense of the shrink, probably seeing if they could enlist Rosen in the cause of his demise.

What they did, however, no longer seemed to be of consequence to him. On the contrary, it only strengthened his resolve. With each passing day, he was more convinced that his suicide attempt had been a desperate and foolish act. At the time, he had been afraid that they were on to him. But now he was certain they were only fishing. If they had anything concrete, they would already have taken him.

He thought about his suicide attempt, and loathed himself for such an aberrant sign of weakness. He had tried likening himself to a brave soldier, ingesting cyanide rather than being captured by the enemy, but in his heart he knew that the analogy was weak. He had simply been afraid of being discovered and shamed in front of his family and the world. There was nothing about it that was brave.

In any event, his fears were now behind him. He was no longer preoccupied with his hunters. He could almost laugh at the great lengths they went through to track him, as if he were some master spy, ready to elude them at the first opportunity. In truth, however, his movements were rather predictable and he was simply too old to run. If they were looking for something, they weren't going to find it.

Now all that mattered to him was his own plan, the first step of which he had just taken. Dr. Rosen had been put to the test and, so far, was displaying unshakable integrity. But Benoît would yet see how far this extended. He had examined Rosen's financial records and had found that, between Katherine Rosen's life insurance and the recent best-selling book, there was a good liquid $300,000. The information he had given Rosen could easily turn that into a million overnight. Who in his right mind could resist?

Of course, the doctor had declined, but this meant nothing. Jacques Benoît knew that men seldom did as they said. He would wait and see if the doctor actually used the information, and if his guess was right, everything would soon fall into place.

chapter 17

STEPHANIE GIFFORD RUMMAGED FRANTICALLY through the front-hall closet. It was 8:35 in the morning and her son had insisted she find his Yankees cap for him to wear to school. The Yankees were having another great year, and Dan Jr. was among their staunchest fans. For the past month, regardless of the weather, the 6-year-old donned the navy-blue jacket and hat his father had gotten him at an early summer game. "It's not here and you're going to miss your bus," she said to her son.

"But Ma, I can't go without it," Dan Jr. responded, his eyes about to tear.

She rubbed the back of his head. "We'll ask your father, he'll get you a new one."

"But I had it yesterday."

"Well, where did you put it?"

He shrugged his shoulders.

She knew how this was going to play out. They would search until they found the cap, he would miss the bus and she would have to drive him to school, winding up late for her own job. Since her separation from his father, she'd found it more and more difficult to say no to him. It was that guilt thing, trying every which way to keep him happy under the circumstances.

She also realized that his attachment to the baseball cap was his way of staying connected to his father. Even though Dan Sr. hadn't spent much time at home before the separation, at least the boy knew that his father had been sleeping in the house. Now, with Gifford's upcoming drug trial, father and son were seeing each other once a week at best.

"You sure you didn't leave it at a friend's?" she asked.

"I'm sure."

She stuck her head back in the closet. "Why don't you go check upstairs?"

He looked at her, as if to say, *That's a dumb idea, we already looked there.*

"Please go up and check again."

Without answering, he begrudgingly started toward the stairs.

Just like his father, she thought.

"Wait a minute," she said, "I know where it is." She grabbed her keychain and ran out to her car. As she exited the house, she saw the school bus pull away from the end of the block, and released a frustrated groan.

A minute later, she came back into the house with the hat in her hand. "You fell asleep on the way home from the pizza place last night and I carried you in. The hat must've fallen off in the car."

He took the hat and put it on his head. "Thanks, Mom."

"You're welcome." She couldn't help but just love him in that cap. She looked at her watch. "Come, I'll drive you to school."

The two of them got into the car and she pulled out of the driveway. As she turned the corner from her street onto the main road, she noticed through the rearview mirror an unfamiliar car coming out of her street and turning in the same direction. This was strange to her, considering that she lived on a dead end and knew all her neighbors' cars, none of which resembled this brown sedan. She drove about a half-mile and turned another corner. A few other cars were now behind her, and she was about to discard her paranoia when she saw the sedan again, three cars back.

She stepped on the gas and made a sharp right.

"Ma, what're you doing? School's the other way!"

"I know, honey," she said with feigned calmness. "Just taking a little detour."

The boy shrugged.

She sped up to the next corner, screeched a left, then a quick right back onto the road to the school. A few seconds later, with fresh traffic behind her, she heard a screech from another car, looked in the rearview mirror, and saw the brown sedan emerge once more.

She kept her cool, so as not to scare Dan Jr., and pulled up to the school. As she kissed him goodbye, she saw the sedan drive past them. *Two men. Cops.* She was sure of it. After all these years married to an assistant DA, she could smell them. She figured they knew they were made and that replacements would soon follow.

"You okay, Ma?"

"Sure," she said, trying to be believable. "Why not?"

The boy gave her a strange look.

"I just got new brakes," she explained. "Wanted to try them out."

"They work good," he said, wearing a wise-guy grin.

"Yes, they do." Her heart was pounding. "Now, go to school. We've had enough dilly-dallying for one day."

They kissed again, hugged, and Dan Jr. got out from the car. She watched him walk into the school with the other kids, waved to the security guard, then pulled away. She searched for the sedan. It was gone.

There was no doubt in her mind they were cops. She figured they were courtesy of her husband, that something dangerous was going on. She decided to head back home before going to work. She was going to be late anyway and there was something there she needed.

She pulled into her driveway and instinctively looked around once again. She saw nothing, but figured it was only a matter of time before a new car appeared. She thought of calling Dan, asking him what this was about. But she knew what he would say: "There's no reason to worry, it's only a precaution." He always downplayed that aspect of his work. He downplayed a lot of things. She had learned in her Al-Anon meetings that this was typical of alcoholics.

She ran upstairs into her bedroom and opened the closet. The box she wanted was on the top shelf and she needed to pull over a chair to reach it. She and Dan had kept it there so that Dan Jr. wouldn't be able to get at it. She took the box down and began turning the combination – her wedding date.

She lifted out the gun and held it in her hand. A silver-plated .38 that Dan got her about three months after he was promoted to major crimes, one week before his first trial. He had taken her to the range and trained her well. Since their separation, she had continued practicing, figuring one day she might need it.

She opened the cartridge, checked the bullets and put the gun in her bag. If the cops were watching her, then she and her son could be in danger. And if that was true, she couldn't depend on the cops.

chapter 18

DAN GIFFORD HAD JUST FINISHED packing his briefcase and was about to leave the office for the evening, when an unfamiliar man appeared in his doorway.

Gifford was surprised; although the secretaries and clerks had departed hours ago, the security guards should have informed him that he had a visitor.

"Can I help you?" Gifford asked, keeping his calm. The stranger was a burley-looking sort, balding, with a face that was marred from what must have been a terrible case of adolescent acne. But the cheap gray suit was the real giveaway.

Gifford had been working with cops long enough to figure that this guy was either "on the job" or served some other such function yielding him enough clout to get past security.

"Daniel Gifford?"

"Name's on the door."

The stranger approached Gifford's desk, reached into his pocket and pulled out an ID. "Richard Schwartz, federal agent."

Gifford made no effort to conceal his displeasure. It was past

10:30 in the evening and Schwartz had caught him off guard. "And what exactly is it that I can do for the FBI, Agent Schwartz?"

The FBI agent appeared unflinching, as if he had anticipated a less than warm welcome. The turf wars, power games, mistrust and mutual lack of respect between feds and locals had a rich heritage. He glanced at the chair in front of Gifford's desk.

"I wouldn't bother to sit, Agent Schwartz," Gifford said, eyeing his watch. "It's very late, you don't have an appointment and – to be quite honest – I'm anxious to get home."

"Then I guess I'll get right to the point. My office received a call from some bigwig at the Israeli consulate today. It seems two of your guys were rousting two of their guys."

"Rousting? I would hardly characterize a mere conversation as 'rousting.' And since when is the FBI interested in this sort of thing? I thought complaints from international diplomats were matters for the State Department."

"Normally," Schwartz responded, as though he expected this question. "This situation is sort of… unusual."

"Unusual? How so?"

"Let's just say that these two Israeli gentlemen are working with the bureau on a very delicate matter."

"The details of which you are, no doubt, unable to provide."

"You know how it works."

Gifford contemplated for a moment. "Tell me," he said, "how did you get to *me*?"

"Easy, the Israelis got your plate number."

Gifford wasn't surprised. In fact, when he had driven past the Israelis' car, he knew exactly what he was doing, hoping that whatever was going on would eventually come back to him. And here it was. "You're right, Agent Schwartz, I do know how it works. And let me tell you how I work. First, you are presently in the offices of the elected district attorney of Queens County, and these offices pursue crimes as we see fit. We serve the people of this county, not Uncle Sam and his emissaries."

"I understand all that, Mr. Gifford, and allow me to tell you what else I understand. First, your men were in Nassau County, not Queens County – *that's* out of your jurisdiction. Second, you aren't investigating any crime. Third, once we ran your plate and got your ID, your picture was very familiar to those Israeli gentlemen. You've been seen entering and leaving that building. We also did some investigating and we know about your problems. There's a shrink on the first floor. Put one and one together and…" Schwartz stopped himself.

Gifford waited for more.

"Now, if you want my take on things," Schwartz continued, "I'd guess your intelligence background makes you paranoid, not a bad thing to be in your line of work. So, I figure you spotted these guys, got curious, maybe thought they were after you or something, and so you launched a little independent investigation of your own. Just let me know when I'm getting warm."

Gifford wasn't rattled. He had already guessed that Schwartz knew all this. "What exactly is it that you want?" he asked.

"Look, Gifford, I'm not here to quarrel with you, only to tell you that this situation has nothing to do with you or your offices. I believe it would be best if you backed off and left it alone."

"It being…"

"I can't say."

The two men stared at each other.

"I'll certainly consider what you believe would be best," Gifford said.

"Do that."

The staring continued.

"And one more thing," Schwartz said. "This whole situation is not for public knowledge. If that shrink, or anyone else in that building, were to get wind of our presence, it would compromise a federal investigation and it would have serious national and international consequences, to say nothing of the effect on your career."

Gifford didn't enjoy being threatened, but he realized that it was best he keep quiet until he knew what he was dealing with. "If you don't mind, it's late and I'm tired," he said.

Schwartz simply nodded, turned on his heel and carried himself out of the office.

Gifford finally sat down in his chair, thinking about what had just transpired. He waited a few minutes, then picked up the phone and dialed Bobby Marcus' home number. Marcus picked up on the third ring.

"It's me," Gifford said.

"Surprise, surprise. Who else would it be this time of night?"

After sharing the details of the meeting with Schwartz, Gifford said, "I want you to get everything you can on this guy. I want to know what he's working on, where he lives, who he sleeps with, everything. And I don't want him to get wind of it." Gifford knew he was asking a lot of Marcus and that his tone betrayed his determination. He felt somehow violated by Schwartz and wanted to return the favor.

"Consider it done," Marcus said.

chapter 19

ELIZABETH ROSEN WORE A CURIOUS expression. She was accustomed to watching her father shave in the morning but never at night. Martin, oblivious to his daughter's presence, struggled to steady his hand while he stroked the blade. He couldn't recall ever having felt so nervous about a dinner date.

"Daddy, why are you shaving now?" Elizabeth asked.

"Ouch!" Martin yelped as the blade drew blood. He reached for a tissue and brought it to his cheek.

"You okay, daddy?"

He examined the wound in the mirror; it appeared superficial. "I'm fine, princess, just a little cut." He ran water over it, but the bleeding continued. He opened the medicine cabinet and began searching for his styptic pencil. "I'm shaving because I have a special appointment tonight."

"Why's it special?"

He knew he should have anticipated that question. "Because I'm seeing a special friend and I want to look nice. Just like sometimes you want to look nice when you go to see your friends." He found the styptic pencil, opened it, and moistened the tip.

She thought about his response and said, "Do girls ever shave?"

He hesitated, wondering how to answer that. It occurred to him that his patients were often easier to deal with than a 4-year-old. "Yes, they do," he began, "but usually only their legs."

"Their *legs?*" She laughed. "Do any girls shave their faces?"

"None that I know," he said.

"But some do," she reacted, as if she knew this to be a fact.

"I suppose so," Martin said, wondering what was coming next. Whenever these things got started, there was no telling where they might lead.

"When I get bigger, I'm going to shave my face just like you!"

In his mind, Martin chastised himself: *What a great psychologist you are!*

A lump formed in his throat as he placed the razor on the sink, rinsed his face, picked her up and hugged her. "When you grow up, you're going to be very special," he said, trying not to say anything stupid. "I'm happy that you love me so much that you want to be like me. That's a good thing. But there'll be a few things that you might *not* want to do, and shaving your face may just be one of them."

"No, I'm going to, just like you!" She was adamant. "I'm going to do *everything* you do."

He carried her into his bedroom, put her down on the bed, looked into her eyes and said, "If that's what you want. But just remember, if you should change your mind, it's okay with me."

"I'm not going to change my mind."

He simply kissed her on the forehead, smiled, then opened the closet to choose his clothes.

"Daddy?"

"Yes, princess?"

"What time will you be home?"

"Probably after you're asleep." He placed a pair of khakis on the bed with a light blue pinpoint oxford button-down shirt. He then reached for a reddish-brown Harris Tweed blazer. The weather report had promised a nippy night.

"Will you come in and kiss me goodnight?"

"Don't I always?"

"I don't know. I'm asleep."

He took her head in his heads, kissed her again and said, "Well I *always* do, and I *always* will."

"Even when I'm married?"

"When you're married, I may not always be there to kiss you goodnight, but you'll always be my little princess."

"I don't want to get married."

"That might be another thing you'll change your mind about."

"No I won't."

"We'll see."

"I really won't."

"Why not?" He knew he shouldn't have gone there the instant the words slipped from his tongue.

"Because I want to stay with you."

"You will *always* be with me, even if you marry someone else. You see, it doesn't matter where you are or who you live with. When you love someone, they're always with you."

A moment of silence descended as they each digested the exchange. Martin continued dressing and Elizabeth sat on the bed, watching, seeming to have run out of questions. He thanked God – or whomever he usually thanked at times like this – though he knew his reprieve was only temporary. There would be more to come, of that he was certain. But he wasn't so sure how much longer he could get by with such clumsy answers.

For now, all he could do was turn his thoughts to the evening that awaited.

chapter 20

MARTIN ROSEN WAS NERVOUS AS a schoolboy while he waited for Cheryl Manning to answer the door. He painted on a broad smile as he heard her footsteps from inside the apartment. The door opened and she was smiling back at him, her eyes on the bouquet of red roses in his hand.

"Hi," Martin said, handing her the flowers.

"Hi yourself," she replied as she took the roses and smelled them. "You shouldn't have."

She took his hand and led him into the living room.

The décor immediately struck him as very much "single woman on the run." The floor was oak, natural finish, slightly worn and covered with a simple black-and-brown-checkered area rug. The couch and loveseat were cloth, ivory-colored, and separated by a faux redwood coffee table. There were two end tables flanking either side of the couch, same style as the coffee table, a few framed reproductions of famous paintings, and a wall-unit bookcase, also faux wood, with a TV, stereo, some hardcover books and a bunch of paperbacks. He noticed that there were no special ornaments or tchotchkes, nor any hint that someone had gone to great lengths to put all this together. It appeared somewhat expedient, though he had to admit that it somehow worked.

He glanced at the book titles, hoping they would tell him something about his hostess, but there seemed to be no particular theme to her interests. As one who enjoyed getting the jump on others by analyzing their literary proclivities, he found this somewhat unsettling. And there was something else about the collection that bothered him, something he couldn't exactly put his finger on but felt was there. It was akin to what occasionally happened to him with patients: he would find himself uneasy, yet unable to pinpoint why.

Suddenly, he stopped himself, realizing what he was doing. Though it was as natural for him as breathing, it was a certain hindrance to his enjoyment. He turned around to her, the smile back on his face.

She gestured to the couch and they sat down. "Can I get you something to drink?" she asked. "I have wine or diet coke."

"Wine sounds good."

She got up, went into the kitchen and returned with a bottle and two glasses. "I guessed you would opt for the wine," she said. "I'm not always right, but it is good to know that some things are predictable." She put the glasses down on the coffee table and began tearing the wrapper from the top of the bottle.

"By the way, what's that I smell cooking?" He inhaled deeply, smiled and said, "Veal Marsala?"

She kissed him gently on the lips. "Such a smart man."

He looked at the label on the bottle, assuming it would be a Merlot, and was surprised. "Pinot noir?"

"You like?"

"I don't know."

"You've never had it before?"

"I'm a Scotch man, remember?"

"Yes I do. That's why I got the wine."

He looked at her curiously.

"To celebrate *new* things," she explained.

"Aha."

She handed him the bottle and corkscrew. "Would you like the honors?"

"If you insist."

She smiled as he struggled with the corkscrew, but eventually he got it.

"Not bad for a beginner," she said.

"I'm a fast learner."

She took the bottle from him, poured some into a glass and handed it to him. "I believe it is the man's job to taste the wine."

"A bit chauvinistic, aren't we?"

"A traditionalist."

"Oh." He smirked as he held the wine up to the light. "I suppose this is how they do it."

She giggled.

"Nice color."

"You know the difference?"

"Shh, I'm trying to look sophisticated."

He brought the glass to his mouth, took a sip and swished the wine with his tongue. "Not too shabby," he said, surprised at how pleasant it was.

"I'm glad you like it." She poured for both of them.

"To *new* things," he said, holding out his glass.

"To new things."

Watching her drink was sensual, as was everything about her. He sat back on the couch, sipped the wine and said, "Who are you, really, and what were you before? What'd ya do, and what'd ya think, huh?"

"That line sounds awfully familiar. I think I've heard it in a movie."

"You have, have you?"

"I thought we said no questions," she said with a grimace and the best Swedish accent she could muster.

"Did we?"

"*That's* not your line! Come on, you know what comes next."

"I do?"

She frowned.

"Yes, I suppose I do," he admitted.

"Well then, let's hear it."

"Okay," he said, raising his glass. "Here's looking at you, kid."

She chuckled. "That's more like it."

"But in all seriousness, I do have questions."

"As do I."

"How about we each reveal one thing to the other," he suggested.

"But it has to be significant," she added, feeling an inexplicable urge to step out of role and say something honest. Quite dangerous, she knew, and a complete violation of all the rules, yet with him she knew she could. And the most unnerving thing of it was that she wanted to.

"Okay, you first," he said.

"Not a chance. It was your idea, so you start."

He hesitated. "It has to be significant?"

She nodded. "Your idea."

"All right." He thought for a moment. "My parents are Holocaust survivors who have never met their granddaughter."

"That sounds like a quite a story." It was a story she already knew, yet hearing him say it somehow moved her in a way she hadn't anticipated.

"It is, and the rest of it would probably take the entire evening and then some."

"I understand," she said, sensing his discomfort. "We said one thing, and that certainly qualifies."

"Thanks," he said, doing a somewhat poor job at hiding his relief. "Now you!"

"Me?" She was pensive, realizing that she was about to break her cover. A small break, but a break nonetheless. And there was nothing she could do to stop herself. "Me too," she said.

"You too? What?"

"My parents are also survivors."

"Survivors? Are you Jewish?"

She nodded. "Also a long story."

He saw that she too would prefer not to go any further, at least not for now. "That's okay. We did say one thing."

"Yes. We did."

The veal Marsala was served with roasted new potatoes and broccoli sautéed with mushrooms and garlic. Martin was impressed. The food was better than he'd anticipated and, after two glasses of wine, he stopped feeling the need to turn away from her whenever things grew intense.

After dinner, he helped her clear the table and do the dishes while they indulged in a pint of coffee Häagen-Dazs. They shared a single spoon, passing it back and forth, observing each other carefully, until she took an entire spoonful for herself.

"Where's mine?" he protested.

"Here," she said as she pulled him into a cold, silky sweet kiss.

He awakened a few hours later, bathed in sweat, jolted into consciousness by a dream he couldn't recall. His heart racing, he wondered where he was until he felt her hand on his arm.

"Are you all right?" she asked, half-dazed.

He wiped his forehead with his hand. "Yes," he responded hesitantly, suddenly realizing it was the middle of the night. "What time is it?" He turned to the night table and saw that it was 1:15. Earlier than he'd thought but later than he'd hoped.

"One-fifteen," he announced as if it should mean something. He pulled the sheet off and sat up on the side of the bed. "I really should go."

"Yes, I suppose you should." Her disappointment was evident.

"I'm sorry, it's just that…"

"I know," she interjected, maneuvering herself up behind him. "You don't want to have to explain to your little girl why you were out all night." She wrapped her arms around him and rested her chin on his shoulder.

He was surprised to feel himself once again aroused. They had already made love twice, and now his body was telling him that he still wanted more. He was beginning to worry about this power she had.

She began kissing his ear. "Do you have to leave this minute?"

she whispered.

"I suppose I could stay a while longer."

He made love to her again, yet still it didn't seem enough. Nothing could quite bring him to where he wanted to be. Trapped in his physicality, all he could do was follow his cravings. It was the only way he knew to join her, to become part of her. And when it was over, he was left once more with emptiness and the certainty that separating from her would grow ever more anguishing with time.

He dressed as she lay in bed, listening to the sound of her breathing. When he was finished, he looked at her. She lay naked on top of the sheets, facing him.

"I'll call you later," he said.

"Wait!" She got up, wrapped herself in the sheet, took his hand and led him to the front door. "A lady should see her visitors out."

They reached the door. She put her hands on his face as the sheet dropped to the floor. They brought each other closer and fell into a long, hard kiss.

"Good night," she said, turning the door latch.

"Yes, it was," he replied.

He turned to leave, when a sudden unsettled feeling came upon him. He figured it was probably a reaction to the dream that had awakened him, though he still couldn't recall its content. Then, from the corner of his eye, he saw the bookcase in the living room, remembering that something about it had bothered him earlier, though he was still at a loss as to what. He wondered for a moment if the dream and the bookcase were somehow connected.

"Are you all right?"

"Yeah, sure." He hesitated. "Just tired."

She looked at him with a curious expression, as if she didn't quite believe him. "Really?"

"Really."

"Okay then, talk to you later."

"Yes," he agreed. "Later."

They parted with an awkward embrace, reflective of the abrupt, inexplicable turn in his mood. And as he walked down the hallway, he wondered what exactly had happened – whether his mind was playing tricks on him for fear of a relationship, or if there was something else that he didn't have a handle on. He was angry with himself; it was just like him to bring a lousy end to a perfect evening.

Once again, it became apparent that it was indeed time to consult his own shrink.

She closed the door behind him, confident that, despite her revelation, she had given away nothing that could compromise her. And yet, she still wondered what had bothered him. Could it have been something in the apartment, or something else that happened during the evening? She drew a blank.

Bewildered, she walked to her bedroom. Maybe a hot shower and a good night's sleep would help her figure things out. Maybe Martin Rosen simply had an acute case of the jitters and was freaking out over the intensity of the evening. That might be it, she mused; after all, it made perfect sense. Especially to someone who was having a few unsettled feelings of her own.

She came into the bedroom, tossed the sheet back on the bed and stood naked for a moment, observing herself in the mirror. She was 29 years old, as fit as she'd ever been. She worked hard to look this way, to have something she could use to her advantage. She thought about some of the men she had been with, many of whom had nauseated her. But she always did whatever was needed to get the job done.

She took her fingers and gently ran them down her torso, from her shoulders to her thighs. The feeling excited her; she shivered and felt warm all at once. An image of the man she'd said good night to just a few minutes earlier entered her mind and her excitement grew. She tried to fight it, to see this as merely another mission, but this time she knew something *was* different. She was used to clarity, had thrived on it her entire life, and here she was, for the first time, leery. She turned from the mirror and walked to the bathroom.

She stepped into the shower; the warmth and pressure of the water felt soothing. She closed her eyes and breathed deeply, trying to thwart the strange wave of sadness that was slowly gaining ground. Disheartening thoughts raced through her mind, thoughts of the life she'd been leading all these years; questions about her future, what awaited her as she grew older and alone. Usually, she was able to ignore such notions, but this time they'd caught her off guard. She sensed something happening within, an uncertainty she'd never known.

She cursed herself for weakening, for succumbing to a silly, fleeting instinct to let go. But something about the man had seemed to grant her permission. She would have to be more careful; simply seduce him like all the others, get what she needed and be on her way. Yes, that was *exactly* what she would do.

Convincing herself of this, she swallowed hard and silenced any doubt that she would succeed.

GALIT STEIN WAS THE ONLY child of Nathan and Eva Stein, two Polish war refugees who had survived the Dachau concentration camp, having escaped the crematoria, and found a new life for themselves on kibbutz *Kfar Giladi* in the north of Israel. Nathan was 12 years old when he first set foot on the shores of what was then called Palestine; Eva was 10. Although each had spent at least two years in Dachau, they hadn't met until after the liberation, in a Red Cross infirmary in Switzerland where they were nourished back to life. They had both lost their entire families, a commonality that drew them to each other and eventually rendered them inseparable. Within six months, Nathan was tall, muscular and restored to health with a resilience unusual even for the young and strong. Eva, however, remained frail and vulnerable.

Nathan had sworn to protect Eva, to stay by her side and never leave, but the Red Cross had other plans. Eva had distant cousins in London, and arrangements were made for her to be sent to live with them. Nathan had no one, but the "do-gooders" were exploring adoption possibilities in America. Their only chance of remaining together was with a man named Mordechai Katz, a representative of the Jewish Agency who was secretly recruiting refugees to be smuggled into Palestine.

At first, Katz had been hesitant; Nathan and Eva were on the young side for the Agency's operation. Transit for Jews to Palestine was illegal and fraught with all kinds of danger, not the least of which was confinement in a British internment camp if apprehended. But Nathan's determination knew no bounds, and Katz eventually came around to see that the boy was exactly what the Zionists needed.

They traveled on a boat with hundreds of refugees through the Mediterranean and, after several weeks of evading British cruisers, they finally came ashore one late-June evening in 1947 on a deserted beach called Nahariya. From there, they were taken to a small kibbutz near the northern border, shown to their quarters, and given food, baths, and cots to rest out what remained of the night. With daybreak, they were sent directly to the fields.

In the years that followed, their existence was challenged by the earth, disease and their Arab neighbors. The fighting never seemed to cease. But the kibbutz also had its joys, the sense of family, belonging, purpose. Midnight campfires, song and dance – anything to drown the despair.

Some left, seeking passage to America in hope of something better. But Nathan and Eva remained. Together, they were determined to make this place their home. Eight years after they had arrived, they were married.

Eva had healed some and had grown stronger in body and spirit. Yet still, on their wedding night, the first time Nathan came to her, she reacted with terror. He was soft with her, as he always had been, offering to leave their consummation for another time. She cried in his arms for hours, and then spoke of things she had never before revealed.

Her voice filled with shame, she recounted how it was that she had been able to stay alive in the concentration camp, how one guard in particular had singled her out for his pleasure. The first time it had happened, she was lying with her mother in a small bunk when the guard came for her. Her mother resisted, holding her tightly, but the guard decided to take her mother also. Outside the barracks, the guard pulled Eva from her mother's grasp and shot her mother in the head. From that moment, there would be no more resistance.

Nathan stayed silent, holding her, wishing he could extinguish her agony. But all he could do was listen and understand. And understand he did. He had his own stories, though he would never bring himself to recount them.

In the weeks that followed, the young bride and groom slowly found their way with each other beneath the sheets. They had been lovers long before they had ever made love and, while their pleasure was inevitably marred by ghosts, they would remain lovers forever. They created their way, grew comfortable, and were at home together.

They lived for each other and for the family they hoped to make. Yet, despite their determination, nature defied them. After almost two years of trying to conceive a child, it became apparent that something was wrong.

The kibbutz doctor delivered the news with a morose expression on his usually spirited face. Eva's internal organs had sustained permanent, irreparable damage from trauma. The doctor asked no questions, he had known Nathan and Eva since they had arrived, knew where they had been. The rest remained unspoken.

The following year, Nathan and Eva fought and survived yet another war against the Arabs, while many of their friends weren't as fortunate. Whatever their travails, they chose to be thankful, to abide in their faith that God had kept them for a reason. They clung to each other yet again, finding joy in what they had, in simply being alive.

In 1967, the worst war of all came, at least for them and their neighbors. The Syrians hit the kibbutz hard. There were many casualties. Several women were widowed and many children orphaned.

The kibbutz continued to care for these children as it always had. It was an integral part of their structure that all children, regardless of family, be provided for by the community. There was no need for private adoptions or anything of the sort.

But Nathan and Eva had an idea of their own. It concerned the youngest of these children, an 8-month-old baby girl named Galit, whose mother had died during her delivery and whose father had just been killed on the northern front. The father had been a close friend of the Steins, and Eva had already developed a surrogate relationship with Galit since birth. For all intents and purposes, Eva was as close to a mother as Galit had ever had.

The kibbutz council agreed, for Galit's sake, and because this was a fitting consolation for two of their finest. The adoption was legalized within a few months and the infant, whose name means "small wave" in Hebrew, became for Nathan and Eva a small wave of bliss in a largely wretched sea.

From her earliest years, Galit was well acquainted with strife. The kibbutz was only a few miles from the northern border and surprise attacks by enemy rockets were commonplace. Barely a month passed without a casualty. When she was 4 years old, a band of terrorists attacked her school and killed two of her friends. Galit's injuries were superficial, and she was home from the infirmary by nightfall. That was the day the strife turned into hatred, the moment that Nathan and Eva Stein began teaching their daughter about good and evil.

The lesson crystallized in 1973, when the Syrians again attacked the kibbutz on Yom Kippur day. Galit, her parents, and most of the kibbutz members were caught off guard while praying in the synagogue. They were not religious, not in the traditional sense, but Yom Kippur was still a holy day to them. Until that year.

The destruction was unmatched, more than half the kibbutz was wiped out, and Nathan lost his right leg to a shrapnel wound. Galit and Eva were safe, but the trauma and desolation would forever haunt the young girl.

When Nathan Stein returned from the hospital, he was a different man. Aside from the loss of his leg, the attack on Yom Kippur had been too poignant a reminder of his childhood, when the Nazis, too, had attacked the Jews of his small Polish village and herded them away on the High Holidays. His strength now transformed into bitterness, he could no longer hold his tongue about the worst things he had known. He began to speak openly to his daughter of all that had happened. He became obsessed and believed it his duty to pass that obsession on to her.

In the beginning, Eva objected and admonished her husband. But soon Galit began asking about her adoption, why her parents were older than her friends' parents, and why she had no brothers and sisters. Eva herself could no longer evade the truth.

In their divulgence, both Nathan and Eva found an unexpected sense of relief. The burden was no longer theirs alone, the suffering could be shared. For Nathan, there was no question about the self-serving nature of his actions. He had convinced himself that he was behaving in Galit's best interest, for her betterment as a Jew and a human being. For Eva, there remained a conflict between the guilt she felt over tainting Galit and her belief that only the tainted survived.

By the time Galit was 10 years old, she understood more about life's travails than most grown-ups. She also understood that there was little she could do to bring her parents true happiness. Her father's every breath and action were imbued with venom, her mother's sadness unending. And her own helplessness fostered within her the singular purpose to one day capture and smite the terrible demons who had wrought all this ruin.

Kibbutz life stressed discipline, fraternity, hard work and perseverance. Everyone was equal, no one special. But when Galit entered the military at 17, as all Israeli women, that changed. Aside from her obvious physical beauty and charm, which attracted the attention of her superiors, her uncanny ability to learn new languages and pass for a young woman of several nationalities made her an excellent candidate for certain foreign intelligence operations.

For her, the choice was simple. She could do an ordinary three-year stint in the army, like most of her peers, return to the kibbutz, find a husband and raise a family, or she could at last pursue the dream for which she had longed. In this decision, and in every subsequent step she took, she became more the daughter of Nathan and Eva Stein than she could have been had she emanated from their own flesh.

JACQUES BENOÎT WORE HIS SATISFACTION in his smile. He couldn't help himself, Martin figured. The news about the Gamatron/LMI merger was a day old, and no one who read the newspapers would have missed it. The stock had almost tripled in value.

"Good morning," Martin said.

"Good morning to you, my dear doctor," Benoît replied.

"You seem to be in an up mood."

"Observant of you to notice."

Not really. "An occupational hazard," Martin replied.

"Ah."

"To what should we attribute your jubilation?"

"Nothing much, just that the stock I told you about took a little jump yesterday."

"So I saw."

"You watched it?"

"I read the financial section every day."

"Oh," Benoît said.

"I'm glad you brought that up though. I think we probably need to talk more about it."

"What more is there to say?"

"It's important to our work together that you understand where I was coming from," Martin said.

"I believe you made yourself perfectly clear. It would be unprofessional of you to confuse our relationship by accepting a favor from me, especially a possibly illegal favor."

"Was it illegal?"

Benoît seemed to consider the question. "It's a gray area. The information I received was just speculation, of course, but my sources are usually well placed. It goes on all the time – certain individuals have an advantage over others by getting more reliable and timely information."

"And if it's 'insider' information, it's illegal?"

"Precisely."

"So, was it?" Martin asked the question matter-of-factly, as if he were asking if it was raining outside.

"I received the information from one of my brokers."

"Then it wasn't?"

"I cannot be held responsible for where others get *their* information."

Martin noted the defensiveness in Benoît's tone. "Even when they pass that information on to you?" he asked.

Benoît appeared unnerved. "We all have our ethical shortcomings, doctor. I am sure that you are no exception to this."

"You're probably right. But to the extent that I can, I try to leave my ethical shortcomings out of this room. That was why I couldn't accept your offer."

"I understand perfectly well."

"I hope you do, because it wasn't personal. Nor do I judge you for your choices, including the choice to share your information with me."

"Ah, but now you *are* making an ethical compromise!"

Martin looked curious. "In what way?"

"By not being completely honest with me."

"How so?"

"In claiming that you don't judge me, you are certainly being less than truthful. Of course you judge me, doctor. Men always judge one another, regardless of what room they are in."

"I suppose you have a point, but you see, I make every effort not to be judgmental, and if at times I fail, I'm probably unaware of it."

"Not very different from what I do with my investing. As I said, I am *unaware* of the exact sources of the information I get. And perhaps, like you, I want to believe that everything is proper."

Martin saw no purpose in continuing this. The more he would enumerate the differences between Benoît's rationalizations and his own, the more Benoît would point out the similarities. It could go on endlessly.

"You see, my dear doctor," Benoît continued, "the world is filled with moral ambiguity."

Martin nodded. "I can't argue with that."

"So," Benoît said a bit awkwardly, "where do we go from here?"

"Where would you like to go?"

Benoît hesitated, then said, "Why don't we continue from where we left off last time?"

"That's always a good idea."

"I believe I was talking about my first wife, the war, all those very unpleasant things."

"Did it upset you to discuss them?"

"Upset me? That's an interesting question. It was so long ago, it is hard to tell how I feel about it."

"I would imagine that it's hard for you to tell how you feel about a lot of things."

"Very good, doctor."

"You know, Jacques, I'm sitting here wondering why it is that you seem to enjoy this so much."

"You mean our repartee?"

"I suppose you could call it that."

Benoît smiled. "It is simply that I find you to be a formidable adversary."

"Why do you find me to be an adversary at all?"

"Because you are. Here again, we have an ambiguity: your job is to help me, but in doing so, you must dismantle my defenses, invade my psyche and uncover my secrets. I, however, have always lived by these defenses, and – as you can see – in some ways they have served me quite well. To my mind, that sounds adversarial."

"I suppose that's one way to look at it," Martin said.

"Which means that you don't agree."

"No, I don't. I never see *myself* as the adversary of a patient. On the contrary, I see each man as his own adversary, myself included. As a psychologist, I facilitate you in becoming aware of your own destructive tendencies, and then, hopefully, you gain more mastery over them. Admittedly, that is often painful, but – to use an analogy – I would hardly characterize a doctor who injects an antigen into a patient's body as an adversary."

"I agree that he is not, from his point of view. But to me, because I am the recipient of the pain, the perpetrator's intentions do not matter. He is still an adversary."

Paranoid, self-absorbed, Martin thought. "It seems to me that you have arrived at your conclusion without considering all the facts."

"Perhaps so. But then again, don't we all give more weight to some aspects of a situation than to others."

"Yes, but when doing so creates psychological distress, it is healthy to entertain alternatives."

"Psychological distress, doctor, isn't always the worst thing."

Martin looked at Benoît curiously.

"What I mean is that sometimes psychological distress aids in our survival."

"That's a very astute comment, Jacques," Martin admitted while wondering where Benoît was going with this.

"I have read about the 'fight-or-flight response,' that it is a feeling of distress when a person feels threatened."

Martin smiled. The *fight-or-flight* response was a popular explanation of why people experience anxiety. The senses perceive a threat, and the heart beats rapidly to pump more blood to the skeletal muscles to prepare the body to either flee or fight. This reaction, however, occurs because the mind believes there is danger, even though there may be none in actuality. In a case in which there is no real peril, the individual remains still. And since the body has prepared for action but doesn't act, the physiological changes bring about hyperventilation, dizziness, nausea and other common symptoms of anxiety. If this happens often, it can be detrimental to one's physical well-being.

"That's correct," Martin responded, "but there are clearly times when that reaction is neither healthy nor useful."

"Ah, but how am I to know if this is, or is not, one of those times?"

"By asking yourself some questions."

"What kind of questions?"

"Like, in what way could I possibly pose a threat to you?"

"You have never heard of doctors injuring patients?"

"I have. But you speak as if I intend to hurt you."

"Maybe you do, maybe you do not. Or maybe you simply don't care and are just out for your own gain."

"And what would that gain be?"

"Perhaps you derive satisfaction from uncovering things, like a voyeur? You will do whatever it takes to satisfy your own needs, regardless of how it impacts your patients."

"Do you see me that way?"

Benoît hesitated. "Not really, but one can never know for certain."

"I suppose one can't, and that's where trust comes in. It must be hard to trust in your world."

"Yes, that is quite accurate."

Martin glanced at his watch. It was always important to keep track of the remaining time in the session.

"Worried about the time?" Benoit snapped.

"It's an unfortunate pitfall of the process that our time is limited," Martin explained.

"And also beneficial, so I am told." Benoît said.

Notwithstanding the derision, Martin appreciated Benoît's understanding of how the time limitation can make the patient and therapist use the session more wisely. "You're well informed," he said.

"I try to be."

ASHOK REDDY SAT ACROSS FROM Martin in the hospital cafeteria. The two had been there for a while, and Martin, practically wordless, had barely touched his lunch.

"Is something wrong, Marty?" Reddy asked.

"Why would you think that?"

"You are awfully quiet. And frankly, I have never seen you so disinterested in food."

"I just have a lot on my mind."

"Woman problems?"

"Perhaps."

"Same girl?"

Martin lifted his eyes and looked at his friend.

Reddy looked at his watch. "If my memory is correct, Marty, you requested this luncheon."

Martin nodded.

"I even recall you saying you had something you needed to discuss."

Another nod.

"Well, in case you were wondering, I *do* have a department to run, patients to see, a stock broker to call, just a few minor chores for the afternoon."

"I'm sorry, Ashok."

"Save your contrition for church, my friend. Or synagogue, or wherever it is you go these days. Just tell me what is on your mind."

"That's just it. I'm not quite sure."

"Aha, so it's one of those vague premonition-type things. You have a sense that something is not quite right, but you just cannot pin it down."

"Exactly!"

"That isn't so unusual, it happens to me all the time."

"Me too, with patients. But not in my private life."

"You forget, Marty, you have not had a *private* life for quite some time."

Martin shrugged. "True."

Reddy seemed to be contemplating. "Do you have a clue?"

"I know it's something about her. At least I think it is. Don't get me wrong, she really grabs me, but when I was looking around her place last night, something just didn't feel right."

"You were at her place? That seems rather fast."

Martin smirked. "She cooked me dinner."

"I can just imagine."

"Ashok..."

"Yes. Sorry, Marty. Sometimes I just like to live vicariously."

"You don't need to. You have a perfect life."

"Nothing's perfect, my friend, but I will take it."

The two men smiled at each other.

"Getting back to you," Reddy continued. "Maybe you are just frightened about getting close to someone new. It is quite normal to feel that way in your circumstances."

"I've thought about that. It's true, I am scared, but I think I'm dealing with it. *This* is something else."

"Well, Marty, everyone has secrets. I am sure she has a few. In time you will learn what you need to know."

"You're probably right. But I just had a sense that there was something else." Martin thought for a moment. "I had a disturbing dream while I was there."

"How did you manage to dream during dinner?"

Martin's eyes told his friend to cut the sarcasm.

"Okay," Reddy said. "Do you recall the details?"

"That's just it. I can't remember anything about the dream."

"Then how do you know it was disturbing?"

"Because I woke up feeling troubled, even agitated."

Reddy's beeper sounded. He removed it from his waist, looked at it and said, "Shit! I am late for a meeting with the administration. I forgot all about it." He looked at Martin apologetically.

"It's fine. Go!"

"I'm really sorry, Marty. It is about budget nonsense, but I have to be there."

"Don't worry about it. We'll catch each other later."

They stood up, took their trays, and started toward the conveyer belt.

"You know, Marty, there are two things we could try."

Martin looked at him curiously. "What're you thinking?"

"Well, the first, and simplest, is for you to bring her by for dinner. Savitri's quite eager to meet her, and I will have her sized up in no time."

"Thanks, but I think I'll spare her the scrutiny for now."

"Who said anything about scrutiny? She would just be meeting friends."

"Yeah, sure. What's your other idea?"

"Hypnosis."

Martin stopped in his tracks and stared at Reddy. "Are you serious?"

"Sure. Why not? If I can get you in a good trance, there is no telling what we will uncover. I won't even charge you."

Martin looked like he was actually considering the idea.

"Why don't you think on it," Reddy said.

"I'll do just that."

chapter 24

DAN GIFFORD'S MIND WAS IN overdrive. He gulped his coffee, not realizing how hot it was until it was too late. It would be days before he would be able to taste his food again. "Are you sure?" he asked Bobby Marcus.

"I have this friend at the bureau, owes me a few favors," Marcus explained. "That's what he says."

The information on Richard Schwartz was puzzling, but it definitely fit; Israeli agents in cahoots with one of the FBI's foremost experts on Nazi war criminals. Only, what were they doing outside Martin Rosen's office?

Gifford entertained the possibility that they could be after someone in a neighboring building or in one of the other apartments in Rosen's building. Maybe a resident, guest, or even one of the professional tenants. The possibilities were plentiful.

Either way, Gifford realized that Schwartz was right; it really wasn't his problem. He already had enough on his plate with the upcoming drug trial. Yet, having to keep all this from Rosen irked him. What if Rosen was somehow unwittingly involved, whether through another patient or in some other way?

Gifford was knee-deep in this thing. He couldn't continue his therapy, business-as-usual, while keeping this a secret; he couldn't divulge the secret either, until he knew it was safe to do so; and he couldn't imagine quitting therapy, one of the few things in his life that was working. "You seem to have a lot of people owing you," he said to Marcus.

They were sitting at their usual corner table in Starbucks. They spoke quietly beneath the noise of the crowd, assuring their privacy. "Don't fret, Danny boy. You'll join the club soon enough."

"I'm already there. You've done a lot for me, Bobby. I don't forget things like this."

Marcus ignored the comment. He was uncomfortable with accolades from friends. "So, what do you want me to do next?"

Gifford weighed the question. It wouldn't cause any harm to dig a little deeper, especially with Marcus doing the digging. Gifford trusted his instincts about Marcus, as he did about most things. Marcus was good, always covered his tracks well. It was highly unlikely the FBI would get wind of anything. "Do you think you could find out exactly what Schwartz is working on?"

"That's a tall order, boss."

"I know."

The two friends looked at each other.

"I'll see what I can do."

chapter 25

GALIT STEIN SAT NERVOUSLY, WONDERING if the place she had chosen for her meeting with Richard Schwartz would make a difference. She wanted a frank discussion with her FBI compatriot, something that was generally impossible between people in their respective positions. Notwithstanding what they had in common, she and Schwartz worked for different governments with different agendas. They shared only what they needed to, and would easily turn on the other if circumstances necessitated. Her intention now was to try to get past that, to engage him, Jew-to-Jew.

She, Arik, and Kovi had spent the morning at the Israeli consulate, meeting with a member of the Israeli delegation to the UN, who was really the local Mossad commander, to update the mission's status. She wondered if the commander had noticed some tension among the three agents, particularly between her and Arik. The commander had already known about the incident with Gifford from his own sources, leaving her to guess that the FBI and the consulate were somehow in contact. She was hoping that the meeting with Schwartz might short-circuit that line of communication.

The sanctuary of Congregation Emanu-El on Fifth Avenue and 65th Street in New York City was open every day for tourists and those seeking a place to meditate. It was the world's largest synagogue, erected in 1929 on the former site of the John Jacob Astor mansion. The Gothic sanctuary was massive, softly lit, and quiet. Galit was neither a religious nor particularly observant Jew, but she chose the synagogue because it was a place where Jews gathered in worship, a place with an ark containing sacred Torah scrolls, and perhaps in some intangible way, a place where God dwelt. It was a place she figured neither she nor Schwartz would be likely to lie, and a place where they might feel somewhat akin to each other. And it was far enough from the consulate, from the FBI's New York headquarters, and from Long Island's North Shore, for them to be on equal footing.

She sat at the end of a wooden pew toward the back of the sanctuary and looked at her watch. Schwartz was already twelve minutes late. She knew he would keep the appointment, because he had said he would. He must simply be caught in traffic or held up for some other reason, she told herself.

She looked at her surroundings and tried to remember the last time she'd been in a synagogue. It was probably when she was 15 or 16, before she had entered the army, she decided. The kibbutz was not a religious place, but it had a small synagogue for High Holidays and special occasions, such as bat mitzvahs, weddings and funerals. It was a funny thing, she thought, even the most secular Israelis celebrated the High Holidays, and the same was generally true of American Jews as well. She wondered if Martin Rosen cared about such things.

Her eyes scanned the sanctuary. There were only a few other visitors, all far enough away to permit complete privacy for her rendezvous with Schwartz. Sunshine crept in through the stained glass windows, casting multicolored rays of light across the room, and shadows of mysterious shapes on a far wall. She wondered if God was actually in this place, and thought back to the stories of the concentration camps that she had heard growing up. They had been as integral to her rearing as butter to bread. And they had shaped the essence of her being as nothing else. They had caused her to wonder if God could actually have been in those camps. Or anywhere.

A familiar voice broke her meditation. "Hello, Galit," Schwartz said quietly as he took a seat next to her. "Strange place to request a meeting." He looked around.

Agent Richard Schwartz was one of the FBI's leading specialists on Nazi war criminals. He was a seasoned agent, nearing retirement, tired, cynical, and aware that he had caught this detail because of his German-Jewish background, while most of the Bureau's higher-ups couldn't give a shit. Throughout the Nazi-hunting community, however, he was legendary.

Schwartz' career launched in the '70s on one of the most difficult Nazi war criminal cases in history, involving a Romanian-born U.S. citizen named Valerian Trifa living in Grass Lake, Michigan. Trifa had been an active member of the infamous Romanian "Iron Guard," and had participated in pogroms against thousands of Jews in Bucharest. What had made the case tricky was that Trifa was an archbishop and leader of the Romanian Orthodox Episcopate of America. After years of dogged investigating, and resisting intense political pressure from his own and other governmental agencies, Schwartz saw to it that Trifa was convicted of entering the U.S. under false pretenses. The fascist archbishop was denaturalized, deported, and ended up in Portugal – the only country that would admit him – where he eventually died a free man.

Schwartz' second big case concerned a carpenter who had lived in Mineola, Long Island, named Boleslavs Maikovskis. Maikovskis, a native of Latvia, had also entered the U.S. during the '50s, by way of Austria. On his immigration papers, he had described himself as a staunch anticommunist, and claimed to have worked as a bookkeeper during the war. His Long Island neighbors saw him as a friendly, docile sort who attended church every morning. Schwartz' evidence, based on a request for extradition from the Soviet Union, told a different story: Maikovskis had been chief of the second precinct of the Rezekne District for the Nazi-created police force in Latvia. In 1941, he had personally ordered the mass arrest of every man, woman and child in the village of Audrini, totaling about 300 people, most of whom were Jews. He also ordered that every house be burnt to the ground, after which thirty of the villagers were publicly executed in the middle of the town, while the rest were taken out to the nearby woods and slaughtered.

Maikovskis was eventually sentenced to death in absentia in a Soviet Latvian court for his crimes. As a result of Schwartz' efforts, he was denaturalized and deported from the U.S. in 1987, and fled to West Germany to avoid Soviet justice. The German government, after years of prodding by Schwartz and the Israelis, eventually indicted him, and was set to try him in 1994, when he became ill. The trial was suspended, and Maikovskis died two years later of a heart attack. Another free man.

But of all Schwartz' cases, the most harrowing was the one against John Demjanjuk, the Cleveland, Ohio, autoworker accused of having been "Ivan the Terrible," a notorious Treblinka concentration camp guard who personally supervised the extermination of thousands of Jews. Schwartz had worked closely with the Israelis, who sought extradition of Demjanjuk to Israel for trial. Demjanjuk was eventually convicted of lying on his U.S. immigration papers, denaturalized, and extradited for what was to be the second-largest Nazi criminal trial in history, next to Eichmann's. There was testimony from five eyewitnesses, and a resulting verdict of guilty, which was eventually overturned by the Israeli Supreme Court on grounds of reasonable doubt. The higher court's decision had emanated from the release of previously secret KGB files identifying a supposedly different Ukrainian, one Ivan Marchenko, as Ivan the Terrible.

Though there was other evidence supporting a claim that Demjanjuk, while not Ivan the Terrible, may actually have been a guard at another concentration camp, the Israeli court chose not to convict him on that charge either, because he had not been given ample opportunity to defend himself from it. In the end, Demjanjuk reapplied for his U.S. citizenship, and was still awaiting a decision from the U.S. District Court on that matter, while the entire Nazi-hunting community had been left lost and demoralized.

"If you're not comfortable, we can go somewhere else," Galit whispered.

"No." Schwartz was defensive. "This will do just fine."

"I thought it was a good idea. Neutral turf, so to speak, and it also reminds us why we do what we do."

"I suppose you could look at it that way."

There was a brief silence between them.

"When was the last time you were in a synagogue, Richard?"

Schwartz looked her in the eye. She could tell he felt uneasy with the question, partly because, through the years they had known each other, she had never before called him by his first name. He remained quiet for a few seconds, thinking, and then said, "My son's bar mitzvah."

"You never told me you had a son."

"You never asked."

"You're right, I guess there is much about our lives that we don't discuss."

"If we even have lives."

She digested the comment. "Where is your son now?"

"Law school. Yale. No thanks to me, however. His mother divorced me when he was 3. I don't know if it was me she couldn't stand or the job. Either way, I didn't see much of him as he grew up. Paid what I had to, but was too busy with other things. You know how it is."

She nodded.

"So," Schwartz continued, "you asked for this meeting. What's it about?"

"I understand you are upset with us."

"It was a pretty stupid thing, your boys getting caught outside that psychologist's office with their pants down like that. Caused a lot of unnecessary complications."

"You knew what we were doing. You authorized it."

"I didn't authorize getting caught."

"It was nothing we did. Who could have known that someone like Gifford would be going in and out of the building regularly? He's ex-naval intelligence, trained to see things that normal people don't. You can only hide from an eye like that if you are prepared for it."

"And what do you think Jacques Benoît is, blind?" Schwartz whispered angrily. "Let me tell you, he's every bit as observant as Gifford, and every bit as smart as we are. If Gifford saw them, then Benoît did too."

"What does that matter? Benoît knows we are onto him. What difference does it make if he sees us following him?"

"All the difference in the world. Right now, we have very little on him. At best, there are only three or four eyewitnesses, a circumstantial trail, and a few old, worn photos. You know how that sort of stuff turned out in the Demjanjuk thing. We need more. I was hoping that if he felt safe for a little while, maybe he would do something stupid or lead us someplace."

Her eyes asked for an explanation.

"Look Galit, it's a reach, I know, but we're both aware that these guys sometimes consort with their cronies, keep one another abreast of happenings, dangers. They even help one another out financially. It's hard to believe that a man of Benoît's resources hasn't been approached. We only started watching him closely a few months ago, so we're not sure who he's been in touch with over the years. If we could catch him on camera with some other guy who looks familiar to us, we could start to build a stronger case, maybe get someone to turn against him, or maybe even find a bigger fish to fry."

This wasn't the first time Galit had heard this strategy, though she knew that things never quite worked out this way. Rumors of a "brotherhood" of Nazi fugitives had been rampant in the Nazi-hunting world for the past five decades but never proven. And even if such an organization had existed, the fact was that most of its members would be dead at this point. "I doubt that Benoît will be meeting with anyone," she said.

Schwartz didn't disagree; on the contrary, he wore his frustration. "So, what do you propose?"

"I say we stay on Rosen. I know it is a long shot, but he is the best thing we have."

"I hear you're getting very close to him, perhaps too close."

"Why don't you let me worry about that."

"And what do you think you can possibly get from him? Even if he learns something, it's unlikely he'll give it up, and even if he does, it wouldn't be admissible in any court."

"I know."

"So why are we wasting our time with him? Aside from your own personal amusement."

She ignored the gibe. “It is possible that he could give us something that doesn’t require testimony.”

“Like what?”

“Look, Richard, we both know that Benoît is different from the others. He is bolder, more egotistical. Instead of laying low in some blue-collar neighborhood with a menial job, he has put himself in the public eye. Of course, he has avoided photographers, but aside from that, he acts like a man with no fear. He *is* calculating and cunning, and his choice of Rosen is not an accident. I don’t know why, but I do know that he is dying to tell someone. Martin Rosen is going to learn things, and just maybe one of those things will prove useful to us.”

“It’s a lot of resources to spend on a hunch.”

“It is all we have.”

Schwartz looked at her, then shifted his eyes around the sanctuary. “Tell me, Galit, what keeps you going?”

“The same thing that keeps you going.”

His eyes landed on the Ark. “You really think we make a difference?”

“Sometimes.”

“You know, we’re becoming obsolete.”

“After this, we *will* be obsolete.”

He turned back to her, a sympathetic expression on his face. “This is it for you, isn’t it?”

“For us all, my friend.”

He considered her response. “Then let’s go out with a bang.”

“Yes, let’s.”

chapter 26

JACQUES BENOÎT HASTENED FROM HIS limousine into the bank. He was taking chances, but he gave himself no choice. He knew it shouldn't bother him that he was still being watched; after all, he went to the bank all the time. Still, he was nervous. This visit was different.

The manager met him at the entrance, as usual. "Good afternoon, Mr. Benoît. How are you today?"

"Fine, Charles, and how are you?"

"Very well," the manager answered uncomfortably. Numerous times, he had asked Benoît to call him Chuck – *My friends call me Chuck* – and never had Benoît obliged. "What can we do for you today?" he asked, trying to remain businesslike.

"The vault, please."

"Yes, of course."

The manager escorted Benoît to the vault. As he opened the file drawer for the signature card, he turned to Benoît and whispered, "Which one?"

Benoît looked at the man oddly. True, the presence of a second, and secret, vault box was a private arrangement between him and the manager – an arrangement for which the manager had been aptly rewarded – but there was no reason to whisper when they were the only ones in the room. No reason other than the manager trying to accentuate the fact the he and the billionaire shared a secret. Realizing that it was getting harder for him to suffer fools, Benoît recomposed his face and smiled. "My own," he replied, excluding the box that he shared with his wife.

The manager turned the keys and extracted the box. He carried it as he led Benoît to a private room. "If there is anything else, Mr. Benoît…"

"Thank you, Charles, that will be all."

Benoît stared at the box. It had been decades since he had opened it. A wave of dread came upon him, a feeling he didn't understand. He was alone and no one knew what he was doing. He was simply going to open the box, remove the object, place it in his pocket and leave the bank. What was there to worry about?

But deep down he knew it wasn't his fear of getting caught anymore. In fact, it wasn't fear at all. It was disgust, his own personal abhorrence of what he had done, who he had been, and his desire to somehow erase it all. Contained in this box was the one thing he had saved, his sole connection to the past. It was strange to him how his motives for keeping it had changed over time. At first, it was a trophy, a symbol of the power he'd had over others to take whatever he wanted. And now it signified his greatest weakness.

He opened the box and looked at the small manila jeweler's envelope contained within. He took the envelope and held it for a moment, thinking that perhaps he should just put it in his pocket and leave. There was no reason to torture himself needlessly. Or was there?

It dawned on him that at some point he would have to face himself; otherwise, there was no way he could complete his plan. Suddenly, with determination, he opened the envelope and removed the brooch. He stared at it, his heart beating rapidly. He grasped it and held it up, scrutinizing it beneath the light. It was just as he had remembered, exactly as he had pictured it through the years.

Until this moment, his debauchery had been cloaked in

darkness, hidden in the confines of his memories. Now it glistened vividly before his eyes.

DAN GIFFORD SHIFTED UNEASILY IN his seat. He was finding therapy increasingly difficult, considering Agent Schwartz' demands for secrecy, as well as his own decision to keep Dr. Rosen out of the loop until something concrete developed. He had been sitting for over a half hour, updating Martin about the latest developments in his case against the Colombians, doing what the psychologist called "past-timing," a therapy term for avoiding.

"Is something bothering you, Dan?" Martin said.

Gifford had anticipated the question. "Why do you ask that? I think I'm doing fine, really!"

"Well, for starters, you seem fidgety. Last week, you cancelled your appointment for the first time since we've been working together, and now we're not talking about anything meaningful."

Gifford hadn't realized he was fidgeting. It irked him that he, a seasoned pro, could be such a giveaway. He had simply become so used to letting his guard down in this room that he was no longer able to reestablish it, even at will.

Suddenly, it occurred to Gifford that a part of him must have wanted to let Rosen know that something was wrong. He had been conflicted about keeping Rosen in the dark to begin with, reluctant to compromise what was probably the only pure, honest relationship he'd ever had. He understood that his time in this room was valueless unless he somehow resolved this.

"I suppose you're right," he said.

"Have you been feeling like drinking?" Martin figured he was probably off base, but it was the first question to ask nonetheless.

"I always feel like taking a drink, Doc. That's nothing new."

Martin understood that Gifford was still too early in his sobriety to lose the thirst. It embarrassed him to have needed the reminder. "So then, what exactly is it?"

"I'm just stressed over things."

"Your separation?"

"That, and the job."

"So, talking about the Colombians isn't completely afield, I guess."

"No. Not completely."

Martin sensed the evasiveness, but the session was too close to the end to continue exploring. "I guess we'll have to pick things up here next time."

Gifford stood, dreading what he was about to say. "You know, Doc, I've been thinking..."

Martin looked at him curiously. Such words at the close of a session were usually the prelude to quitting therapy, a way for the patient to break free without any discussion. He would never have expected this from Gifford, though he had learned over the years not to be surprised by anything a patient did. Still, he found himself shocked, so much so that he could have sworn that Gifford was going to say something else completely.

"I feel like I need a break from this," Gifford continued.

"Don't you think this is something we should have talked about at the beginning of the session?" Martin tried to contain his disappointment.

Gifford was silent. He was angry with himself, despite his belief that he had no choice but to handle things this way. He couldn't just keep coming here with a secret, and he couldn't divulge his secret until he knew what it was all about. His paranoia, and Schwartz' warning, had landed him in a pickle, and now he had to see it through. For his own mental health, if nothing else.

"Look, Doc, I'm sorry for not bringing it up sooner. It's just that we're getting closer to trial and I'm not going to have time for anything else for a while. I'll be back, I promise, as soon as the trial's over. Maybe sooner if things go okay."

Martin heard the outer door open. His next appointment: Jacques Benoît, prompt as usual. Martin knew he should be used to this by now; patients left treatment abruptly all the time. It was rare, in fact, when treatment actually ended according to plan. Part of that was because many therapists never had a termination plan, and would keep their patients forever unless the patient made the break. The other part concerned the patients, who, because of their fear of chastisement as well as other issues around separation, frequently resorted to such tactics.

But Martin had always regarded himself as different, and found himself acutely disappointed that Dan Gifford didn't seem to see that. He had even frequently joked with colleagues about the interminable nature of therapy, gibing them with a little-known passage he had once read in Jung's book, "Psychology and Religion," saying that therapy ends only "when the patient runs out of money." That there was nothing he could say in the time remaining to influence Gifford was the most frustrating thing of all. "Why don't you give me a call so we can discuss this further?" he said in an unusually clinical manner.

"Sure. Okay, I'll call you."

Martin believed Gifford was lying, and still he couldn't do anything about it. Gifford held out his hand and the two men shook. Martin felt the sweat in Gifford's palm and wanted to reach out and shake the man back to his senses. But, as always, another patient was waiting.

Later in the afternoon, Martin dialed for the third time that day the phone number for Jacob Lipton Associates. On his previous calls, he had asked for Cheryl and was immediately fed to her voice mail. He had chosen not to leave a message.

Once again, he got her voice mail, a simple outgoing message: *Hi, this is Cheryl Manning. I am either away from my desk or on another line. Please leave a message, and I will return your call shortly. If you'd like to speak with the receptionist, please press the star key.*

Martin held the receiver to his ear, looking out the window, wondering what to do, reluctant to respond.

Perhaps it was his insecurity, he reflected, the feeling that once he left a message he would relinquish control, giving her the opportunity to choose when to call back. But he knew it wasn't that. On the contrary, he was fairly certain that she wanted him as much as he wanted her.

Clueless to the cause of his reticence, he forced himself to get past it. "Hi Cheryl, it's Marty. Give me a call as soon as you get a chance. Bye."

chapter 28

MARTHA BENOÎT WATCHED HER HUSBAND stare out the window. They had been riding in the back of the limo for close to half an hour and he had barely uttered a word. She looked at her watch; it was 7:18. The fundraiser for the American Red Cross was scheduled for 7:30 at the Hilton on Sixth Avenue, and they were just nearing the Queens entrance to the Midtown Tunnel. They would be more than fashionably late at this point, a position that normally would have Jacques on edge, especially because he was one of the honorees. But he seemed oblivious, his mind elsewhere.

"Is everything all right?" she asked.

"Yes, everything is fine," he responded, still gazing out the window.

"Do you see anything interesting?"

"I'm sorry," he said, turning to her. "I was just thinking about something."

She decided not to intrude, though this had become more difficult since the suicide attempt. She was now the constant worrier, the very sort of wife she'd always sworn she'd never be. She'd tried convincing herself that things were okay, that he was in good hands with Dr. Rosen, but at times like this, she wondered.

"Don't worry, dear," he said, putting his hand on her lap and a smile on his face. "We are going to have a splendid evening."

She returned the smile, pretending to be mollified. It was the best she could do at the moment. But she knew something was wrong.

The sound of footsteps behind Dan Gifford would have caught his attention earlier, had he not been so preoccupied. He had just left his office and was walking in the garage to his car. The first thing he noticed was that the steps sounded like there were two people; the pace and heaviness suggested males. If they were simply two other night owls heading toward a car, they would likely be chatting, which they weren't. Hence his conclusion that they were there for him.

He reached into his blazer, removed his Glock from its shoulder holster and held the gun against his chest, out of sight from his pursuers. He felt anxious. It had been years since he'd been in a position like this. He took a deep breath and told himself he was prepared. This was turning out to be one hell of a day.

There was a time when he had believed he was finished with guns, before his promotion to major crimes and his dealings with criminals from whom the law offered little protection. Now, carrying a weapon was as ordinary as wearing his wristwatch, and while it felt familiar in his hand, he hadn't actually needed to use one since his days in Vietnam.

The garage was dimly lit, with a few security cameras. But it was late and he was sure that whoever was at the other end of those cameras was either sleeping, on a break, or doing something other than watching. As far as he could tell, there was no one else in the garage except for him and the men following him.

He turned a corner and quickly slipped out of sight behind a row of cars. The pace of his pursuers hastened. He slouched down, both hands on the 9 mm, trying to get a glimpse of them without being seen. No one. He figured they split up and would try to surround him.

He was as good as blind now, so he used his ears, catching some movement at five o' clock about twenty feet away. Then, a muffled click, more familiar to his instincts than his consciousness. He hit the ground just as the window directly above him exploded and the car alarm started blasting. They had his position and were using silencers. Definitely professionals.

He quickly removed his shoes and fired off three rounds in the direction of the shot, setting off two more car alarms. He began maneuvering between the cars, staying low for cover. It wouldn't be long before help would come; meanwhile, he just had to stay alive. The noise from the alarms made it impossible for him to track them without using his eyes. He lifted his head slightly, and pulled down just in time to miss another bullet.

He knew he was trapped, that these guys weren't apt to leave empty-handed. He needed to retreat toward a wall or partition. With two of them out there, he definitely had to have his back against a wall. He began crawling when, suddenly, a voice called out.

"Mr. Gifford?"

He noted the characteristics of the voice – deep, raspy, accented, definitely Spanish, most likely Colombian – but he didn't respond. He wasn't about to give up his position.

"You do not have to answer us, we know you are there. We are not here to kill you. Otherwise, you'd be dead already. We only want to talk to you about Roberto Alvarez. We will let you live and even pay you a sizeable sum of money if you tell us where he is."

So that's what this was about; they were Colombians. He wasn't surprised. He had known that it would only be a matter of time before Miguel Domingo made a move against Alvarez. He let his silence be his answer.

"If that is how you want it, Mr. Gifford, we are sorry we cannot let you live. We have to send a message to Roberto, I am sure your wife and son will understand."

Gifford had to admit, these guys spooked him. And that's exactly what they were trying to do, psych him into something stupid.

Suddenly, he heard the sound of screeching tires, a car entering the garage one flight up. Could be cops, or reinforcements for the goons. Either way, he was staying put. Let them come to him. However this was going to end, he wasn't going out alone.

More screeching as the car turned a corner. Red flashing lights. The good guys. Gifford felt pangs of relief, until all at once a barrage of car windows started shattering around him. Glass flew in every direction. The silencers letting loose.

He then heard standard gunfire, someone else in on the action. The silencers still firing, but no longer in his direction.

He crawled away from the wall, toward the end of the row of cars, stuck his head out from behind the rear wheel of a car and saw a brown Chevy with a flashing red bubble on the dash, blown out windows, abandoned. Bobby Marcus' car.

What was Marcus doing here?

The gunfire subsided.

Was Marcus injured?

"Bobby?" Gifford yelled, no longer caring about revealing his position.

No response.

Gifford swallowed hard, thinking that Marcus was either down or reconnoitering.

"Your friend is dead, Mr. Gifford, but you still have a chance to get out of this alive," the Spanish voice said.

"Fuck you!" Gifford yelled.

"Have it your way."

Suddenly, loud gunfire rang out. Gifford looked again and saw Marcus crouched, moving between cars, approaching the goons, a gun in each hand. It was time for him to go on the offensive as well.

He eased out, under cover from Marcus' shots, and began firing in the same direction. The two of them gave each other cover as they closed in on the Colombians. Luckily, no one hit a gas tank. Yet.

Gifford caught up with Marcus when, abruptly, his Glock emptied. They both ducked behind a car. Marcus handed Gifford his second piece and an extra magazine. The silencers began returning fire.

"Something's going to blow up," Gifford said nervously.

"Not a bad idea," Marcus responded.

"Are you crazy? You'll kill us all!"

"It's better than letting them win, don't you think?"

Gifford looked at him, expressionless.

"It's your call," Marcus said as he dropped out his empty magazine and slid in a new one. "You're the boss."

"Go for it."

Marcus took the low, picking off two shots at the tank of the car shielding the goons. Gifford went from above, firing in the same direction. They heard sirens from afar, reinforcements on the way.

The silencers stopped. The Colombians were yelling, this time in Spanish.

"Speak Spanish?" Marcus asked.

"Not a word."

"Me neither. Bet they can't believe what we're doing. Probably think we're suicidal."

"They're right. They also know that our guys are coming. They're running out of time. Now let's see what they're made of." He raised his voice, and said, "Drop your guns and give it up, or we're all going out together!"

He knew they wouldn't comply; in their world, that would be suicide. But it was obvious that their plan had failed. Men like this were always used to easy targets, and never prepared for the unexpected. They were desperate; it was only a matter of seconds before they would do something stupid. He picked off another shot at the tank, just to raise the ante.

The Colombians emerged from their cover, firing their silencers, trying to make a break for it.

"Let's get them," Marcus said.

"Let them go! The blue and whites will get them."

"Sorry, boss, can't do that," Marcus said as he darted in pursuit.

Gifford had no choice now, he couldn't let Marcus go it alone. He followed behind, firing at the Colombians. The Colombians returned fire, but out in the open they were no match. Within seconds, they were down.

Marcus and Gifford walked over to the bodies. Marcus bent down and felt their pulses.

"Dead?" Gifford asked.

"As doornails."

The two men looked at each other. Gifford didn't know what to feel. Marcus had defied his directive but had also saved his life.

"What's with the two guns?" Gifford asked. Carrying more than one gun was against departmental regulations.

"It always pays to be careful."

"Ballistics will figure it out when they analyze all the shells."

"Ballistics won't be analyzing shit here. With your story, these creeps dead, and us alive, no one's gonna spend the time or the money. This isn't even gonna make the papers." He looked back down at the bodies. "Assholes won't be missed by anyone."

Marcus had a point, Gifford reflected, however disturbing it may have been. The two of them walked away from the bodies toward Marcus' car.

"What were you doing here anyway?" Gifford asked.

"I came by to update you on the Schwartz thing, was just pulling up in front of the building when I heard shots from the garage." He reached into the glove compartment, took out a pack of cigarettes and held it out for Gifford.

"No thanks. Thought you quit?"

"I did. Always keep a pack around for emergencies though." He lit a cigarette and inhaled deeply, as if for his last breath.

"It's a good thing you were around," Gifford said.

"I'll say."

"I wonder where security was."

Marcus looked at him sardonically. "The square badge? Probably called the cops then sat and waited."

"Probably." Gifford looked back at the bodies. Regardless of who they were, he felt nauseated. It had been years since he'd killed anyone. "So, what'd you find out about Schwartz?" he asked, trying to collect himself.

"Nothing."

"Nothing?"

"Seems this Schwartz fellow works with a small team, no one talks, and he reports directly to the top."

"The top?"

"Deputy director."

"No leaks?"

"Not a one. Would you believe it? We oughta have this guy work for us."

"You wouldn't like him."

"Probably not. I don't like anybody." He drew on his cigarette. "Let me ask you something. Why go worrying about this Schwartz character? You don't got enough on your plate with this thing here?"

Gifford nodded.

"You got the biggest trial of your career in three weeks and a bunch of Colombian badasses after you. Who gives a shit about some Nazi thing on Long Island?"

"Point well taken," Gifford said, though he knew it was contrary to his nature to give up like that. He was tired and didn't want to justify himself to anyone right now.

They heard the sirens of police cars entering the garage above.

"Come," said Marcus, placing his hand on Gifford's shoulder, "let's go meet the cavalry."

chapter 29

DAN GIFFORD FOUND HIMSELF FLUSTERED by the inquisitive expression of the bartender.

"Haven't seen you for quite a while," the man said, waiting for Gifford to say something.

Gifford eyed the selection. Gin had always been his drink of choice, usually some cheap house brand, but on special occasions Beefeater or Tanqueray. He wondered what this particular evening called for.

"Need a minute?" the bartender asked.

Gifford nodded, staring at the bottles as if he were alone. The bartender took the cue and wandered away.

Gifford's thoughts were racing. From the moment he had stopped drinking, he suspected that he would never be completely beyond this. And now it was clear.

The bartender returned with a shot of gin and a chaser of club soda.

"I didn't ask for that," Gifford said.

"It's a gift from Marjorie."

Gifford shifted his gaze to the other side of the bar, and there sat Marjorie Phillips, one of his old drinking cronies. She was as thin as ever – the product of years of drinking her meals – and her face was encased in makeup to hide its wear. Her blouse was tight, her nails bright red, and her hair bleached glistening blond. Sadly enough, at that moment she looked tempting.

She smiled and held up a glass to toast, as if to say, "Welcome back, Danny boy." He lifted his shot glass, painted on a polite grin, then sat the glass back down on the bar. He knew he had but a few moments before she walked over and offered to sit with him, and the next thing he would remember would be waking up beside her in that shoddy SRO she called home. It scared the shit out of him that he could even consider this.

He thought about Martin Rosen. Boy, he really screwed up that one. Maybe he should follow Bobby Marcus' advice: just forget this Schwartz thing, erase it from his mind. If he did, then he could return to Rosen and get his life back on track.

He felt a tap on his shoulder.

"Hi, Dan," Marjorie said as she eased onto the stool beside him.

"Marj," he responded. The power of her perfume was enough to make him wish he had a facemask.

"Long time no see."

"A while," he said. "Thanks for the drink."

She ran her nails down his neckline, onto his chest. "I see you haven't touched it."

He looked at the shot glass.

"Shame to let good booze go to waste."

He nodded.

"So, where you been?"

"Here and there." He wasn't being evasive. She was asking for the hell of it and any answer was fine.

"Really? I've been there too," she said.

He feigned another smile.

"So, you gonna drink or what?"

"I haven't decided."

She moved her hand down to his lap, then up the inside of his thigh. "Wish you would."

He swallowed. "I bet."

She stroked a little harder and felt him rise. "Nice to know you're still healthy."

"You always do it for me, Marj."

"Then why not let old Marjie take care of you now?"

No response.

She rose from the stool, pressed her body close to his. "You know I can," she whispered. No one in the bar seemed to notice.

He took a deep breath, moved her back a bit, and looked into her bloodshot eyes. "I'm sorry, Marj. I just can't."

Her mouth was open. It was hard for him to tell if she was angry or stunned. But he decided he wasn't going to stick around long enough to find out. "Thanks again for the drink," he said as he turned on his heel and left.

He put the key in the ignition and sat in his car, staring at the door to the bar, wondering if he should go back in. He knew that even when he got home and was lying in bed, the temptation to get dressed and return would still be with him. Marj would still be there, she would always be there. And never with hard feelings or resentment, at least none that couldn't be washed away with a drink or two.

He pounded the dashboard with his fist. Would it always be this hard, he wondered. Would he ever be able to make a clean break, and never be tempted again? Dr. Rosen had assured him it would get better with time, *lots of time*, and hard work. In AA, they had touted the same line. But he had become a mite too negligent these past few weeks, and had eased up on the meetings. Rosen had brought this up a few times, and Gifford had promised to go back. He just hadn't gotten around to it. Now he was on his own.

He reached into his pocket, took out his phone and dialed. Depending on one's perspective, it was either late in the evening or early in the morning. He didn't care. He had to make the call.

A woman's voice came on the line. "Hello?"

He didn't respond.

"Hello?"

Nothing.

"Danny, is that you?" Stephanie Gifford asked.

He knew she would figure it was him; he had done this so many times before, only never sober. "Yeah," he said, his voice laden with vulnerability.

"Where are you?"

"Outside McNally's."

Silence.

"I'm sorry," he said, "I shouldn't have bothered you."

"Wait!" she said.

He waited.

"Did you drink?"

"Not yet."

He sensed relief from her end, and wondered if she still cared for him or if her concern was strictly the byproduct of his being the father of their child.

There was some interference on the connection.

"Dan, you still there?"

"Yeah."

"You okay?"

"I guess."

She hesitated, then said, "Do you want to come by?"

He was surprised by the offer. "That's all right, I'll be fine."

"I'd like you to."

"Steph, you don't have to…"

"I'm not feeling sorry for you. I just think you should come home tonight."

Home. It struck in him a sense of longing, yet the thought of actually going there brought wariness. Was he ready? Could he return to her arms without telling her what had happened earlier in the garage? He knew he couldn't. Yet he also knew that it wasn't right to burden her with fear. "Maybe another time."

"Dan, are you in some type of trouble?"

"Nothing more than usual."

"There's a policeman sitting in a car down the block. They've been watching and following us."

"I know."

"They're trying awfully hard not to let me know they're there."

"They don't know who they're dealing with."

"I had a good teacher."

He smiled.

"Is there something I need to be concerned about?"

"Yes." He couldn't lie.

She was silent.

"They're on you twenty-four seven," he said, referring to the cops.

"Is that good enough?"

"I think so. They're handpicked by Bobby Marcus."

She didn't ask who the bad guys were, because she knew. She was always aware of his cases and how they intruded upon their lives – that was part of the problem. "Should I go to my mother?"

"No. If these guys wanted you, they'd find you. I really think you're safer the way things are now, and I want you and Danny Jr. close by." There was one more thing he needed to say to her, but he didn't know how to word it. "Look, just to be careful, I think you should…"

"Don't worry, Dan, I already have it. I put it in my bag the moment I made those cops."

"Where is it now?"

"Under my pillow."

"Good."

"Like I said, I had a good teacher."

"I wish you wouldn't say that in past tense."

"Maybe I won't… some day."

"That would be nice."

"Yes, it would."

chapter 30

THE THREE MOSSAD AGENTS SAT around the table, examining fifty-year-old photographs and comparing them with recent ones. The older pictures were weathered and too imprecise for definitive conclusions. But this was all they had.

"We have to be certain it's him," Galit said, her tone betraying her frustration.

"Don't worry," Kovi responded. "Once we have him, plenty of witnesses will come forward, believe me."

"A lot of good the *witnesses* did us with Demjanjuk!" she snapped.

She held up a dated photograph of Benoît that had appeared in an Israeli newspaper a year earlier, when the tycoon was negotiating to build a resort on the Red Sea in Aqaba, Jordan, adjacent to the Israeli border. Since Benoît had been adept in avoiding photographers over the years, the enterprising young journalist who authored the article had managed to dig up an old copy of a passport photo. A week later, an elderly Israeli gentleman came to Yad Vashem, Israel's Holocaust museum and research center, claiming that the photograph in the paper was of one Theodore Lemieux, former captain in the Vichy police in Lyon between 1940-1944, who had personally supervised the roundup of thousands of Jews for deportation to Nazi concentration camps. Because such accusations were common, and because Lemieux was believed to have been killed in the summer of 1944 during the Allied liberation, the old man's claim was noted, filed, and ignored. That was until two other witnesses also came forward with the same assertion.

The case was then referred to a particular Hebrew University professor, a Holocaust historian who had been writing a book on Vichy France's collaboration with the Nazis during World War II. The professor, compelled by the witnesses' accounts, traveled to France, where he toiled through piles of official state archives searching for a connection between Theodore Lemieux and Jacques Benoît. While he had managed to find an old photo of the Vichy police captain, it was too tattered to make an absolute match to Benoît.

In searching through employment records, however, the professor discovered that Lemieux's parents owned a small inn on the outskirts of the city and that, surprisingly enough, there was a young man of Theodore's age named Jacques Benoît who happened to work for them. He also learned that the first hotel that the billionaire Jacques Benoît had built was on the French Caribbean island, Guadeloupe. There were no records of how Benoît obtained his financing, but there were travel documents showing that he had arrived on the island in the fall of 1944, shortly after the reported death of Theodore Lemieux. Taking the eyewitnesses' claims seriously, the professor surmised that the real Benoît was killed during the Allied liberation, either by Lemieux or by some other means, and that Lemieux switched identities with the dead man and fled to Guadeloupe where no one would recognize him.

Documents revealed that the new Benoît remained in Guadeloupe, married there, had a son, and hadn't ventured off the island for several years. When he finally did begin to travel, he visited France only sporadically and steered clear of Lyon and its vicinities, fearing he might be recognized. The professor wondered why the French government hadn't adequately investigated the supposed death of this potential war criminal, and concluded that its embarrassment over its ineffectiveness and complicity during the war had created within its ranks a strong desire to close the history books for that period. The politicians had probably turned their eyes away from several similar scenarios.

"It may be circumstantial, but I'm convinced," Arik said.

"You being convinced isn't enough, we need hard evidence, something concrete, identifying Benoît as the Monster of Lyon," Galit responded. "Has there been any information from his house?"

"Schwartz has it wiretapped, every room and telephone. They're also running constant surveillance outside. Nothing yet," Kovi responded.

"Why don't they bug Martin Rosen's office?" Arik asked.

"Because no judge would allow that, and Schwartz would never do it without a warrant," Galit said.

"Maybe *we* can tap it?" Arik said.

"That would be a very bad idea," Galit answered. "The Justice Department is watching this investigation very carefully. They're tired of these Nazi cases, and eager for any reason to pull the plug and send us home. If we go breaking their laws, they've got one."

"I don't believe that anything we might get from the shrink's office would even be usable in an Israeli court," Kovi added.

"Probably not," Galit said. "We're just going to do this one the old-fashioned way."

Kovi offered an agreeable look. "I still wonder why Benoît is going to a Jewish shrink," he said.

"Stop wondering," Galit replied. "He is simply trying to confuse us, to make us question if he is who we think he is."

"Do you really believe that Rosen will help us in the end?" Arik asked her.

"I don't know," she answered. "His father is a rabbi and both his parents are survivors. On the other hand, he has the rules of his profession." She pondered a moment, then added, "He is quite independent-minded, only I don't know whether that will work for us or against us."

MARTIN ROSEN GRABBED THE PHONE on its first ring. He let out a drowsy "hello," then looked at the clock and realized it was 7 a.m. He had been up most of the night, ruminating about where Cheryl Manning might be and why she hadn't returned his call.

"Marty, hi, it's Cheryl."

Even on half throttle, he could sense tension in her voice; perhaps guilt over not getting back to him sooner. He didn't want to make an issue of it. There were no strings between them. She had a right to do whatever she had been doing.

"I'm sorry I didn't call you last night," she said. "I got in late and didn't want to wake you."

"That's okay," he lied. He was bothered by his jealousy. "Hey, are you ever in that office of yours? I must have gotten your voice mail three or four times before I left a message."

"Actually, I've been out coddling my latest client."

He was silent.

"When am I going to see you?" she asked.

"I was hoping for tonight. Elizabeth has a playdate with her cousins after school today. We'll probably spend a couple of hours at the park, get some kosher pizza, then I'm all yours."

"Kosher pizza?"

"Elizabeth's cousins are Orthodox. It's a long story."

"And an interesting one, I'm sure."

"That too."

"I look forward to hearing it."

"Then why don't we meet for dinner, say around 8?"

"Sounds good to me. Where?"

"Millie's okay?"

"You're such a creature of habit."

"That I am."

"Then Millie's it is. Eight sharp."

"Good. See you there."

"Marty," she said, changing her tone. "Is everything all right?"

"Yes," he answered defensively. "Why do you ask?"

"Only because you seemed a little strange the other night as you left."

"It was just a moment. I'm over it," he said, troubled by his own duplicity.

"Okay," she said, adding her own pretense, "I'll see you tonight then."

"Looking forward to it."

"Me too."

BOBBY MARCUS STRUTTED INTO DAN Gifford's office and dropped two manila files on the desk, each with a photo clipped to the cover.

"These the guys?" Gifford asked. It was hard for him to connect the pictures to the dead Colombians in the garage the night before.

"That's them."

Gifford lifted the first file, opened it and examined the contents. The rap sheet was long, and the guy was a recent parolee for what appeared to have been a plea bargain down to manslaughter. "Nice record. Good thing the taxpayers can sleep at night knowing we keep our hardened criminals behind bars."

He tossed the file on his desk.

"Take a look at the other one," Marcus said.

"Why? I'm sure it's more of the same."

Marcus eyed his boss. "Something wrong?"

"Of course something's wrong. I killed two men last night."

"Whoa, wait just a minute there! First of all, they tried to take you out. Second, what makes you think *you* killed them?"

"I guess we'll never know, considering there won't be any ballistics."

"You want ballistics? Order it."

Gifford stared into space. He knew a ballistics test could mean trouble for Marcus. "Let's forget about it."

"Look, Dan, you don't owe me because I saved your ass. That was part of the job."

"I know. I owe you because you're a friend."

Marcus smiled. "Gee, does that mean you wanna go out dancing tonight?"

"All right, cut the shit."

"Whatever you say. You're the boss."

Gifford got up from his chair and walked toward the window.

"Where'd you go after the shoot?" Marcus asked in a tone that pretty much indicated he knew the answer.

"A bar." Gifford was looking out at the view.

"Did you drink?"

"No."

"But it's not over."

Gifford thought for a moment. "It's never over."

Marcus was way over his head in this discussion. While being on the job for so many years had given him more than enough exposure to alcoholism, he still couldn't claim to understand it. "You still go to those meetings?" he asked.

Gifford turned away from the window and looked askance at Marcus. It took him a moment to realize that it was Bobby Marcus, and not some nosy, intrusive acquaintance, who was asking. The man cared about him and deserved an honest response. "No, I haven't," he said, his expression softening.

"Maybe you should."

Gifford turned back toward the window. "Maybe."

"What about the shrink? Does he know about the shoot?"

"No. I cut that off for a while."

Marcus gave Gifford a concerned look. "Because of the Schwartz thing?"

"Precisely."

"Look, Dan, since I'm already prying beyond the limit, I'll

come out and say what I gotta say. First, I know that killing someone isn't completely novel to you. It isn't for me either. But that doesn't matter, because regardless of how many times you do it, it never gets easy. And it also doesn't make that much difference if the dead guy's a dirtbag who didn't deserve to live in the first place."

"What's your point?"

"My first point is that you don't look so good. My other point is that I'm headed to the department shrink this afternoon, partly because they're making me, and partly because I think it's a good idea."

"The DA's office doesn't require psychological debriefing after a shooting."

"Bullshit. The reason there's no policy is because it never happens. How many ADA's you know that have been involved in shootings?"

"None," Gifford granted.

"You know what I think?"

"I'm sure you're going to tell me."

Marcus smiled. "I think that maybe you should forget all about that Schwartz stuff, which isn't any of our business to begin with, and give that shrink of yours a call."

Gifford knew his friend was right. He sat down on his chair, looked Marcus in the eye and responded, "Maybe I should."

chapter 33

ELIZABETH ROSEN'S HAIR FLEW BACK as she soared toward the sky. "Higher, Daddy, higher!" she demanded, her hands wrapped tightly around the swing's chains. She reached her peak, then floated backward into her father's hands for another push, this one even stronger than she'd hoped. She laughed as the chains loosened, then became taut again.

"Marty!" Esther roared, worried for her niece's safety.

Martin reacted with a smile.

"Just do me a favor, slow it down a bit with her."

"Sure, Sis, whatever you say." He lightened up on his next few pushes. "My arms were getting tired anyway."

"Higher, Daddy, higher!"

"Sorry, princess, I've been overruled."

"What's overruled, Daddy?"

"It's when your aunt Esther tells me what to do."

Elizabeth's cousins came running over. The eldest, Michali, was holding a soccer ball. "Can we have a drink, Ima?" Devorah, the younger one, asked.

So far, the outing had been a dismal failure. Neither Esther nor Martin knew quite what to do to get all three children to play together. They couldn't blame the kids. They were practically strangers. Michali was 7 years old, Devorah 6, and sadly, all they knew of their cousin and uncle was a single visit two years earlier, and stories their mother had shared with them. The same was true for Elizabeth.

The discomfort was apparent.

"Of course," Esther answered. She reached into her bag and took out a juice box, stuck in the straw and handed it to Michali. "Why don't you offer this one to your cousin?" she whispered.

"But Ima, I'm thirsty!"

"Don't worry, honey, I have plenty of juice boxes. It's a mitzvah to offer other people first. Remember the story of Abraham and the three strangers?"

"Yes, Ima, I remember," the girl responded, rolling her eyes.

Martin was still swinging Elizabeth, pretending not to overhear. Michali walked around the side of the swing, her younger sister dutifully following. "Would you like something to drink, Elizabeth?" Michali asked.

"Yes," Elizabeth answered shyly.

Martin slowed the swing so Michali could hand the juice box to Elizabeth.

"Thank you," Elizabeth said, looking at both girls.

"You're welcome," the sisters responded in unison, then ran back to their mother.

"Elizabeth," Esther called out, "I have cookies too."

Elizabeth turned to her father, who nodded his approval. She slowly came off the swing and inched over to her cousins and aunt. This time, Esther had Devorah hand her cousin a cookie.

"Thank you," Elizabeth said.

"Tell me, Elizabeth," Esther said, "do you play soccer?"

"Yes, my daddy showed me how."

"I play in a league," Michali jumped in.

"And so do you, Devorah," Esther said, trying to goad the younger sister to participate. "Why don't the three of you go play together?"

The two sisters looked at each other, then at their cousin.

"Okay," Michali said, taking the lead as if she knew it was her job.

The girls ran off with the ball, leaving Esther and Martin sitting on a bench.

"Good job," Martin said.

"They just needed a push."

"Elizabeth has really been looking forward to this for a long time."

"So have the girls. But you know how it is, the reality is always different than the fantasy."

"I'll say."

"Speaking of reality and fantasy, how are yours?"

"Things are good."

She elbowed him in the side. "Come on, Marty, tell me about her!"

"What makes you think there's a her?"

"You said there was."

"That was more than a week ago."

"Don't tell me you're becoming a love 'em and leave 'em type!"

"Not quite."

"Then what's going on?"

He didn't want to discuss the topic, especially considering recent developments. Yet he knew he couldn't get away without telling her something. "What's going on is that I met someone nice, I've seen her a few times, and that's about it."

"*That's about it?* You don't expect to get away with that, little brother. When was the last time you saw someone more than once? A few times! For you, that's going steady."

"Going steady?"

She elbowed him again. "Don't make fun of my terminology. So I'm a little behind the times."

"I just don't get what's so important about my social life."

She looked at him soberly and took his hand. "Look, Marty, for the past two years you've been in a daze. I don't mean to minimize Katherine and Ethan's deaths, and God knows I can't imagine what it's like to have something like that happen. But two years is an awfully long time for someone your age not to meet someone. At times, I've thought that you would never again get involved with anyone. I guess I'm just excited for you and I care about you."

"I know you care." He squeezed her hand.

"And if you don't want to tell me, you don't have to."

He nodded.

She smiled, then simultaneously, as if in sync, they turned to watch the children playing. "Looks like they're getting along nicely," Esther said.

He thought about that for a moment, how easy it would be for the kids to relate to one another at this point in their lives and how difficult it would become for them in the future. They would lead lives as distinctive as his and Esther's, perhaps more so because Elizabeth had never had any exposure to the religion. And in the end, her cousins wouldn't even regard her as Jewish. He wondered why he was bothering in the first place, what kind of pain this might one day bring his daughter. And then he reminded himself of the other side of the equation: life is long, full of surprises, and one never knows what it will bring. Hearing Elizabeth's laughter, watching her rollick with Esther's children from afar, reassured him that somehow she would find her way, just as he would find his. Only now, he was on a detour unsure where he might end up. He had always been a person of little faith, but now he was wondering more and more if there might be something beyond himself and this moment. Just what that something was, however, he wouldn't speculate.

"It's nice to see," he said.

"We should do this more often."

"I'd like to." He turned to her. "The reason I'm being cryptic about this other thing is simply because I don't understand it. You know how important it is for me to understand things. After all, I'm in the business."

She nodded. "Maybe you're trying too hard."

"You're probably right. But I can't help myself, it's my nature."

"I wonder what you tell your patients when they say that."

He smiled. "Point well taken."

"Why don't you try relaxing, let it happen and see where it takes you."

"It's just that it's going so fast. I find myself absorbed with this woman, and I hardly even know her. I'm... lost in her." He was surprised at his honesty. He hadn't been this forthcoming with Reddy.

"Isn't that the best part of it though? The trick isn't to avoid getting infatuated, it's to sustain the infatuation even after you know the person like the back of your hand."

"This from a woman who met her husband through a matchmaker!"

"Ah, but that's exactly the point. You see, I met many men through the matchmaker – all suitable on paper, at least as far as Mamma and Papa were concerned – but I married the one I was infatuated with. Did I know him when I married him? Of course not! And when I did get to know him and, as in all marriages, discovered things about him that annoyed me, what kept me going was that infatuation. If you have that, so intensely and so soon, I think it's a good thing."

"Interesting. Surprising though, coming from you."

"You disappoint me, little brother. You should know better than to pigeonhole me like that."

He considered her point. "You're right. I'm sorry."

"Apology accepted. So, you want to tell me more about this lady? I'll bet she's gorgeous."

"I think so."

"And smart, probably very smart."

"That too."

"Yet there's more, something else that's bothering you."

"Is it that obvious?"

"With you, Marty, nothing's obvious."

He bent over and seemed lost in thought for a moment. She rubbed his shoulder.

"So, what is it?" she asked.

"Nothing, I suppose. I'm probably scared, that's all."

"That's okay, it's a good sign."

"I suppose you could look at it that way."

"You *should* look at it that way." She got up from the bench and held out her hand. "Now, let's go play with the kids."

He pulled himself up and fell in stride beside her. As they walked, he wondered why she let the conversation end so easily. Was it that she knew he was throwing her a line of bull? Of course, it had to have been. She had always been able to read him as no one else could. Well enough to know when not to push. He looked at her out of the corner of his eye as they approached the children, and a smile came to his face.

chapter 34

CHERYL MANNING GAZED INTO MARTIN Rosen's eyes, imagining the suspicions he might be having. Her heart was laden with the fear of losing him once he learned the truth.

They had been sitting in the restaurant for over an hour and things seemed fine on the surface. She wanted to be with him again. He was able to get to her in a way that no man ever had. And she was eager to invite him back to her place again to see if whatever had hit him the other night would recur, and perhaps learn what it was.

"So, what's next on the agenda?" he asked.

"I don't know." Coy. "What did you have in mind?"

"Gee," he responded, "beats me. That's why I asked you."

"My apartment?" she asked.

"Exactly what I was hoping you'd say." He signaled the waiter for a check.

They sat together on the couch in her living room, holding

hands, gazing at each other, engaging in the prerequisite rituals to the inevitable. Much of their thoughts remained unspoken.

"I have a confession," she said.

His eyes opened widely.

"You sure you want to hear it?"

"I want to hear anything you have to say."

She squeezed his hand tighter. "It's just that... well, I know we've being seeing each other for such a short time, but... I want to tell you that you make me feel special."

He smiled. "You make *me* feel special." He hesitated. "You make me feel alive again."

"I've never said that to a man before. I suppose I never met the right person."

Her last statement sounded a bit cliché to him, and he figured there had to be more to it. A woman of her intelligence and beauty must have had lovers before, and if not, there would be a better reason than the one she had just offered. His reservations gnawed at him even more.

"Is something wrong?" she asked.

"No, nothing. I just... think too much, that's all."

"I've noticed that."

"You have?"

"Like the other night, as you were leaving, the way you drifted off, it felt strange to me."

"It was really nothing," he said, wondering why she was bringing it up again. "I just get spacey now and then."

"I'll try and get used to it. If that's the only strange thing about you, I think we can work it out." She moved closer to him.

"You know what they say about us shrinks?"

"That you're all voyeurs?" she said, kissing his neck.

"That wasn't exactly what I was referring to, but it'll do."

He lifted her head to his, brought their lips together, and was once again struck by the same staggering intensity of their first kiss. All he wanted was to have her, then and there, for as long as they could stand it. And whatever doubts that still lingered in his mind he cast aside, as he was powerless in the wake of his need to surrender.

"Tell me about Elizabeth," she said, sitting up in bed, stroking his hair.

"Now?" he mumbled, his face in the pillow. He turned to her. "Aren't you exhausted?"

"Yes. But if I go to sleep, you'll leave."

He sat up and kissed her gently on the cheek.

"I hate it when you go," she said.

"So do I."

"So, tell me about her!"

Martin considered his response. "Well, for starters, she's the most beautiful creation in the universe. She's smart, precocious, fun, bratty, spoiled and delicious."

Cheryl smiled, though inside she felt some jealousy. *Is he describing his daughter, his ex-wife, or both*? "I'd like to meet her," she said, not fully believing that the words had actually slipped from her tongue.

Martin's face turned serious. "You think that's a good idea just yet?"

"It doesn't have to be tomorrow," she responded, her tone guarded. "I meant eventually."

"Why don't we talk more about it next time we see each other?" he suggested, sounding more like a therapist than a lover.

"Okay," she said, appearing eager to let the topic drop.

He looked at the clock on the night table, then back at her. He didn't have to say it; they both knew it was time for him to go.

chapter 35

MARTIN ROSEN NOTICED THAT JACQUES Benoît appeared more pensive than usual.

"I have something to show you," Benoît said.

Martin lifted his eyebrows.

"It's really not that exciting, just something I've held onto for several years."

Keen as he was to Benoît's knack for understatement, Martin knew that if the billionaire was bothering to show him something, it would prove to be important. He watched as Benoît reached into his pocket and took out a jeweler's envelope.

Benoît handed the envelope to Martin. "Go ahead, take a look."

Martin opened the envelope and slid the brooch out into his palm. He examined it for a minute, then looked at Benoît. "It's very pretty. What is it?"

"A piece I saved from the war. I've kept it in my bank vault since."

Martin hesitated, wondering what was going on. "Why are you showing it to *me*?"

"Because I would like for you to have it."

"Jacques, you know I can't really..."

"If you'll just hear me out," Benoît interrupted, "you might look upon this gesture a little differently."

Martin nodded.

"You see," Benoît continued, "this piece once belonged to a Jewish woman whom I had met briefly. My unit was hiding her and her two children from the Vichy police in the hills of Lyon. I believe the husband was a banker and had hidden assets, if memory serves me. Anyway, the Vichy thought he would be a big prize for the Nazis. He managed to get his wife and children out of the city but was captured before he could join them.

"My men and I kept his family for two days before our scouts informed us that the Vichy were closing in. I ordered two men to escort the family to another safe location, while the rest of us stayed to fight. The woman, to thank me, gave me this piece before they fled. I refused it at first, but she insisted. It was the only thing of value she had, and she wanted me to have it rather than to have it fall into the hands of the Nazis. I didn't quite understand it myself, but I suppose people in desperation do desperate things. In any event, I never saw her, her children, nor my two comrades again."

Martin looked at the brooch more closely and saw the insignia on the back.

"Do you understand French?" Benoît asked.

"No."

"It says, 'To Leila, all my love, Philip.'"

"Her name was Leila?"

"Yes. I imagine Philip was her husband."

Martin scrutinized the brooch again. "That is a very powerful story," he said. "Still, why would you want to give this away? Clearly it was given to *you* as a sign of your righteousness in helping those people."

"Righteousness is a funny word, doctor. I prefer to think of my acts in terms of humanness."

Martin nodded. It was a point well taken.

"And as for my giving it to you," Benoît continued, "I think that this is the proper thing to do."

Martin's eyes asked *why*.

"I assume you've heard about the recent Senate committee hearings on how the Swiss government hid enormous sums of money over the past fifty years that had belonged to Jewish families during the Holocaust," Benoît said.

Martin nodded.

"Well, *I*, for one, find that whole business reprehensible. It will most certainly be recorded as a very dark episode of history, much like the Holocaust itself."

The direction this was taking was becoming clear to Martin. How to handle it, however, was presently beyond his grasp. He remained wordless.

"I want to give this to you simply because you are a Jew. I know that may seem bizarre, but it is the only way I can do my part in righting a despicable wrong. Believe me, if I could ever find that woman, I would return it to her. Under the circumstances, ***you*** are the only candidate I have."

"Surely you know other Jewish people," Martin said.

"Of course. But in our brief time together, I have grown quite fond of you. I hope I am permitted to say that, and even if not, it is still the truth. You have impressed me as a person of integrity. Your refusal to avail yourself of that stock tip, for example, was most unusual." Benoît stopped himself, seeming to consider what to say next.

Martin waited.

"Maybe I cannot articulate exactly what is in my heart," Benoît said, "but as far as I am concerned, you are the person to whom I should give this."

"I appreciate your feelings on this, Jacques, but I honestly don't..."

"Feel comfortable with this?" Benoît interjected.

"I don't really know how I feel," Martin responded, betraying a rare moment of confusion in front of a patient.

"Then why not hold onto it for a while, then decide if you want to keep it. Perhaps you know a survivor, or a lady friend to whom you might want to give it?"

Martin was suddenly suspicious. Could Benoit possibly know

about Cheryl and his parents? Was it far-fetched to think that this man was investigating him?

Martin decided not to raise the issue. There were three minutes remaining in the session – not nearly enough time to get into it – and he thought it best to wait and see if Benoît dropped any more hints about his personal life in the future before acting on what might be nothing more than his own paranoia.

Martin examined the brooch, observing its elegance, feeling eerie just to have it in his hand. But mostly, he was struck by the irony that *he,* of all people, would be chosen by anyone as the keeper of such a thing. He looked up at Benoît, still not sure of what to do.

Benoît handed him a check as payment for the session. "Can I take your silence as agreement?" he asked.

"I need to think more about it."

"I hope you will hold onto it while you think. You may even become used to the idea of having it."

"I'll agree to do that, only so long as you know that I may decide to return it."

"That would be fine," Benoît replied.

"Good then, I'll see you next time."

Benoît held his hand out for Martin to shake. "Have a good week, doctor," he said.

Martin felt strange taking Benoît's hand. They had shaken at their first meeting, but not since. Doing so now felt as if he were acquiescing in some deal when, in reality, he had committed to nothing. Then again, there was reality, and there was Jacques Benoît's mind. And Martin couldn't help but wonder which was truly more compelling.

A few hours later, during a break, Martin picked up the phone and called Cheryl at her office. He was expecting her voice mail, yet he still felt uneasy when he got it. *Why isn't she ever in her office?*

"Hi Cheryl, it's Marty. I was thinking about our conversation last night. I'm still not completely comfortable with introducing you to Elizabeth, but I do have another thought. I won't be in the office this afternoon, but you can reach me on my cell phone. The number is 363-3640. Call me as soon as you can. Bye."

ASHOK REDDY LOOKED AGHAST. IT was the third time in a row Martin had topped the ball, and they were only getting started. Sure, every golfer had a bad day now and then, but this was ridiculous.

The ball dribbled about ten yards, Reddy and Martin both watching in dismay. Martin didn't bang his clubhead into the ground, nor did he yell any profanities – as many golfers would have. All he did was softly say, "Ouch."

"Something's still on your mind," Reddy said as Martin approached the cart.

"Yeah, yeah, yeah." Translation: *Put a lid on it, Ashok.*

Reddy took the hint, stepped on the accelerator and drove the cart to Martin's ball. At this rate, it would be a while before they reached Reddy's 230-yard drive.

Martin stepped off the cart, grabbed a club from his bag and walked to his ball. He was an awfully long way from the green to be hitting his fourth shot, but the hole was par five. With any luck, he could get on the green with two more shots, one putt, and end up with a bogey. It would be close to miraculous, considering his performance thus far, but as they say in the PGA: *Anything* can happen.

He took a deep breath and tried to clear his mind of everything but the task at hand. That is the liberating force of golf; it reduces all of life's concerns to one thing: hitting a little white ball. And to do it properly, nothing else could matter. Whether Martin was able to attain such liberation at this point would soon become apparent.

He swept the club back, turning his shoulders counterclockwise, then reversed the motion, bringing the clubhead through the ball. It might have turned out perfectly, had the stress he'd been under not found itself in his wrists, causing him to unintentionally open the face of the club. He watched as the ball took off to the right, and kissed that bogey goodbye.

Martin sat down next to Reddy, feeling forlorn.

"Maybe this is just not a good day to play," Reddy said.

"No, I need to play."

Reddy hit the gas. "Is it the girl?"

"And a few other things."

"You want to talk about any of them?"

Martin considered the offer. His apprehensions about Cheryl felt less pressing than the matters of Benoît's brooch and Gifford's sudden termination of treatment, both of which he was eager to explore with Reddy. Only, there was the small dilemma of patient confidentiality. With Gifford it was easier, because Reddy didn't know Gifford and would have no way of guessing his identity. With Benoît, however, Reddy had been the referring doctor. Even if he disguised the details, Reddy might still figure it out. But Benoît was Martin's most recent conundrum, and the issue he felt most compelled to air. He decided to take a stab at presenting the problem as generically as possible.

"Tell me this, without getting into specific details: What do you think about gifts from patients?"

"Receiving them or accepting them?" Reddy asked.

"Good distinction. Let's start with the former."

They pulled up alongside Reddy's ball. Reddy gently slapped Martin's knee and said, "To be continued."

He returned two minutes later, after hitting another good shot.

"You're going to clean me out today," Martin said.

"Consider it a consulting fee."

Martin smiled for the first time all day.

"Anyway, back to your question," Reddy said. "First, you and I do different things. I write prescriptions, you listen to heartaches. The relationship I have with a patient is different from the one you have."

Martin nodded.

"So, when I receive a gift from a patient, I usually take it at face value, as a sign of appreciation for whatever help I have provided. I don't interpret it any further. I'm not saying that there may not be some additional underlying meaning, only that I do not concern myself with such things."

"And you don't think you should?"

"Perhaps I should, perhaps I shouldn't. You must *always* analyze why a patient is giving you a gift. And that includes not only the patient's intentions but also the specific nature of the gift."

Martin already knew all this, but discussing it with Reddy still seemed helpful.

"And there's also context," Reddy said. "At holidays, a lot of patients give gifts, as well as when they terminate treatment. In these instances, there is less to interpret than if a patient gives me something out of the blue."

They came upon Martin's ball, which was in the wrong fairway, about thirty yards from another green. "Not a bad shot," Reddy said, "if you were playing the fifth hole."

"Who says I'm not?" Martin said, grabbing his eight iron to get his ball back into play on the first hole.

Reddy looked at the row of trees separating Martin's ball from the first fairway. "Those trees look pretty high. You might want to take a more lofted club than that."

"The green's far away. I have to go for the distance." He swung his club smoothly and connected for the first time.

Reddy clapped as the ball flew over the trees toward the first green. "You may be on."

"May even be close enough for a double bogey."

"Wishful thinking."

"A positive outlook is a healthy thing."

Reddy smiled and Martin climbed back on the cart.

"It seems you are feeling a bit better," Reddy said. "Have we come close to solving your problem?"

"No, not really," Martin said. "But I do have more perspective."

"In what way?"

"Well, now I understand what bothers me about this particular patient. It's not the gift, per se, but the fact that I don't feel I really understand him. If I understood him and his motivations, my decision would be easy."

"It's a him?"

"That's all you're getting."

Reddy chuckled at the rebuke. "A gift from a male patient you don't understand," Reddy reflected. "Sounds intriguing."

"It is."

"Speaking of intrigue, what is happening with the woman?"

"I'm glad you brought that up."

"You've decided to let me hypnotize you?"

"Not quite. But I have decided to give you and Savitri a crack at her."

"You mean we are going to meet her."

"I'm waiting for a call as we speak to see if she's available tonight."

"That isn't a lot of notice."

"We could do it another time," Martin said nonchalantly, fully knowing that his friend wouldn't want to wait.

"No, no, no! Give me your phone. I will call Savitri and clear it."

Martin smiled and handed Reddy his phone. "How come you never bring your own phone?"

"Because you always have yours." He patted Martin on the shoulder and dialed his home. "Hello, Savitri, I am on the golf course, so I have to keep it short." Pause. "Uh huh… uh huh… I am calling to find out if we have any plans this evening, because Marty has offered to introduce us to his significant other." Another pause. "It isn't definite. He has to see if she is available…"

Reddy gave Martin a thumb's up.

"Good, good," he said to Savitri. "I will call you as soon as I know."

He hung up, turned to Martin and said, "She is intrigued, as am I."

Amused by his friend's eagerness, Martin chuckled.

Martin's cell rang about twenty minutes later. He had lost the first hole, pushed the second, and was now working toward a win on the third. "Hello," he whispered, trying to keep his voice down because Reddy was about to putt.

It was Cheryl.

He walked off the green in order to talk in privacy.

"You've got me burning with curiosity," Cheryl said.

"It's nothing, really. Just that my friend Ashok and his wife demand to meet my mystery woman, and I was wondering if you were up to it tonight."

"These were friends of yours and Katherine's, I take it?"

He had considered she might be anxious about that. "Yes."

There was a moment of silence on the other end, then, "I suppose I should be flattered?"

"I was hoping you'd see it that way."

"This is quite different than meeting a 4-year-old."

"I know. But we have to start somewhere."

"Okay."

He wasn't completely sure he'd heard her. "Okay?"

"That's what I said."

"Then I'll pick you up at your place at 7."

"Where are we going?"

"Their place. I hope you like Indian food."

"I hate Indian food."

"Ha. So do I. I'll see you at 7."

Martin hung up the phone, placed it in the cup holder on the golf cart and walked back onto the green with his putter.

"So?" Reddy asked.

"It's on. Just tell Savitri to go easy on the spices."

"Don't worry, we have plenty of bathrooms." Reddy laughed.

Martin squatted down behind his ball to get a read of the terrain of the green. "Looks to me like it breaks left," he said, realizing that he should hit the ball toward the right of the hole.

"If you wanted to know, you should have watched my putt," Reddy said.

Martin stood square to his ball, about ten feet from the hole. It was a difficult putt, but he had to make it to win. More than that, he was dying to give Reddy some just deserts. He pulled his club back a few inches and gently eased it forward, hoping to strike the ball with just the right speed and accuracy. His eyes followed as the ball rolled toward the right side of the hole, then turned slightly on its approach. The line appeared perfect, but it looked as if the ball was going to stop dead at the lip of the hole. Which was what it did, before it fell in and created what was, for Martin, the sweetest of sounds.

Galit Stein sat in a daze as she hung up the phone.

"What is it?" Arik demanded.

She didn't answer.

"We are wasting our time with this psychologist," Arik said. "In fact, I think we are wasting our time with this whole operation. In the end, we will have nothing!"

Kovi looked at her for an answer.

"He wants me to have dinner with his closest friends."

"You mean the psychiatrist and his wife?" Kovi asked.

Galit nodded.

"So what?" Arik snapped. "He wants you to have dinner. What the hell does that mean? He is in love with you. You are in love with him. Everybody is in love and Benoît goes free. Great plan."

"What is it that you want?" Galit asked.

"I want something on Benoît," Arik answered. "If we can get something from the shrink, let's do it. If not, then let's look elsewhere. But what I do not want is to sit and wait while you figure out your life."

"Is this what it all comes down to, that we care nothing for each other? All we care about is getting Benoît?"

"That's a lot of shit," Arik said. "We have always given our all for each other. We have risked our lives for each other. How can you say that?"

She knew he was right. Until the past few weeks, no one in her life had been closer to her. "I'm sorry, that was out of line," she said.

"It's all right," Kovi jumped in. "We will figure it out."

Arik appeared unconvinced.

"No," she said, "it's not all right. Arik is correct, I have lost control and perspective, and I think it may be too late."

"Too late?" Kovi asked.

"For me," she said in a resolved tone.

The three of them looked at one another.

"Don't worry," she said unconvincingly, "Schwartz will dig something up. Anyway, we are technically here only to observe."

Arik cast her a look of disbelief.

"You really think so?" Kovi asked.

She didn't respond.

"Look," Arik said, "maybe you should just push a little harder with the shrink."

"He knows nothing. Benoît has him duped," she said.

"How can you be sure?" Kovi asked.

"Do you think if he knew he was treating a Nazi butcher he would be playing golf and planning dinner parties? Trust me, the only person he is suspicious of is *me*."

"Then you have to tell him the truth," Arik said. "Tell him about yourself and all about Benoît. Maybe he will turn the cards on Benoît and help us get something."

"I don't think it would work."

"Is that the reason," Arik said, "or is it your fear of losing him once he learns you have been lying?"

"He is going to learn that at some point anyway," she said.

"I'm sorry, Galit," Arik said, "but I just cannot believe that this man, *a Jew*, wouldn't help you capture someone like Benoît."

She read the jealousy in his voice but didn't want to go there. "It's more complicated than that."

"How so?" Arik said. "You mean to tell me that his ethics as a psychologist are more important to him than his obligations as a

Jew?"

She gave him a blank expression.

"That's enough, Arik," Kovi said.

"Is it?" Arik said, looking at Galit. "Is it enough?"

Silence.

"Maybe I need more time," she said.

"How much time?" Kovi asked.

"I don't know. A few days, maybe?"

"A few days and what?" Arik said.

She stared into space for a moment, then turned back to her friends. "I will tell him."

chapter 37

CHERYL MANNING DRIED HER FOREHEAD with a tissue as she looked in the mirror. The lighting in the Reddys' guest bathroom was too dim for her to tell if her perspiration was obvious. She'd felt unnerved all evening. It wasn't the Reddys. They had been perfectly pleasant. It was her anticipation that soon everything would change.

The Reddys were just as Martin had described. Ashok was tall, thin, and handsome, with youthful olive skin and no signs of graying or thinning in his jet-black hair. Savitri seemed equally immune to the effects of time. She was shapely, dressed tastefully and conservatively and, though she comported herself with an aristocratic demeanor, she was not the least bit pretentious. Like her husband, she was born in India. Unlike him, she had been raised and educated in the U.S., with a degree from Berkeley College, and a Master of Fine Arts from the Pratt Institute. Her vocation was interior decorating, and Cheryl noted from the surroundings that she was obviously good at it.

Dinner had come off nicely. Cheryl and Martin had been

expecting Indian food, but were surprised by a simple continental menu: poached salmon, scalloped potatoes, and asparagus with hollandaise sauce. Martin had been overtly thankful, as his feelings about Indian delicacies were well known to his hosts. Savitri Reddy's explanation for the change, however, had nothing to do with Martin's preferences. She simply hadn't had sufficient notice to come up with anything more elaborate.

Cheryl took a deep breath, came out of the bathroom and walked through the foyer to the dining room. The sound of her footsteps on the oak floor softened as she neared the conversation.

"Ah, Cheryl," Ashok Reddy said, "we were just discussing the impact of public relations on medicine these days. Right up your alley, I bet."

"Well, actually," she said, "I've never represented any hospitals." She picked up her coffee and sipped it.

"How about doctors?" Savitri Reddy asked.

"No doctors either," Cheryl said.

"I have been thinking about getting someone," Ashok said.

Martin looked at him incredulously. "*You*? What for?"

"One needs all the help one can find. Not everybody has the benefits of a best-selling book." He smiled at Martin. "When an ordinary person sees a doctor on a television show, he thinks the doctor must be the best. People have no idea that the only reason the doctor is there is because of a good PR agent."

"Ashok is just talking," Savitri said, looking at Cheryl. "He enjoys needling Marty."

"I'll drink to that," Martin said, raising his coffee cup.

"So, Cheryl," Ashok said, "Marty tells me you went to Oxford."

Cheryl nodded, wondering where this was leading.

"Did you enjoy it?"

"Very much so."

"I visited there once," Reddy said. "I actually delivered a paper there at an international conference on psychopharmacology a few years ago. A beautiful place."

"Yes. That it is."

Savitri Reddy rose from the table and began clearing the dishes.

"Let me help you," Cheryl said, picking up her and Martin's

plates, eager to escape any more questions about a place she'd never actually been. She followed Savitri into the kitchen while the men got up and went into the den.

"They will probably help themselves to some brandy," Savitri said, placing the dishes in the sink. "Would you like something?"

"No thank you," Cheryl replied.

Savitri smiled, sensing Cheryl's preference to be with her at that moment. "We're a difficult crowd," she said.

"Not that difficult."

"But it's hard for you, meeting Marty's friends?"

"You two are the first friends of his I've met."

"We are probably the only ones you will meet. Marty is somewhat of a loner, he spends his time on his career and with Elizabeth, but doesn't do much socializing."

"So I gather," Cheryl said. She waited a beat, then added, "I take it things were different when Katherine was alive."

Savitri looked at her, seeming to realize how difficult it must have been for her to broach this subject. "Katherine was very different," she said sadly.

"I'm sorry..."

"No, no, no. There is nothing to be sorry about. Your curiosity is natural."

Cheryl thought for a moment. "It's hard to ask Marty about her."

"I'm sure it is."

From the den, Ashok called, "Savitri!"

"We'll be right there," Savitri answered.

"The two of you were friends?" Cheryl asked.

"We were the *best* of friends."

"She must have been quite a woman."

Savitri looked sad. "And from everything I can see, so are you," she said.

"Thank you."

Savitri put her hand on Cheryl's shoulder. "Come, let's join them."

"You're awfully quiet," Martin said, his eyes glued to the road in front of him. It had been a few minutes since they'd left the Reddys' house.

"I'm sorry, I was just thinking."

"About what?"

"Things."

They came to a red light. He turned to her. "You're being cryptic."

"Is that what you say to your patients?"

"When I have to."

She smiled and pointed to the light. "I don't think it's going to get any greener."

He grinned and started driving again. "You haven't answered my question."

"I was just thinking about us."

"What about us?"

"Nothing in particular. Just about where we are headed, I suppose."

"And where is that?"

"You tell me."

"Right now, we're on our way to your place."

She hit him in the side.

"Sorry, bad joke," he said.

She waited for a better response.

"I don't know," he said honestly, "but I'm really enjoying it. I haven't enjoyed anything this much in a long time."

She put her hand on the back of his neck. "Neither have I."

He thought for a moment. "There's something I need to tell you."

"Okay," she said, trying to contain her apprehension.

"Before I met you, I had met someone else."

Her nerves relaxed. She had thought he was going to reveal whatever he had seen in her apartment the night he had acted strangely.

"I was in Chicago," he continued, "at a conference, giving a paper."

"Was she a psychologist?" she asked, trying to conceal her

jealousy.

"Yes, from San Francisco."

"Did you sleep with her?"

"No. That's sort of what I wanted to tell you. I couldn't."

"Couldn't what?"

He pulled the car to the side of the road and looked at her. "I couldn't sleep with her." He hesitated, then added, "I couldn't sleep with anyone."

She was wordless, struck by a strange amalgam of gladness, guilt and trepidation. *She* was the one, the only one, since the death of his wife.

"You don't have to say anything," he said.

"I know," she responded, moving toward him. She placed her lips on his, wishing that everything else would somehow disappear. But inside, her anguish grew, knowing that *he*, too, was the only one for her, and that she was destined to lose him.

chapter 38

DAN GIFFORD STARED AT MARTIN Rosen for a good while without saying anything. It was hard for him to admit the need to be back in this room again, but he was resigned to the fact. For now, he couldn't go it alone.

Martin looked concerned and seemed to be waiting for Gifford to start. An explanation would be the first step, Gifford knew, not only for Martin's curiosity but also for therapeutic soundness. There could be no skirting or avoiding the point.

"I'm surprised you didn't call me," Gifford said.

"Surprised or offended?"

"I'm not sure. I suppose you guys have ways of handling these things. Like, protocols that tell you under what circumstances you should or shouldn't call a patient."

"There are rules, but to me it's an individual thing. I *was* going to call you, eventually, but thought it best to give it a while. You obviously had your reasons for doing what you did, and I didn't want to push just yet."

"I understand."

"Which gets us to the next thing: your reasons. What were they?"

"My reasons for quitting, or returning?"

"Both."

"It's a long story."

"We have time."

Gifford hesitated. He understood that he had to come clean. He had considered Schwartz' warning, as well as the possibility that Rosen might somehow be connected, but decided: to hell with it. Whether what he was about to do was self-centered or ignoble could no longer concern him. His very survival was at stake, and the only thing that mattered was getting the help he needed to stay sober. After that, the other pieces would somehow get sorted out.

"It began a few weeks ago," he said uneasily, "after leaving your office. I was walking to my car and noticed another car, a black Mercedes, across the street, down the block. There were two men sitting in it and it struck me as suspicious. I suppose I was paranoid because of the case I'm working on."

"The drug dealers?"

Gifford nodded. "Anyway, I didn't see them following me as I drove off, but that didn't mean they weren't. I didn't notice anything after that, but I put some guys on you, just in case."

"You had people watching *me*?"

"For a while. Sorry, Doc, but I thought they could just as well have been after you."

"For what?"

"They might have thought I told you where Roberto Alvarez was, or maybe they just wanted to kidnap you to get me to give up Alvarez."

Martin looked at him incredulously.

"I know it sounds ridiculous, but in my world you can't be too careful."

"You're not in Navy intelligence anymore," Martin said.

"You're right, I'm not. At least back then there were rules. With these creeps, there aren't. They'll come after your family, friends, whatever. They don't give a shit about anything."

Martin seemed to back down some, indicating for Gifford to

continue.

"Anyway, nothing happened for a week. No cars outside your office, nobody following you or me, at least not that my guys could see. So I figured, if they're after me, the best time to catch them would be right before or after my session with you."

Martin raised his eyebrows.

"You see, Doc, you're the only steady gig I've got. All the other times I'm alone – at home, on my way to work or on my way from work – they aren't predictable, considering my schedule. My apartment's also pretty impenetrable."

"I can imagine," Martin said.

Gifford took no offense; he understood that it was hard for Martin to relate. "The long and short of it is that I missed my session with you the following week to see if I was right. I showed up with one of my men and someone from Nassau County to keep things kosher."

"You mean you believed whoever it was would return, so you were outside to watch."

"Exactly. And they showed, just as I'd figured."

Martin's eyes lit up.

"My guys got out of the car and confronted them," Gifford continued, "and it turns out they're Israelis."

"Israelis?"

"Better yet. I get a visit from an FBI special agent later that night telling me to back off. It's none of my business what these guys are doing." Gifford searched Martin's eyes for some indication that he knew where this was headed, and found nothing but inquisitiveness. "After this FBI guy leaves, I did some research on him, and guess what he's into."

Martin appeared bewildered. "Dan, do you think *I* know something about this?"

"To tell you the truth, Doc, I don't know what to think."

"Is that why you decided to stop coming?"

"Not really. It wasn't that I suspected that you actually knew something, but there was the possibility that you were somehow involved in something that you didn't know. Get my meaning?"

"Sort of."

"There was also the fact that I couldn't tell you any of this."

"Why not?"

"Because the FBI guy said so, which also led me to believe it had something to do with you."

Martin did a poor job concealing his dismay.

"Look," Gifford said defensively, "for all I know, they were listening to our conversations. Maybe they still are, and I'm getting arrested as soon as I leave."

"Dan, what are we talking about here?"

"Nazis."

"Nazis?"

"Not the neo kind either. The real McCoy."

"You mean the FBI and the Israelis have been outside this building on Monday mornings looking for Nazis?"

"Probably one Nazi, as in war criminal."

Suddenly, Martin clammed up.

"You okay, Doc?" Gifford asked.

"I'm fine," Martin said haltingly. "It's just so… unbelievable."

"Why do you think this was on Monday mornings?" Gifford asked, suddenly realizing the import of his question. *Holy shit*, he thought, *it's* another *steady appointment*.

Martin just stared.

"I can't offer any speculation on that," Martin said, apparently struggling to remain poised.

"I guess not," Gifford responded. It was obvious to him that the bond between them was getting shaky.

"Why did you decide to return to treatment?" Martin asked, eager to stay on subject.

Gifford swallowed hard. He wanted to answer the question; after all, that was why he was there. Yet, a feeling of reticence overcame him. Suddenly, it occurred to him that this was the crossroad: he had to decide here and now if he and Martin had a future. Moreover, he had to decide just how important his sobriety was, and all that came with it. In this, he would not only have to leave Martin's problems – whatever they were – to Martin, he would also have to trust Martin even more than he already did.

"I went to a bar a few nights ago," he said.

Martin didn't seem surprised. "Did you drink?"

"No. But I came close."

"What was it about?"

"The stress, I suppose. It's not an excuse. It just is what it is."

"Aside from the situation you just described, was there something else?"

"Oh, I'd say so."

Martin waited for more.

"I got shot at by two Colombian hit men."

Martin's eyes opened wide. "What happened?"

"They came at me in the garage where I work, late at night as I was leaving. So much for being unpredictable." Gifford felt himself tremble. "If it wasn't for Bobby Marcus – I think I've told you about him – if not for him, I don't think I'd be here right now."

"Is he okay?"

"Better than me."

"And the guys who shot at you?"

"Dead."

Silence filled the space between them.

"You went to the bar after the shooting?" Martin asked.

"Right after I gave my statements."

"I could see why you did."

"Just talking about it makes me want to…" Gifford stopped himself.

"So, why haven't you?"

Gifford considered his response. "I don't know." The words came out softly, as if he had spoken them to himself.

"I'm glad you came back," Martin said.

It amazed Gifford how Martin was able to seemingly dismiss his own dilemma and focus on his patient. It was almost as if they'd never discussed the first thing. Almost.

"I am too," Gifford said.

Dan Gifford exited the office and nodded to the man sitting in the waiting room as he walked past. It was awkward for each of them, but it would have been more awkward, and certainly impolite, for two strangers who crossed paths week after week to simply ignore each other. This time, however, Gifford was glad for the exchange. It reminded him of how, back in his intelligence days, he had been able to completely scrutinize another person with a mere glance, and, though he was recently a bit rusty, he would now pay more attention.

He left the building, once again convinced that he recognized the stranger but still unable to put a name to the face. He could procure the services of a sketch artist, but that might be going too far – unless Rosen was actually in danger.

Gifford approached his car, looked around before getting in, and saw nothing suspicious. If the surveillance was ongoing, he mused, they were doing a better job at staying out of sight. He opened the door, got in, and stared out the window before starting the engine, wondering if he was completely off-base about all this.

Was it possible that he had misread Rosen's reaction? After all, anyone would be shaken by what he said, especially a Jew. And could it have been merely coincidence that the black Mercedes appeared only on the same day and time that he would be leaving the building. If so, then Rosen and the stranger in the waiting room might have nothing to do with any of this.

He turned around and looked back at the building. It consisted of four stories. By the length of it, he estimated there could be as many as fifty apartments. There were two other doctors' signs in front, one for an internist, the other a urologist. He had to admit that there could be other explanations.

He put the car in drive, pulled out, and ignored the sign in front of him that said, "No U-turn." As he drove past the building, his original suspicions took hold again. Sure, there were other possibilities. But his instincts wouldn't allow him to discard the ones he was certain were true. The only thing he wasn't certain of was what to do about it.

After Gifford left, Martin took a few minutes before ushering Benoît into his office. He opened his desk drawer and looked at the brooch he had placed there. *What kind of game is he playing?* Martin wondered as he removed the brooch from the drawer. He read the inscription once again, and it sent a chill through his body.

He hadn't wanted to lie to Gifford, but there was no way he could have taken the matter any further. He could not, and *would* not, discuss one patient with another, regardless of the circumstances. And was he even certain that Benoît was the key to all this? Maybe it was just a coincidence, and someone in another apartment was the target of the investigation. Or maybe Benoît was in fact the man being watched, but the Israelis and the FBI were mistaken about his being a war criminal.

He stared at the brooch, more bewildered than he'd ever found himself.

Why, in God's name, did he choose me?

MARTIN ROSEN GATHERED HIS COMPOSURE as he opened the door. For a multitude of reasons, he had decided that the worst thing he could do at this point would be to confront Benoît. First, all he had were suspicions. Second, a confrontation, valid or not, would be certain to drive Benoît away. And most important, Martin thought, if his suspicions were true, he needed to learn more before deciding on his next step.

"Good morning, my dear doctor," Benoît said as he rose from his seat.

"Good morning, Jacques."

The two men entered the office and took their places.

"You look a bit stressed," Benoît observed.

"No, I'm fine," Martin responded, angry with himself for not having hid it better.

Benoît appeared unconvinced.

"How are things?" Martin asked.

"I can't complain."

Silence.

"So, have you thought about my gift?" Benoît asked.

Martin waited a beat. "Yes, I have."

"And?"

"I'm still considering it."

"Good. I guess that means you're not returning it yet."

"That's correct, for the time being."

Benoît smiled.

Martin now understood that smile more fully than he had before. It was a cat-and-mouse thing with Benoît, a sign of enjoying the competition of who's going to get whom. Only now, the stakes were higher.

"You know, Jacques, in thinking about the brooch, I'm still not sure why you gave it to me."

"But I told you."

"I understand what you said, but it seems such an unusual thing to do."

"I'm an unusual man." Again, the smile.

"I can't help wondering if there isn't some other reason."

"There you go, playing psychologist. It must be taxing, not being able to take what anyone says at face value."

"It has its disadvantages. And its benefits."

"You think I have some hidden reason for giving you that brooch?"

"I do," Martin said.

"Well, I can't imagine what it is."

Martin observed his patient's discomfort. "Neither can I."

"Why do you doubt me?"

"It's not that I *doubt* you, it's that I believe that things can often have multiple meanings. Take, for example, your statement that you were giving the brooch to me because I am Jewish. However, I'm also your therapist, meaning we have a special relationship, and that makes me think that there was more to your choosing me than simply my religion."

"But I told you that I chose you because of my fondness for you."

Martin sensed anxiety in Benoît's tone. "Yes," he said, "you did. Only, it doesn't make sense to me. The Swiss, in the example you used, stole money from the Jews. Therefore, it's only right that they make restitution. You, however, were given this brooch as a token for your heroism. One would think you would cherish it and display it proudly, rather than keep it locked in a safe-deposit box for decades and then decide to give it away." Martin hesitated. "Unless, of course, there's something else."

"Something else? And what, my dear doctor, could that possibly be?"

"Guilt, perhaps?"

"Guilt? What kind of guilt?" Benoît asked defensively.

"I don't know. That's what I'm trying to find out."

"What could *I* have to feel guilty about?" Benoît repeated.

Martin noticed a slight tremor in Benoît's hand that hadn't been there before. He opted for silence.

"I think you are mistaken, my friend, and frankly, I am offended at your implication."

"Implication?"

"That I somehow had something to do with that woman and her family's death."

"Death? You never said anything about death," Martin said.

Benoît stared at him. "I was just assuming," he said softly, shifting in his seat.

"Oh."

They looked at each other in silence.

"Do you think me an imposter or some such thing?" Benoît asked.

"I don't know how we got here, Jacques, but I haven't accused you of anything. I simply raised the possibility of guilt having played a role in your decision to give the brooch to me. That guilt could come from many places, from things you may have done, to things you regret not having done. People often feel guilty, for example, because they believe they didn't do enough. Regardless of whether a person is truly pure and righteous, he can still blame himself for something that was completely beyond his control."

Benoît looked off into space, then fixed his eyes on Martin. "I am sorry," he said, appearing to regain his composure. "I believe I overreacted. Perhaps you are correct. Perhaps there are some things that have made me feel… guilty."

Martin nodded. "And whatever your guilt may be about, it could be playing a more significant role in your life than you think."

Benoît offered a curious expression, inviting Martin to clarify himself.

"It may help us understand your suicide attempt a bit better," Martin said. "I've always had my reservations about your explanation for that as well."

"I'm sure you have."

RICHARD SCHWARTZ LOOKED UP FROM his pastrami on rye to the man standing over his table. Although his reaction to being disturbed during lunch would typically be frustration, his curiosity had the better of him.

"How did you know where to find me?" he asked.

"I have my sources," the man responded.

Schwartz bit into his sandwich. "Good stuff," he said, "you really should try some."

"Jewish soul food?"

"Well it ain't any good for the heart, that's for certain," Schwartz said as he delivered a forkful of potato salad to his mouth. "This isn't bad either."

"I'll remember that."

Schwartz finished chewing, swallowed, and said, "So, Mr. Gifford, what is it that I can do for you?"

"May I sit?"

Schwartz held his hands up as if to say, *whatever*. "I don't own the place."

Gifford took a seat.

Schwartz waited for an answer to his question.

"I want to know what kind of protection the doctor has," Gifford said.

"The doctor?"

"As in Rosen."

"And what makes you think that Dr. Rosen needs protection?"

Gifford swallowed hard. "He knows."

Schwartz feigned curiosity. "Knows? Knows what?"

"He knows that one of his patients is the guy you're looking for."

"And how does he know this?"

"I told him."

"Seems you've been a busy beaver," Schwartz said.

"I did what I had to."

"You did everything I warned you not to do," Schwartz said, stabbing Gifford with his eyes. "Tell me, counselor, are you aware of the consequences for obstructing a federal investigation?"

Gifford didn't flinch. "Look, as far as I see it, we're on the same side here. I'm sorry if you can't understand why I had to get into this, but Martin Rosen is important to me. If there's something going on that involves him, I have to know about it. It's that simple."

"It's never that simple."

"It is for me."

The two men scrutinized each other.

"So, where do we go from here?" Gifford asked.

"How much do you know?" Schwartz inquired, softening his tone a bit.

"I know that your gig is Nazis. Put that together with the two Israeli goons, and voilà."

"That's it?"

Gifford had wondered how far he was going to take this before he had even entered the restaurant. He knew that if Schwartz was to give him anything, he would have to come clean.

"I think it's the guy who sees Rosen after me," he said.

"And you figured this how?"

"The Israelis. They were only there at the time I was coming out, the same time the other guy was going in. My guess, they weren't watching Rosen or the building. They were following the other guy."

"That's a nice theory," Schwartz said.

"I'm glad you like it."

Schwartz grinned.

"Look, Agent Schwartz, I didn't come here expecting you to confirm or deny my suspicions, only to find out if Rosen is in any danger."

"This Rosen fellow, he must be good."

Gifford nodded.

"Maybe I could use a guy like that."

"I think we all could."

"How much does he know?" Schwartz asked nonchalantly.

"What I know."

Schwartz sipped his Dr. Brown's Cel-Ray soda. "You really stuck your nose somewhere it don't belong," he said.

"Depends how you look at it."

"I suppose."

"What about Rosen?"

Schwartz looked Gifford in the eye. "I'm not saying your story has any merit at all, you understand?"

Gifford nodded. He knew he was going to get what he came for.

"What I can say," Schwartz continued, "is that the guy I'm looking at, I don't think he's really a danger to anyone at this point."

"But if he finds out that Rosen knows who he is, wouldn't he want to protect himself?"

"Still speaking theoretically?"

Gifford nodded again.

"He might, except for one thing. Our guy knows we're onto him. My guess is, he even knows we're watching. He's smart, and probably figures that the reason we haven't picked him up yet is because we don't have enough to make it stick. If I were him, I'd just bide my time till the good guys give up. It would be awfully stupid of him to do anything, much less kill anybody. And one thing this guy ain't is stupid."

Gifford considered the point.

"Now let me ask you something," Schwartz said.

Gifford was afraid that this might happen, but the exchange of information had to be even, those were the rules. "Theoretically?"

"Absolutely."

Gifford waited.

"In your scenario, what do you think this Rosen guy's gonna do?"

Gifford considered the question that he'd been pondering all day. "I don't know."

"Maybe he won't do anything," Schwartz reflected. "Bit of a quagmire for a shrink to be in, don't you think?"

"Yeah, you're right about that," Gifford agreed. "But you couldn't be more mistaken about the first part. You see, I know Rosen. And while I can't predict exactly what it is that he's going to do, I can assure you, he *is* going to do something."

"Hmm… could get interesting," Schwartz mused.

Gifford considered the possibilities. If Schwartz' people really didn't have enough evidence on the Nazi, who knew what Rosen stirring things up might yield? "It seems, Agent Schwartz, that I may have actually done you a favor," he said.

"Yeah, sure, I owe you one."

MARTIN ROSEN WALKED OVER TO the window and peeked through the vertical blinds at the park across the way. "Nice view," he said.

"You burst in on me in the middle of the day to tell me I have a nice view?" Reddy asked.

Martin turned around and looked at his friend. Reddy was leaning back in his burgundy executive chair, his feet comfortably resting on a redwood desk. "I don't know why I came here," Martin said.

"You sound like you have something on your mind."

"I have a lot on my mind. I just don't know if you can help me with any of it."

"You are acting like a patient."

"Maybe I ought to be one."

"Maybe we all should. It would probably do us and our patients some good."

"Amen to that." Martin made his way to the chair and dropped into it.

Reddy scrutinized his friend's face. "I sense I am about to hear something unsettling."

"To say the least."

The two men looked at each other. Reddy waited for Martin to continue.

"It's about a patient," Martin said.

"The same patient who gave you the gift?"

"Good guess."

"No guess at all. When you told me about that, it was obvious that trouble was coming."

"Obvious?"

"Call it ex-psychoanalyst's intuition."

Martin smiled. Once again, he was trying to figure a way to present his dilemma without revealing anything that might lead Reddy to suspect Benoît. "What would you do if you knew that a patient of yours committed a truly heinous crime?" he asked.

"In the past?"

Martin knew where Reddy was going with this. The law, or Tarasoff Decision, as it was known in the mental health community, stated that a patient's privilege of confidentiality didn't apply if the practitioner had sufficient reason to believe that the patient posed a serious physical or life-threatening danger to someone else. On the other hand, if a practitioner becomes aware of a patient's past acts, regardless of the severity, but has no reason to suspect any specific future act that would entail a serious physical or life-threatening danger to another, the patient's confidentiality must be protected.

"Yes," Martin said.

"Then there is no question. You wrote the book on confidentiality, Marty – the law is clear."

Martin had already entertained the irony of being caught up in a situation in which he was a supposed expert, yet hearing it articulated made it all the more jarring. "What if I didn't learn this information from the patient himself?"

Reddy looked at Martin askance. "Then how did you come by it?"

"Let's just say, for argument's sake, that it came to me by way of another patient."

"And how did that happen?"

"It's… a bit complicated."

"I would say it is." Reddy stopped for a moment. "Let me ask you this: How can you be sure that the information you have is true?"

"I just know it is."

Reddy took a deep breath. "What did your patient do?"

"I can't say."

Reddy looked miffed. "What do you mean, you can't say?"

"Look, Ashok, there are some things I can't tell you. I know that I'm speaking to you in a consulting capacity and that everything we say is confidential. But there are things about this situation that could possibly reveal the identity of my patient." Martin felt safe enough in saying this; Benoît was one of a number of patients Reddy had referred to him.

"Fair enough," Reddy said.

"The truth is, I don't really know *what* he did. All I know is that he was somehow involved in something gruesome. Exactly what his role was, I'm not sure. Though I would imagine it must have been pretty bad."

"And how do you come to that?"

"By the nature of things." It was obvious to Martin that, in order to have drawn an FBI and Israeli investigation, Benoît must be suspected of having perpetrated significant crimes.

"That is certainly a vague answer."

Martin sighed. "Sorry."

"Tell me, Marty, why do you think your patient hasn't told you anything himself?"

Martin considered the question. "Maybe he has, sort of. He keeps dwelling on the time period in which the crime was committed, but he distorts and lies. I know he isn't deluded. In fact, I suspect he wants to come out with it."

"What about confronting him?"

"You know I can't do that, at least not directly. What am I supposed to say, 'Patient X has given me information that implicates you in thus and such'? Aside from the fact that I'll look like an ass, it's not very professional."

"What about indirectly?"

"I already have."

"And?"

"That's what leads me to think he's guilty, he became highly defensive, even had me accusing him of things I hadn't said."

"But you do not know for certain?"

"No, I don't."

"Well, there is your answer. You are asking about what to do with information that you don't really have. All you have is hearsay and suspicion. You cannot know anything for sure until your patient tells you, and once he tells you, it is…"

"Protected," Martin interjected.

"Unless, of course, you feel that he is going to do it again, and he reveals a specific plan to you indicating such."

Martin's look said, *I was hoping you'd tell me something I don't already know*. "That's not the issue."

"Then you don't really have an issue, do you?"

"Not from a strictly *legal* perspective," Martin reflected.

"Aha! So it is the *moral* question you are grappling with."

"Precisely."

"It always gets interesting when morality enters into the equation. We are not supposed to judge our patients, you know?" A tinge of sarcasm.

"Yeah, well, that one's always been difficult. Here, it's virtually impossible."

"Must be something rather disturbing," Reddy said.

"It doesn't get worse."

"Well, at least you see that you can't be nonjudgmental. Many of the sanctimonious asses in this business would never even admit to that."

"No one would be able to be purely objective with this."

They looked at each other again, both realizing that they'd taken this about as far as they could.

"So, what are you going to do?" Reddy asked.

"That's a good question," Martin responded.

RICHARD SCHWARTZ ADMIRED THE COLORS of autumn as he sat on a park bench, waiting for his Israeli associates. He had purposely arrived early at Grace Avenue Park in Great Neck to enjoy a few moments with nature before attending to business.

The Great Neck peninsula was replete with parks, trees and hills, juxtaposing God's hand on this otherwise saturated residential and commercial area. In this sense, it was quite unlike the Lower East Side of Manhattan where Schwartz had been raised, or his current Georgetown residence where he spent little time. The scent of green in the air coupled with the sounds of chirping birds made him long for something different. It was time for him to move on to the next stage of his life.

This was it, he had been telling himself the past few weeks, his last hurrah. The people he chased were old and dying, and the world no longer cared. Some tribute, he mused, to a career that had sapped his blood and wrecked his family.

He heard footsteps, turned, and saw the Israelis approaching.

He exchanged brief niceties with them as they sat down, Galit to his right, Arik and Kovi to his left.

"There have been some developments," Schwartz said.

"What do you mean?" Arik asked.

"It seems that our Dr. Rosen knows about Benoît," Schwartz responded.

"How did you learn this?" Galit snapped.

Schwartz figured the Mossad agents assumed that he must have been tapping Rosen's office behind their backs. "Gifford," he answered.

The Israelis' expressions changed.

"Gifford?" Galit said. "What the hell is going on?"

"It's a long story," Schwartz replied. "Suffice it to say that Gifford did his own searching, for his own reasons, found out who we are and what we're doing, and told Rosen."

"What exactly did he tell Rosen?" Kovi asked.

"He didn't tell him about Benoît. He doesn't actually know about Benoît. He told him about us, and he believes that Rosen put the pieces together himself. The good news is that neither Gifford nor Rosen know about Galit."

The Israelis were silent as they digested the information.

"This is all a surprise to you?" Schwartz asked Galit.

She glared at him furiously. "What kind of question is that?"

"One that I had to ask."

"Look," Arik interjected, "we have to decide where we go from here."

"This changes things," Schwartz added.

They all turned to Galit.

"Since when does he know?" she asked.

"Past day or so," Schwartz responded.

"I haven't spoken to him in the past day," she said.

"I wonder if he will tell you," Kovi speculated.

"I know he'll say something. It would be hard for him not to," Galit said.

"Considering your relationship," Arik added derisively.

"Listen," Schwartz said, "you folks can have your little frays on your own time. Right now, we need to figure out our next move."

He looked at Arik. "Personally, I think it's helpful that Galit is close to Rosen. Gives us an edge."

Arik responded with a tentative nod.

Schwartz turned to Galit. "What do you think he'll do?"

Galit shrugged.

"I believe the question should be: What are *we* going to do?" Kovi said.

"I agree," Schwartz added. "I suggest that, rather than waiting to see what Rosen's move is, we try to push things a little further along."

Arik and Kovi appeared eager. Galit, wary. The thought of manipulating Martin Rosen any further didn't seem to sit well with her.

Schwartz reached for a large manila envelope sitting in his briefcase under the bench and gave it to Galit. "See that this somehow falls into Rosen's hands," he said.

She looked at the envelope but didn't bother opening it. They all knew what was inside it.

"And what is this supposed to do?" she asked.

"Like you folks have been doing for the past few weeks, I'm just spitting in the wind," Schwartz replied. "It would be interesting to see what develops if we shake things up a bit though. Don't you think?"

Arik and Kovi nodded. Galit remained still.

Schwartz looked at his watch. "Well, I gotta go."

Galit understood. The decision had been made, and if she wanted to continue playing on his field, it had to be by his rules.

Okay, she told herself with a deep breath. After all, she, more than anyone, wanted this thing done with.

chapter 43

CHERYL MANNING GOT OUT OF the cab and walked up the path toward the house. It was a fairly mild evening, yet she couldn't help shivering. She rang the doorbell with an unsteady hand and waited.

She heard footsteps from inside the house approaching the door, swallowed hard, and somehow managed a smile as the door opened.

"Hi," Martin said, wearing his enthusiasm.

"Hi," she responded as she stepped in.

"Well, this is my home." He gestured to the surroundings.

"Very nice," she said, looking around.

"I'm glad you're here." Earlier in the day, he had told her that he still wasn't ready for her to meet Elizabeth, but he did want her to spend the night at *his* place for a change. He had given the nanny the night off, which he knew she would spend with her boyfriend, and made a sleepover date for Elizabeth with her cousins in Brooklyn.

"I'm glad too," she said.

Martin had spent the past few hours trying to prepare some

semblance of a dinner, ruminating over the day's events, and confronting the question of whether to collect all of Katherine's pictures and put them away. In the end, the dinner had gotten ruined, and he'd decided to keep the pictures where they were.

His decision regarding the pictures had been mostly instinctive, but upon reflection, he believed it was important for Cheryl to see and understand who Katherine was. He simply couldn't hide or dismiss his past. Beyond that, he was convinced that, had he removed the pictures, Cheryl would most likely have asked to see them.

He moved closer to her, kissed her and put his arm around her. "Come, let me show you around."

He walked her to the entrance of the living room. She stepped away from him and entered the room herself, spun around slowly, and offered a nod of approval. Her reaction surprised him, considering that her apartment was so… different. He wondered for a moment if that difference was merely the result of her being a career woman with no time for domestic considerations, or indicative of something else. *Turn it off, Marty*, he told himself.

As he had anticipated, she carefully perused the artwork, then the photographs. The ones that caught her attention were arranged atop a black Baldwin baby grand.

"Who plays?" Cheryl asked, trying to be subtle about her interest in the photos.

"No one, now," Martin answered. "I suppose Elizabeth will take it up. She likes to bang on the keys and make believe she's playing."

"Katherine played?" The pictures helped her avoid looking at him as she asked the question.

"Yes. It was one of her passions."

"As was decorating, I can see."

"Yes."

"She was very beautiful," she said, turning to him with a picture in her hand.

He nodded.

She smiled slightly.

"Can I show you the rest of the house?"

She returned the picture to its place and reached for his hand. "Gladly."

The rest of the tour went quickly, a formality that both of them were eager to dispense with. Afterward, she sat on the sofa in the den, while he excused himself to the kitchen. He returned a few minutes later with two glasses and a bottle of red wine.

"Wine?" she asked.

"Dostoyevsky said, 'Man is a creature who can get used to anything.'"

She examined the bottle. A Chilean Merlot, very impressive. Her smile widened.

He poured.

"To new things," he said.

"You like that toast."

"It's growing on me."

They sipped and looked at each other.

"So, how was your day?" she asked.

"The usual," he said, hoping to leave it at that. He had resigned himself to forgetting his problems for the evening.

"It must be stressful, listening to everybody's misery and having them expect you to fix it all."

"It can be," he responded.

Their conversation was interrupted by the doorbell.

"Expecting someone?" she asked as he got up.

Donning a slightly embarrassed look, he said, "Dinner."

"I thought you were…"

"I'll explain everything," he replied, already halfway out the room.

She rose from the couch, walked into the foyer and watched him pay the delivery man. He turned around holding two paper bags, one with a menu stapled across the top that had Asian characters on it.

"Chinese?" she asked.

"Japanese," he responded, walking past her to the kitchen.

She turned and followed behind him. "As in sushi?"

He looked at her, wondering if there was a problem. "You don't like it?"

"Raw fish?"

Uh oh, he thought. "I really tried to make steak for dinner, but it ended up getting a little… overcooked."

"Overcooked?"

"Burnt."

Her look said, *How did you manage that*?

"I think my mind just wasn't in it," he confessed.

"Where, then, was your mind?" she asked playfully.

He took a deep breath, still trying to erase Benoît from his thoughts. "Work stuff."

"Now there's a detailed answer."

"Sorry."

He opened up the first bag. "I ordered a lot of odds and ends. I'm sure there'll be something you like."

She came over to help him unpack it. "Let's see what we have here."

A few hours later, she awoke, surprised to find herself alone in the bed. She lifted her head, looked around, but he wasn't in the room. She got up, taking the sheet to cover herself, and walked out to the hallway.

"Marty," she called.

There was no answer.

She searched the two other bedrooms, Elizabeth's and the guest room, but both were empty. She decided to try downstairs. As she descended, her footsteps intruded upon the silence, until she came to the foot of the stairs and thought she heard something from the den. She walked slowly toward the den and called his name again.

"In here," he said.

She entered the den and found him sitting in a chair, looking out a window at the night.

"Are you all right?" she asked.

"I'm fine," he said. "Just couldn't sleep."

"Want company?"

"Sure."

His tone was far from convincing, but she planted herself on the couch anyway. "Are you sure you're all right?"

"I don't know if I'm sure of anything," he said as if he were talking to himself.

She looked down at the floor next to the chair and saw an empty Scotch glass. "You've been drinking?"

"I'm not drunk," he clarified. "Just a few ounces to clear my mind."

"And is your mind clear?"

He thought for a moment. "Not really."

"Anything you want to talk about?"

"It probably wouldn't be a good idea. It's about a patient, and I really shouldn't discuss my cases with…"

"It's okay, I understand," she interjected. "Would you like to be alone?"

"No," he said, seemingly surprised by his own response. "I'd like you to stay."

"Then I will."

They sat silently for a few moments.

"Let me ask you this," Martin said.

She perked up, thinking that he was going to get into it.

"Do you find that people frequently aren't who and what they profess to be?" he continued.

"What do you mean?"

"People. You deal with them all the time. What do you think, are most of them phonies?"

"I don't know," she said, hiding her uneasiness. She reflected a moment. "I suppose in my line of work, everyone is putting on a show."

"It's that way in my field as well," he muttered.

"How so?"

"Patients. They lie all the time. Mostly to themselves, occasionally to me. Every now and then I get a whopper, but it's part of the job. People have defenses. Lying is very common. I've grown used to it over the years, I've even developed the skills to deal with it… until today."

"What happened today?"

"Today I found out that I was being told the mother of all lies."

"And what difference does that make? Why can't you handle this the way you always have?"

He thought about her question. "Because *this* is different."

She looked into his eyes and somehow knew that the moment had arrived. She could no longer handle her own complicity in what was happening to him. It had to come to an end. "Marty?" she said.

He gazed at her.

She hesitated. "I am one of those people."

"What people?"

"People who pretend to be what they aren't."

"I wasn't talking about you."

"But you were." Her eyes became watery.

"Cheryl?"

She put her head in her hands.

He got up from his chair and sat down beside her. "Are you okay?" He stroked her hair.

She lifted her head, faced him, and took his hands. "I have to tell you something, Marty."

"Sure, anything."

Her lips quivered. "I… just need for you to know that I… love you very much."

"I know…"

She put her finger over his lips.

"That no matter what happens between us, I have never met a man in my life that I have felt so deeply for."

He grasped her hand. "Please, tell me, what's the matter?"

She took a deep breath and stood up. Convinced that she was about to spill all, she opened her mouth and suddenly found herself paralyzed. She couldn't do it. Searching for something, anything, to say, the only words she could muster were, "I have to go."

"*Go?* Go where?"

"Please, Marty, don't ask me any more questions. I just can't be here right now."

"This is nuts! You're about to tell me something that is obviously important, then all you say is that you have to leave?"

She stood, silent, looking out the window.

He got up and walked over to her. "Cheryl?"

"I'm sorry, Marty," she said. "We were talking about your problems and somehow ended up here."

"It's okay." He put his arms around her.

"No it isn't. There are things about me that… you don't know."

"So tell me."

She hesitated, then turned around to him. "I will. But not right now. Not tonight. Please, just let me leave. I promise I'll tell you everything soon."

He was about to say something else when she put her hand over his mouth once again.

"Please," she said.

He watched from the window as she got into the cab, wondering what in hell had just happened. After the scene in the den, she had simply gone upstairs, put on her clothes, called the cab and left. He had come out of the den to say goodbye when she was already halfway out the door.

"I'll call you," was all he had time to say.

"Okay."

Now he stood, puzzled, though not completely shocked. He had suspected all along that there was something not quite right, and had known that sooner or later he would have to confront whatever it was. Only this particular evening was just about the worst of all possible times for that.

He turned from the window and went searching for his bottle of scotch.

chapter 44

MARTIN ROSEN ENTERED HIS OFFICE and bent over to pick up the manila envelope on the welcome mat. He reached for the light switch with his free hand and proceeded into his consultation room.

It was just past 7 a.m. and his first patient, a pleasant young divorcee suffering from panic attacks, wasn't due for at least twenty minutes. Outside, torrential rain pounded on the window, leading him to anticipate the patient's tardiness. For a brief moment, he imagined the poor woman screaming and slamming her dashboard, wishing she had called to cancel.

Usually, the first thing he did was pick up the phone and order a bagel and a cup of caffeine from the deli down the block. But his curiosity drew him immediately to the envelope.

He sat down at his desk and tore it open, then pulled out a pile of papers, at the top of which was a picture of a young man in a strange-looking uniform. The picture was black-and-white, and the man seemed in his early 20s. Beneath it appeared the name *Theodore Lemieux*. The face of the man bore uncanny similarities to Jacques

Benoît, and Martin knew what he was about to read. What he didn't know was who had slipped it under his door.

He turned the page and began his education about the collaboration of the French Vichy government in the roundup of the Jews of France for the Nazis, and specifically the role of one Vichy police captain, Theodore Lemieux, in atrocities against the Jews of the city of Lyon. He read about Drancy, the internment camp located just three miles outside Paris, where the Jewish men, woman and children of Lyon were sent until they, along with Jews from all over France, were eventually shipped by freight trains directly to Auschwitz.

Martin had known little of the plight of French Jews during the war. He had, at best, vague notions of the Vichy's role in assisting the Nazis. But nothing had been as poignant a testimony to the connection between these "partners" as the railroad lines running directly from Drancy, eastward through France, Germany and most of southern Poland, straight into the main Katowice-Auschwitz-Krakow line. This tidbit was probably included to give him a clear sense of Benoît's handiwork.

The first part of the dossier chronicled the proclivities of Theodore Lemieux, based on interviews with people who had known him. It portrayed a social-climbing womanizer, a frequenter of brothels and nightclubs who most likely would have wound up an embarrassment to his uniform had he not been so ambitious when it came to the Jews.

The next part dealt with Lemieux's alleged crimes against humanity. There were close to fifteen separate incidents listed. Most of these were brief descriptions, gathered from historical documents consisting mainly of eyewitness accounts from survivors who were no longer alive; only two were based on the testimony of living survivors. Those two, primarily because they concerned children, were the ones that Martin found most disturbing.

The first involved the family of a well-known Jewish banker, Philip Saifer, and described how Lemieux managed to apprehend the two children, who had been hiding in a basement crawlspace. The family had been shipped to Drancy, and from there to Auschwitz. Only the younger brother, Henry Saifer, survived. He presently lived in Jerusalem, working as a writer for an Israeli periodical, and had been the first to pick out a photo of Benoît from the international media years ago and match it to Lemieux.

Martin swallowed hard, recalling Benoît's words about the brooch sitting in his drawer.

I believe the husband was a banker...

It says, 'To Leila, all my love, Philip'...

Sickened, Martin forced himself to read on.

The second incident was a description of a raid on a Jewish orphanage in Izieu, a small village in the hills outside the city of Lyon. The operation was led by Klaus Barbie, the Gestapo chief in Lyon, in April of 1944, only a few months before the Allied liberation of France. The Nazis had apparently been growing restless with the speed at which France was being "purified," so they solicited select Vichy leaders to step up their campaign to round up Jews. At the top of their list, Captain Theodore Lemieux was described as an ideal candidate because of his past "ingenuity and tenacity in dealing with the Jewish problem."

It was Lemieux who stood beside Barbie, supervising his Vichy underlings in assisting the Gestapo's capture of forty-four children and seven adults, all of whom were sent to Drancy. One child escaped during the raid, and one adult was captured but managed to survive. Of the rest, forty-two children and five adults were gassed at Auschwitz-Birkenau, while two other children and the superintendent of the home were executed by a firing squad in Estonia.

The last part of the dossier contained the case against Jacques Benoît, tracing Benoît's roots back to Lemieux and presenting compelling, though circumstantial, evidence that the two men were one and the same. It also contained some early photographs of Benoît, accentuating the similarities to the picture of Lemieux.

Martin placed the pages on his desk and looked at the clock. He had gotten so engrossed in the dossier, he hadn't noticed that his patient was already half an hour late. He knew that at any second, he would hear her enter the waiting room, and he also knew that the last thing he was capable of doing right now was conducting a therapy session. He was thankful that the session would be short.

He opened his address book for the phone numbers of his

remaining patients for the morning. He picked up the phone and started dialing, realizing that, in his fifteen years of practice, the only other time he had cancelled patients was immediately after the deaths of Katherine and Ethan. He continued dialing, gazing again at the papers on his desk and thinking that, once he finished these calls, he would first have to deal with whoever had left this for him.

DAN GIFFORD LOOKED UP FROM his desk at his secretary standing in the doorway. Over an hour ago, he had given her firm instructions: *no calls, no interruptions.* Less than a week away from the trial of his career, he'd gotten sidetracked on this Nazi business to the point where he was far behind, and he desperately needed to get up to speed. Yet, here she was; no doubt about to tell him something that would distract him once again.

"Yes," he said, drawing out the word as if to appear mildly annoyed.

She grinned at his seemliness. "There's a man here who says he has to see you. Says if I told you who he was, you'd want to..."

"And who might he be?"

"Martin Rosen."

Gifford was stunned. "Martin Rosen?"

"Should I show him in?"

"Yes... please."

The few seconds between the secretary's slipping away and reappearing with Martin Rosen passed like a flash in Gifford's mind, leaving him no time to gather his thoughts.

Martin entered the office looking weary. Gifford also had to admit that he was discomfited, even though he was on his own turf. Martin took a seat in front of Gifford's desk. Neither of them spoke until the secretary left.

"I'm sorry to barge in on you like this, Dan," Martin said.

"No, Doc, don't be sorry. If I seem a little..." Gifford struggled to find the right word.

"Surprised?" Martin said.

"Yeah, surprised. It's only because this is... I mean, you, my shrink, coming to *my* office. It's unusual."

"Yes, it is," Martin reflected. "I know I'm breaking all the rules by being here, but it seems a lot of unusual things are happening these days."

Gifford leaned back in his chair. "Rules are sometimes meant to be broken."

"I was going to call you instead of coming by, but I thought it would be best to do this in person."

"Do what?"

"Talk about the contents of the envelope."

"Envelope? What envelope?"

Martin appeared bewildered. "You mean you didn't leave a manila envelope for me under my door?"

"Why would you think I did?" Gifford stopped, considered what was happening, then added, "Unless the envelope contained something concerning what we talked about."

Martin suddenly stood up. "Look, Dan, I'm sorry I barged in on you like this."

Gifford gestured to the chair. "Doc, sit!"

"I can't. I really must leave. In fact, I should never have done this in the first place. It was very unprofessional of me."

"Look, Doc. Whatever is going on, I would guess that nobody could handle it in a strictly 'professional' way. I can assure you that whoever sits up there in that ivory tower and mandates professional conduct *never* had this scenario in mind. Now you know exactly what I'm talking about, and if I'm right, you need help."

Martin considered Gifford's point. "Dan, I like you and I

respect you, and I don't want it to seem like I'm putting you off. But you have to understand, in the relationship that you and I have, it is my job to help you, not the other way around."

"Forget that relationship stuff, Doc, it's all bull," Gifford said, becoming more animated. "The only reason you've helped me is because of *who* you are, not *what* you are. The fact that you're the shrink and I'm the patient is incidental as far as I see it. The fact that you're a good guy who I trust and respect is what it's all about. And now you're telling me *you* can't trust me? What am I supposed to do with that?"

"You're right, Dan, about *most* of what you said, but you're wrong about my not trusting you. As for your claim to trust *me*, that's exactly what I'm asking you to do."

"You're asking me to let you handle this by yourself, even though it's clear that you're in over your head?"

"I'm obviously not alone."

"Yeah," Gifford said, sighing. "It would seem you're not."

Martin turned toward the door. "I know that this whole thing is bound to impact your therapy," he said. "It would be sad to see that end, but if you're having second thoughts about continuing with me, I'll understand."

Gifford stood up and faced Martin eye to eye. "The only thing I'm having second thoughts about, Doc, is your ability to handle this thing without me."

"Like I said, Dan, you'll just have to trust me on that one."

"I guess I have no choice," Gifford said, seemingly resigned. He held his hand out for Martin, and the two men shook. "I'll see you tomorrow," Gifford added, referring to his next session.

Martin responded with a slight but heartfelt smile, then turned and left.

Driving along the Long Island Expressway, Martin was infuriated with himself. He had acted impetuously, jumping to conclusions about Dan Gifford and going to Gifford's office. And he had placed his professional relationship with Gifford in jeopardy. Sure, Gifford's ability to rationalize professionalism out of the picture was compelling, but for Martin it wasn't that easy. Too much of *who* he was was wrapped up in *what* he was.

He thought about tomorrow, confident that Gifford would indeed show and that they would somehow get back on track with what they were supposed to be doing together. Then he thought about Benoît. He already knew how he was going to deal with that; he had come to his decision the moment he had finished the dossier. Gifford was certainly right about one thing: "Whoever sits up there in that ivory tower and mandates professional conduct *never* had this scenario in mind."

As for now, there was still the matter of who had slipped the manila envelope under his door. It could have been the FBI or the Israelis, but *why* would they want to involve him? What could they have had in mind?

His first hypothesis was that perhaps his office was bugged, and they were hoping he would confront Benoît, who in turn would confess. But that was unlikely; such evidence would never be admissible in a court of law. A patient's privilege of confidentiality, as Martin had pointed out in his own book, was actually rooted in the Fifth Amendment right against self-incrimination. Things divulged to therapists, lawyers and clergy were thus deemed "protected" precisely because they had the potential to be self-incriminating.

So what could their intent have been?

Between this, and last night with Cheryl, Martin's head was in disarray, a state that he loathed more than anything in the world. He felt lost, almost paralyzed, until suddenly, something struck him.

He replayed his last conversation with Cheryl:

"Marty… I'm one of those people."

"What people?"

"People who pretend to be what they aren't."

"I wasn't talking about you."

"But you were."

At once, the events of the past few weeks flashed through his mind:

Meeting her the same time he had met Benoît.

His sense from his first time in her apartment that something was amiss.

Never being able to reach her at her workplace.

Last night's scene.

This morning's delivery.

A harrowing picture was taking form as a nauseated feeling began raging through his gut. He sensed himself about to lose control, and pulled the car over to the shoulder of the highway. He sat there for minutes, trying to collect himself, wondering if this was all mere coincidence, if the stress was making him paranoid.

In the end, only one thing was clear: there weren't too many people he could trust. And, for the first time in his life, it wasn't clear to him if he, himself, was among them.

He placed the car in drive and eased his way back into the right lane. It was time to learn the truth.

ASHOK REDDY WAS ROUSED BY the sound of his beeper. The meeting came to a halt as he pulled it from his belt and read the message: Urgent, call Marty Rosen, 363-3640, ASAP.

In truth, he was relieved. He hated these departmental meetings. It was always the same agenda: tightening the budget, filling beds, losing positions. A futile battle to show some stability in a system where it was inevitable for hospitals to lose money. It simply had to be that way, so long as health care was controlled by Wall Street's profit-driven insurance industry, and there was nothing Reddy, nor a thousand departmental meetings, could do about it.

He looked at the others in the room. The hospital's chief administrator and his colleagues from other departments all wore their jealousy as he gathered his things together. "I'm sorry, folks. Seems I have a clinical emergency to attend to."

The meeting continued as if he were already gone. He stood up, his files in hand, and slipped out the door.

Martin Rosen answered his cellular on the first ring. "Ashok?"

"You pulled me out of a meeting."

"Then you owe me."

Reddy chuckled. "Is everything all right?"

"Not really. I need to see you."

Reddy looked at his watch. He knew that if Martin was calling him like this, it was important. "When can you be here?"

"I'm on the Expressway, just past the Douglaston exit. I'd say ten minutes."

"I'll see you then."

"Thanks."

Too wound up to sit still, Martin paced as he spoke, noticing Reddy's skepticism grow with every word.

"You mean to tell me you believe there's a connection between Cheryl and this patient you have been talking about?" Reddy asked.

"I know it sounds crazy."

"Paranoid is more the word that comes to mind."

Martin nodded. He couldn't completely deny the point. "But there are just too many coincidences."

"I will grant you that. You do seem to have an interesting life."

Martin stood still, leaned over the desk, and looked at his friend. "I want you to hypnotize me, like you offered. I'm certain I saw something in her apartment that night. I saw it when I first got there and must have buried it in my unconscious. Then, whatever it was must have come out in my dream. And as I was leaving, it hit me again, still buried but closer to the surface."

Reddy looked askance at him.

"You know that such things can happen!" Martin said.

"In movies, mostly."

"Ashok!"

"You really think that whatever you saw will solve this mystery for you?"

"I can't know that until we find out what it was."

Reddy pondered a moment. "Okay, I will do it. I might even learn your deepest, darkest secrets."

"You already know them," Martin uttered.

Martin sat comfortably in the chair, awaiting his instructions. A skilled hypnotist in his own right, he knew that erasing his own preconceptions from his mind was the key to his success as a subject. At least, as much as he was able.

"Now, I want you to take deep but gentle breaths, inhaling all the way down into your diaphragm," Reddy said in a slow, measured tone.

Martin complied.

"And as you do, I want you to focus on relaxing your body and your mind. Let each breath be as a wave of energy flowing through you, and every time you exhale, you will feel yourself releasing that energy and sinking ever so slightly into the chair."

Reddy waited a beat to assess Martin's reaction.

"Now, Marty," he continued, "I want you to look up at the ceiling, and I want you to pick a spot on the ceiling and stare at it."

Martin raised his eyes and searched for a spot.

Reddy waited until he saw Martin's eyes fixed. "Good," he said. "Now, keep focusing on your breathing and on the spot you have chosen, and just try to relax. You don't have to think about anything. You don't even have to concentrate on what I say. *Nothing* should interfere with your breathing and staring. And remember, each time you exhale, you will feel yourself sinking *deeper* and *deeper*."

Reddy waited again, allowing Martin time to get into it.

"All right, Marty, there is one more thing I want you to do. Continue focusing on your breathing. Continue staring at the spot. And as you exhale, as you feel yourself sinking even *deeper* and *deeper* into the chair, I want you to count backwards from 100, so that each time you exhale, you go down one more number, taking yourself *deeper* and *deeper*, bringing yourself closer to zero.

"Now, remember, there are only three things you must do. Breathe deep but gentle breaths, stare at the spot, and count backwards each time you exhale. And as you do this, you will feel yourself sinking even *deeper* and *deeper* into the chair, into a state in which you will be perfectly responsive to my suggestions..."

Reddy reiterated his instructions a few more times until he saw that Martin was out. He then induced a state of analgesia in Martin's right hand by having Martin imagine the hand sitting in a bucket of ice for a few minutes. He opened his desk drawer, removed a safety pin, unlatched it as he walked over to Martin, and gently poked the hand. When he saw no response, he poked a bit harder, and still Martin remained impervious. Just to make sure, he then pinched Martin's hand tightly. Observing not even a flinch on Martin's face, Reddy was convinced his subject was ready.

"Marty, I want you to take yourself back to that first night you were in Cheryl's home. I want you to use your mind as if it were a camera. Picture everything just as it was. From the moment you enter, the color of the walls, the type of floor, the details of the furnishings and pictures. Focus the lens of your camera so that everything is crystal clear. Can you see it?"

"Yes," Martin answered.

"Good. Tell me where you are."

"In the foyer."

Reddy noted that Martin's words flowed slowly and deliberately, just as they should. "Describe it to me."

"It's a small hallway. Wood floor, a bit beat-up. The walls are linen, or dark white. No pictures, just a welcome mat and a closet." Martin stopped for a second. "A full-length mirror on the outside of the closet door."

"Good, Marty, you are doing well. Now, where did you go next?"

"Living room."

"Describe it."

"The floor is still wood, covered by an area rug. It's checkered, black and… it looks black and brown."

"Go on."

"Ordinary furniture, a couch and a love seat. They're beige, like the walls. And a coffee table, a darker wood, like redwood. Doesn't look like real wood. Same for the end tables." Martin stopped for a moment as if he were looking around in his mind. "There's art.

Posters. Famous artists. I've seen them before."

"Is there anything unusual about them?"

"No." He hesitated. "I don't think so."

"Okay, is there anything else?"

"Yes, there's a… bookcase," Martin answered, his voice growing tremulous.

"What about the bookcase?"

Martin hesitated. "Strange."

"Strange in what way?"

"Also fake wood. Resembles walnut. Build-it-yourself sort of stuff."

"Is that what bothers you?"

"No," Martin responded tentatively.

"Then what?"

"Books."

"What about the books, Marty?" Reddy noted the strain in his own voice, admonishing himself to remain calm.

"There are some hardcovers. Mostly paperbacks. Just there."

"What do you mean by *just there*?"

"No sense."

"No sense?"

"They make no sense."

"The books make no sense?"

"No particular themes or interest. Just there."

"As if someone just found a bunch of books and put them together?"

"Yes," Martin said. He stopped again for a moment. "Something else."

"There's something else that bothers you?"

"The books."

"What else about the books bothers you?"

Martin's hands began to tremor. "The paperbacks… not read."

"The paperbacks weren't read?"

"None."

"How do you know?"

"No creases on the spines. Brand-new. They make no sense. Aren't read."

Reddy considered what he was hearing and was concerned that Martin's agitation might compromise the trance.

"Not real," Martin said.

"What's not real?"

Martin hesitated, then said, "Nothing." His lips quivered as the word came out.

"Was there anything else, Marty?"

"No." His voice returned to normal.

"What about in the bedroom?"

"Bedroom. Dream."

"Do you remember the dream?"

"Cheryl."

"Cheryl's in the dream?"

"Shopping cart."

"What else?"

"Cheryl. Shopping cart. Bookstore."

"What is Cheryl doing with the shopping cart in the book store?"

"Throwing books in it?"

"Any type of books?"

"All types. No sense."

"Was there more in the dream?"

"Katherine."

"Katherine?"

"Katherine is in… bookstore with shopping cart."

"Katherine is in the bookstore with a shopping cart?"

"Katherine," Martin answered, his voice agitated again.

"Is it Katherine or Cheryl?"

"Cheryl. Katherine."

"Katherine and Cheryl?"

"Cheryl. Katherine." Martin's body was starting to shake. "*Cheryl. Katherine. Cheryl. Katherine…*"

Reddy sensed that they had taken this as far as they could. "Okay, Marty." He placed his hand on Martin's. "It's okay. Just relax. I want you to relax."

Instantly, Martin obeyed.

"Now, Marty, in a moment I am going to count you out of

your trance. First, you will remember everything we said here. Second, you will feel like your normal self. Together, we will be able to discuss this all objectively and find out what it means. Okay?"

"Yes."

"And one more thing. Your right hand will return to its normal sensation. It will no longer feel anesthetized. Are you ready?"

"Yes."

"Good, I am going to count forward now, slowly from one to ten. With each number, as I approach ten, I want you to gradually return yourself to a normal state of consciousness. Keep your eyes closed until I reach ten, and *slowly* bring yourself back to my office, back to where we started our journey..."

Martin opened his eyes to a look of concern on Reddy's face.

"How was it for you?" Reddy asked.

Martin shook his head, still trying to awaken himself. "Weird," he answered.

"Do you remember all of it?"

"I think so?"

"Good then, let's talk about the dream. I think that is the key."

"So do I," Martin said, contemplating. "What do you make of it?"

"You became quite upset when you described it, also when describing the bookcase."

"They're obviously related." Martin thought for a moment. "What bothered me about the books – in fact, what bothered me about the entire apartment – was that things didn't seem... authentic."

Reddy nodded in agreement.

"It all had a feeling as if it were, somehow, makeshift."

"Put together for your benefit?" Reddy asked.

Martin threw up his hands, reflecting his own awareness that he sounded crazy. "I don't know. It was just a feeling I had. The style of the place. The things. Everything felt contrived."

"And the books?"

"They clinched it, I suppose. A bookcase full of brand-new,

untouched paperbacks. Not a single crease on any of the spines. And what a hodgepodge, no two books reflecting a similar interest."

"As if they were all just haphazardly thrown into a shopping cart in a…"

"Bookstore," Martin interjected.

The two men looked at each other.

"It does sound curious." Reddy considered his next question very carefully. "What about Katherine?" he asked.

Martin stared off into space.

"What does Katherine bring to mind?" Reddy reiterated.

"Someone who loved me."

"Someone you could trust?"

"Of course."

"Yet, Cheryl seems to be someone you *can't* trust."

"But she's trying to come off as someone I can…"

"Trust," Reddy said. "In your dream, Cheryl and Katherine are one and the same. You put them together and take them apart because you are not sure if Cheryl is fit to replace Katherine in your life. And the reason for this is because you don't trust her. The books suggest deceit to you."

"Precisely," Martin said. "In real life, she is trying to take Katherine's place, or at least I've been thinking about letting her do that. Did I tell you that she asked to meet Elizabeth?"

"Why would she do that if she was out to hurt you?"

Martin pondered the question. "I don't know."

"Maybe she isn't?"

"What do you mean?"

"I mean that maybe this is still all in your head."

"Then what do you make of the books?"

"There could be a lot of explanations. Who knows, maybe she just got them for decoration?"

"Paperbacks?"

"So she isn't the best decorator. That is not exactly what I would call a smoking gun."

Martin thought for a moment. "It wasn't only the books, it was the whole apartment. It all seemed…"

"The word you used before was contrived."

"Exactly."

"So, because of this, you suspect her of some involvement with this patient of yours."

"There's more to it."

Reddy appeared curious, waiting for the rest.

"I still can't give you the details," Martin said.

Reddy threw up his hands. "Then I cannot help."

Martin weighed carefully what he was about to say. "I can tell you this: last night, Cheryl so much as confessed to me that she wasn't who I thought she was."

"People say things like that all the time."

"Not like this. She became hysterical about it, wouldn't explain herself, and left in tears."

Reddy appeared unconvinced.

"This morning, slipped under my door, was a manila envelope containing documents about my patient."

"Documents?"

"As in evidence about things he did."

"And you believe Cheryl had something to do with that?"

"As I said, there are just too many coincidences."

"But they may be just that, *coincidences*. I do not know what to make of any of this, Marty. It seems so… fantastic."

"It is! But I know my instincts are right, and I'm going to find out what the connection is."

"And then?"

"That's a good question."

"You mean you aren't going to tell me what you are going to do about your patient."

Martin looked at his friend. "Ashok, I want you to promise me something."

Reddy nodded.

"Whatever happens, whatever you piece together on your own from things you may hear or learn, we are never going to speak about this again."

Reddy caught Martin's determination. "Okay," he said with hesitation in his voice. "But whatever does happen, whether you are right or wrong about Cheryl, there is one thing I am certain of…"

Martin raised his eyebrows.

"She cares very deeply for you."

"And how do you know this?"

"Let's just say that you aren't the only one here who has good instincts."

chapter 47

GALIT STEIN KNEW IT WAS Martin Rosen the moment she heard the buzzer. She toyed with pretending she wasn't home, but dismissed the idea as quickly as it came. She pressed the intercom button, told the doorman to let the gentleman come up, opened the apartment door and waited.

Martin walked off the elevator, turned, and saw her standing in the doorway. He approached her, a blank look on his face, carrying the manila envelope. Without saying a word, he dropped the envelope in her hands and marched past her into the living room. He stood before the bookcase, giving it one more examination, then turned around.

She fidgeted with the envelope. "How did you know?" she asked, her accent suddenly no longer British, though he couldn't quite place it.

With that, any hope he had of being wrong vanished. He looked at her, almost impassively, and responded, "It wasn't hard once I saw all the pieces. You have lots of books, all unread. And this place, these furnishings, just don't seem to fit your persona, at least not the persona I thought you had."

"That's what bothered you that first night you stayed with me?"

"It might appear trivial to someone else, but not to me, not now. I admit I had dismissed it until last night." He pointed to the envelope. "Until that."

"And now that you know?"

His expression took on a blend of anger and incredulity. "Who are you?"

"Who do you think I am?" She asked, her tone defensive.

"I believe it's time for you to offer answers rather than questions."

"You're right," she conceded, lowering her gaze.

His eyes focused on the envelope still in her hand. "You left that for me."

"Yes," she said, "I did."

"What's this all about? What's your role in it?"

She gestured toward the couch, her hand shaking slightly. "Please sit."

"I don't feel like sitting."

She looked at him, searching for some sign of forgiveness, but found none. "My name is Galit Stein."

He digested the information, appearing stoic. "Galit, that's a Hebrew name."

She nodded.

"You're Israeli?"

Another nod.

He turned away as if he couldn't look at her. Feeling that he needed more support than his legs presently offered, he walked around the couch and sat himself down. Staring into space, he found himself wordless.

"I didn't intend for it to turn out this way," she said.

He lifted his eyes to hers. "And exactly what did you think *was* going to happen?"

"I didn't plan for it to go this far between us."

"Oh," he said, an uncharacteristic bite in his tone. "And how far is that?"

"I didn't think…"

"*What? What* didn't you think would happen?"

"I didn't think... I would fall in love with you."

He struggled to ignore the tears forming in her eyes, convincing himself that she wasn't to be trusted. "And what is it that you were hoping to get from me?"

"Something on Benoît."

"You mean you actually thought I would throw my professional life out the window, betray all my ethics, everything I believe in, for *your* cause."

"There are more important things involved here than what *you* believe."

"What do you know of my beliefs?"

She was silent.

"Oh yes," he continued, "you probably know all about me. No doubt you studied my past and targeted me as just the sort to help you. Must be humbling to learn that your profile was bullshit."

"My parents also survived the Holocaust. I would never exploit that. You were *his* choice, not ours. We simply followed where the trail led."

"But you did intend to get close to me."

"Yes, I did," she admitted. "But not as close as I got. You have to believe me!"

"Why should I believe anything you say?"

She considered the question. "I suppose you shouldn't."

He stared at her. "How could you possibly think I would help you? Even if I had something to tell you, you could never use it."

"Not directly. We were hoping you might give us something, anything that might lead us to something else that we *could* use."

"And what made you think I would?"

"Nothing. It was a shot in the dark."

Silence.

She hesitated. "What happens now?"

His expression turned blank.

She sat down and fixed her eyes on the envelope. "It's all true, you know. Every detail."

Martin didn't respond.

"What do you plan to do about it?" she asked.

"That's all you care about, isn't it? It's not about us, it's about what I'll do for you."

"It's about many things, and as for what you'll do, I only want you to do what is in your heart. You may not trust me anymore, but I still trust you. I know that whatever you choose, it will be the right thing."

"And, of course, you already know what the right thing is," he said with sarcasm.

"I know what the right thing for me is, and I thought I knew what it was for you." She hesitated. "But I am not so sure anymore."

Her admission surprised him, but mostly it left him wondering if this was yet another manipulation. He wanted desperately to believe it was genuine, but his defenses were fortified. He was reverting to the person he had been before she'd entered his life.

"What do you hope to accomplish here?" he asked.

"To bring Benoît to justice, and to remind the world once again of the atrocities against our people."

"Benoît is old, and in the eyes of most people, so is this whole issue. The last time you folks tried to reawaken things, it sort of backfired. What did that teach the world?"

"If you're referring to Demjanjuk, that is *precisely* the reason we need Benoît!"

"So, it's about undoing your own mistakes."

"It is about keeping things clear. Demjanjuk complicated matters, Benoît will clarify them once again – evil is evil and shall be punished!"

"Just like in the Bible."

"Yes," she agreed. "If that's how you must have it: Just like in the Bible."

He thought for a moment. "You know, this whole Benoît thing could work against you. He *is* a popular fellow, quite renowned for his philanthropy, and also employs tens of thousands of people, not to mention the stockholders who depend on the viability of his companies. Now you come along and spoil all that over something that happened more than fifty years ago. Even if he is your man, the world is a funny place these days and there may not be an abundance of support out there. The public may start criticizing you for not forgiving and forgetting, and – poof! – you wind up with just the opposite of what you're looking for."

"Is that how *you* feel?"

"How I feel isn't important. I'm just considering the possibilities."

"Considering the possibilities, or giving yourself an excuse to ease your conscience for letting him go free?"

"He's not mine to free."

She stopped to ponder his point. "Why did you come here tonight?" she asked.

"To see if I was right about you."

"Well, you have your answer."

"I also came to tell you that I can't help you."

"You can't, or you *won't*?"

"It all comes down to the same thing, doesn't it?"

"As far as the outcome, yes. But in terms of what your convictions are, there is a difference."

"I don't have to justify myself to you!"

"That's correct. Tell me though, to whom or to what do you have to justify yourself?"

He took a deep breath and looked away from her again. "I think we're done here."

She stared at him.

He lifted himself off the couch and began making his exit, acutely feeling the weight of his body with each step.

She sat, her eyes watery, still watching him.

His mind retreated inward, rendering him oblivious to everything. He had a faint sense of a voice and the closing of a door behind him, a sense of himself moving from a hallway onto an elevator. But until he stepped out into the crisp air of the night, he hadn't fully realized what had transpired in those final seconds: She had said, "I'm sorry." And he, offering nothing more, had walked out.

chapter 48

MARTIN ROSEN'S EYES WERE FIXATED on the ceiling until he heard the noise. He was startled, like an animal sensing danger. Doused in perspiration, he lifted his head from the pillow, honing his senses for signs of movement from the hallway outside his bedroom.

A figure appeared in the doorway, seeming like a shadow from the way the faint lighting of the hallway hit it from behind. Suddenly, a sense of relief, a slowing of his heart, as Martin recognized his daughter. "Elizabeth?" he called out.

"Daddy," she said, her voice trembling, "I'm scared."

She ran to his side. He scooped her up and wrapped his arms around her. "What's the matter?" he asked as calmly as he could, wondering if the same demons that had kept him awake had invaded her sleep as well.

"I had a bad dream." Tears rolled down her cheeks.

"A bad dream?" He hugged her tighter. "Tell me what it was about."

"I don't remember."

"Then how do you know it was bad?"

"Because I woke up scared."

Martin was no expert in child psychology, but he knew that children frequently had difficulty articulating the things that scared them. And he was only too familiar with the fact that these things often came in the middle of the night. Two years earlier, immediately after Katherine and Ethan were killed, Elizabeth spent many nights running into his bedroom looking for her Mommy. It lasted for almost two months before subsiding, though it had never completely disappeared. Before he had left for Chicago, his first overnight trip away from her, he had been concerned that his absence might cause an exacerbation. Strangely enough, the result was actually the opposite. Since his return, the nights had been uneventful. He had attributed the change to a simple, sudden break in habit. But in truth, he knew that it was really one of those paradoxes of human behavior that defied understanding. And, whatever the reason, her problem had now resurfaced, causing him to wonder if her sense of his own terrors had somehow brought this about.

He stroked her hair. "There's nothing to be scared of, princess. I'm right here. I'll always be here and I would never let anything happen to you."

As he said those words, he realized that he had used them with her frequently since the tragedy, and that it was no doubt a false promise. Still, he could think of little else to allay her fears.

She cuddled close to him.

"Would you like to sleep here tonight?" he asked.

She looked at him, a slight, sudden smile spreading across her face. "Can I?"

"Yes," he said, aware that it wasn't his wisest decision. Many an expert might have disagreed with it, but at that moment, he had neither the strength nor the desire to part with her. He needed her as much as she needed him.

A moment of silence passed as they positioned themselves for sleep.

"Daddy?"

"Yes, princess?"

"Do you get scared?"

Now he was convinced she was onto him. Genius that she was, she had seen him only briefly before she had gone to bed, yet she had read him thoroughly. "Sometimes," he responded.

"And what do you do?"

There it was, the most interesting question she had asked him to date, saying nothing of its timeliness. And, as with all good questions, he hadn't a clue of the answer.

Suddenly, he pictured himself lying in the his childhood bed, asking his own mother the very same thing and, as if transported back to the past, he could hear her response: *God watches over us.*

Faith as the answer to everything, the dogma of his youth. Was he denying his daughter something essential by depriving her of a sense of the divine? Would he, too, be faring better if he simply had reliance on a power beyond? Was Galit right, was there in fact a higher moral purpose superseding his own personal ethics and judgments? And if so, had he been devoting his entire adult life to an illusion, running from the very thing that now offered him his only salvation?

He turned to Elizabeth, pondering how to suddenly invoke the idea of a God who loved and protected her, searching his mind for the right words and thoughts. But all he could come up with was uncertainty, and not even the words to explain that. Looking into her eyes, wondering if she sensed his frustration, he said, "I think about the people who love me, the people who would never let anything bad happen to me, and I know that they'll be there to protect me. Then I'm not scared anymore."

She seemed to contemplate this. "Then that's what I'll do, Daddy." She nestled her head against his chest and put her arm on his waist.

He could tell she had run out of steam, though the dialogue still played in his mind. Back to staring at the ceiling, he was once again ruminating over his own quandaries. And in the end, the only thing he knew for certain was that tomorrow he would confront not one man, but two: Benoît and himself.

chapter 49

MARTIN ROSEN WAS PLEASED WITH the news Dan Gifford had given him: "Stephanie wants me to come home, Doc. She says she wants to try again." Moreover, he was gratified that the session had focused on this development in Gifford's life, giving him a sense that they were back on track. And, although he had detected a slight undercurrent of tension from things unspoken, he was confident it would wane with time.

Now, with Gifford having just departed, Martin sat in his chair, playing with the brooch in his hand, looking at the clock and wondering where Benoît was. It was the first time the man was late and, considering their last session, it wouldn't surprise Martin if he didn't show at all. Martin was accustomed to this sort of behavior from patients, and he admitted to himself that resolving the Benoît dilemma without having to do anything had its appeal. But Martin knew that this could never end so simply.

The silence was suddenly broken by the sound of someone entering the waiting room. Martin had left the door to his inner office open, as he always did with tardy patients – an indication that he was waiting. He quickly placed the brooch in his pocket.

"I am sorry to be late," Benoît said as he came in.

Martin nodded his acceptance.

Benoît closed the door and hastened toward the couch. "There was a business emergency I had to attend to."

Martin raised his eyebrows.

"Nothing really," Benoît explained. "Just a phone call – a crisis in one of my resorts in the Caymans." Benoît sat down and caught his breath. "So, let's get to it."

"Yes, let's."

"Do you have anything in particular you think we should discuss?" Benoît asked.

Martin thought this was an unusual question coming from a patient. It was generally protocol for the patient to set the agenda for the session, not the therapist. He had already surmised that Benoît must have had a plan in mind from the very start of their relationship; thus, he interpreted the question as a fishing expedition on Benoît's part, to see just how far along they actually were.

As for Benoît's tardiness, Martin took that as a tactic, an old business trick – keep the other fellow waiting, make him anxious, gain the upper hand. In this case, it was Benoît's attempt to level the playing field by equalizing the uneasiness. "Actually, I do," Martin answered.

Benoît's eyes opened wide. "And what might that be?"

Martin looked at him impassively. "I'd like you to tell me about the orphanage."

Benoît's face reddened, though his voice remained calm. "You want me to tell you what?"

"About the orphanage," Martin repeated.

"What orphanage?"

"You know exactly what I'm talking about, so let's stop pretending."

Benoît suddenly retreated to silence. He appeared to be to be at a loss, drifting and uncertain, contemplating how to respond.

Martin waited patiently, assuming that the next thing he was going to hear would be the truth.

Benoît reached into his pocket for a handkerchief and began

wiping his forehead. "What is there to tell you? You obviously already know," he said.

"I want to hear it from you."

"Ah, so you want me to wallow in it."

"I want you to tell me the truth."

"You know the truth!"

Martin simply stared at Benoît and waited.

Benoît met his stare, projecting more surrender than anger. Then he proceeded to relate the details, just as he remembered them.

April 6, 1944
Izieu, Vichy France

He opens the car door, tosses his cigarette on the ground, and steps out as the trucks behind him come to a halt. It is the dawn of a spring day; the air is chilled and foggy. He looks around as the Gestapo chief emerges from the second car. The two of them share a brief glance.

There are three other Gestapo agents in the chief's car, and eight Vichy policemen in one of the trucks. The other truck is empty, awaiting its cargo.

He looks at his watch. It is almost time. The place is quiet, secluded out here in the hills beyond the city. A perfect place for refuge, on any other day.

The men gather and stand at attention, awaiting orders. He looks to the chief for a signal. A moment passes while the chief surveys the area. There is always the possibility of a partisan ambush.

The chief appears satisfied and nods.

He turns to the men and shouts, "Begin!"

His command eradicates the stillness of the early morning. Boots pound the ground, whistles blow. Lights go on inside the building. The chief looks at him, offering a faint smile. It is beginning.

The door is kicked in and the men file through, weapons in hand. He is certain that the weapons are needed only to instill fear – if there were partisans, they would already have attacked.

He enters the building last, walking beside the chief. This, more than anything, is his coup – to have been handpicked for this assignment by Klaus Barbie, Gestapo Chief of Lyon.

He hears a confrontation upstairs, some women are resisting. He feels he should intervene before the Nazis do. Bloodshed in an orphanage, even a Jewish one, would be most un-French.

He walks up the stairs and observes three women blocking a doorway that obviously leads to a room filled with children. The women are shouting, and his men, seemingly inept, simply shout back.

He takes out his pistol and fires a shot toward the ceiling. He then steps in front of one of the women and points the gun directly at her head. Now there is silence.

"Madam," he says, "you and your friends have three seconds to step aside, or you will die."

The women obey, as he knew they would. He looks at his men. "You couldn't have pushed past them?" He is not altogether angry – it is another opportunity to demonstrate his prowess to the Nazis. He believes them depraved enough to regard him capable of actually killing the woman. But he is ever the smart one, knowing it would never have come to that.

He surveys the room. It belongs to four young girls, all sitting fearfully on their beds. Avoiding their eyes, he looks them over, guessing them to be 5 or 6 years old. "Take them down," he tells the men as he turns and exits the room.

He hears more clamor from the ground floor – crying, yelling, and what sounds like laughter from the Nazis – as he proceeds downstairs. The children and staff are being gathered and ridiculed by their captors. He glances at his watch. The operation has been in progress just over ten minutes. He is concerned that it will take too long. It is important that these things go quickly; the men shouldn't have too much time to think about what they are doing.

With a gesture of his hand, he beckons his second in command. "Our German friends admire efficiency," he whispers to the man. "We must make haste."

"Yes, Captain," the man replies, then darts away, shouting orders.

He notices Barbie watching him closely. It is a pivotal moment. The war has been good to him thus far. The small fortune he has plundered will serve him well once his country is again free. He knows the Nazi occupation will not last forever, and wonders just how much time remains for him to amass more riches. Already there have been rumors of an Allied invasion.

He notices the room filling up quickly; his men are more aggressive in their task. He knows it is the rewards they anticipate after the war that form the basis for their loyalty. They, like the Nazis, know what he has been up to. The Nazis turn a blind eye; a small price to pay for his assistance. It is all unspoken but quite understood.

Within minutes, the roundup is complete. There are forty-four children in all, and seven adults, one fewer child than the Gestapo report had indicated. *Perhaps the report was faulty*, he contemplates. Either way, there is no time to search.

Several of the children are weeping, clinging to their caretakers. He wonders if things are this warm between them at other times. He has always believed orphanages to be horrible places, not much better than the Nazi camps he has heard about. This, somehow, makes him feel justified.

A few of the older children aren't crying, but the fear on their faces is evident. It is that very fear that has made his job so easy. These people do not resist. They are petrified and do what they are told, hoping that their obedience may afford them a measure of mercy. They are fools.

He steps in front of them and begins to speak: "I am Captain Lemieux of the Vichy police. This building is being seized by the Vichy government because of suspected partisan activities."

He personally considers his comments ridiculous, though they are verbatim what Barbie had told him to say. The Germans have become so habituated to propaganda, he wonders if they have actually come to believe their own lies.

"You will all be sent to a new place to live. There is no need for you to bring any of your belongings. My men will gather them for you and bring them to where you are going. If you cooperate, everything will go smoothly."

He notices a woman bending down and whispering in one of the younger children's ears. "Madam," he says calmly, his expression curious.

"I am just explaining what you said to the boy. He is only 3 and does not understand all your words," the woman responded, her voice quivering.

He nods his head, excusing her, while his eyes reveal that he will not tolerate another interruption. He looks at his men and says, "Proceed."

He watches as the children and their caretakers are led from the building, observing that their fear is not diminished by his speech; on the contrary, it grows by the moment. He believes that those old enough to understand anything know the truth about their destiny. But that is of no concern to him.

Barbie steps beside him. "You have done well," he says.

He nods.

They follow the procession out of the building.

"It seems our partisan friends took the night off," Barbie says.

"Either that or they simply don't care about a bunch of Jewish children."

They watch as their captives are placed on the truck in orderly succession. The Germans appreciate orderliness, and for now, it is all about pleasing the Germans.

"Where will they be taken?" he asks, betraying a momentary lapse in his indifference.

"Drancy, of course," Barbie replies.

"And after that?" He realizes his curiosity is taking over, but can't seem to help himself.

"The usual places," Barbie responds.

He struggles with a desire to probe further. It was foolish to ask in the first place, he tells himself. He knows exactly where the rail lines from Drancy lead. Perhaps he simply wanted to hear Barbie say it, to have the Nazi acknowledge their partnership. But equality with a man of Barbie's stature would always be elusive – for the German sees himself as superior not only to the Jew, but to all. And in the end, superiority is what matters.

His men board the second truck and he watches as both trucks pull away. From a distance, he still hears crying, resounding as strongly as if his victims were right in front of him. And as the trucks disappear from view, the crying persists, leaving him wondering if it will ever stop.

When he had finished, the two men sat, looking at each other, absorbed in a silence more potent than anything either had ever experienced.

"How did you find out?" Benoît asked, breaking the stillness.

"A dossier was left under my door."

"Ah, so it was them."

"Them?"

"The FBI, immigration, Israelis – the usual people who concern themselves with such matters."

"So you knew they were onto you?"

"Of course I did."

"And that's why you tried to kill yourself?"

Benoît pondered. "I suppose that was one of the reasons."

"The other reasons being?"

"There was one other reason. I should think you would have surmised it by now."

"My guess would be that, aside from the shame your exposure would bring upon your family, you may actually have felt some remorse," Martin said, searching Benoît's face for confirmation. "Perhaps you were even trying to punish yourself."

"Bravo, my dear doctor. You have shown yourself to be every bit as smart as I believed you to be."

"Do you really regard this as a time for sarcasm?"

Benoît's face fell. "No, I do not." He hesitated, then added, "I have no idea what this is a time for."

"Frankness," Martin said.

Benoît responded with a slight nod.

"Particularly about the reason you chose me," Martin continued.

"I am sure you have come to understand that as well."

Martin again looked at Benoît, waiting for a more direct response.

"I chose you… because of who you are," Benoît said.

"You checked me out?"

"Yes." Benoît searched Martin's face for some expression – surprise, hurt, even rage – but all he got was a cold stare. "I know about your past, your parents, your wife."

"And what did all that tell you?"

"That maybe you were the one who could help me."

Martin noticed a tear escape from Benoît's eye. "Help you? How?"

The tremor in Benoît's hands spread through his body as he peered into space. Suddenly, he dropped his head and in a quivering voice said, "I have come to you in the hope that you… you might forgive me."

Martin watched as Benoît began to sob, yet he still felt cold. "Forgive you?" he asked, his voice mild and even. "How is it my place to forgive you?"

Benoît seemed to disappear within himself. A few moments passed, then came the words: "You must!"

Martin didn't respond.

"You must forgive me!" Benoît repeated.

Martin waited a few more moments before speaking. "The only things that are in my power to forgive you for are: one, intruding into my past, and two, deceiving me. For those things, I do forgive you. As for all the other things you've done, you didn't do them to me."

"But you know that I am a good man now. I have been for many years."

Martin considered the point. "That, too, is not for me to decide."

Benoît stood and walked over to Martin. He held his hands out, as if pleading. "But you, *you* know me better than anyone, even my own wife. You see the whole person, what I've become despite what I was."

Martin remained still.

"As a man, as a Jew, you see all that."

"It doesn't matter what I see. You think that just because I am a Jew I can forgive you for the things you've done? I do not represent the Jewish people any more than you represent the French or the Nazis. I am one person, as you are, as was each of those children in the orphanage and the people who cared for them." Martin reached into his pocket, removed the brooch and placed it in Benoît's hand. "As was the woman who used to wear this. If it's penitence you seek, find her and plead your case." He dropped his tone. "Though I believe she is no longer alive."

Benoît looked at the brooch, then let it fall from his hand as if it were burning hot.

Martin walked behind his desk and looked at his watch. "Our time is up. I think it is unwise for us to continue working together."

Benoît simply nodded, then handed Martin a check.

"This one's on me," Martin said as he tore the check in two. He looked at the brooch on the floor and added, "Take it with you when you leave."

Benoît bent down, reached for the brooch, then stood and looked once more at Martin. His eyes were watery and his face betrayed a shattered spirit. He couldn't seem to bring himself to leave.

Martin stared him down, as if asking, *Why are you still here?*

"Do you believe in God?" Benoît asked.

Martin was taken aback by the question. "Sometimes," he responded.

"Do you think that God will consider the fact that I've been a good person since then?"

"I can't speak for God any more than I can speak for your victims."

Benoît looked once more at the brooch, then gave Martin a final glance. Seemingly convinced that there was no longer anything to be gained in this room, he turned and went on his way.

chapter 50

MARTHA BENOÎT'S EYES OPENED TO a darkened room, her sleep interrupted by what she could have sworn was a loud noise. She reached for her husband on the other side of the bed, suddenly finding she was alone. She turned to the clock on the night table; it was 3 a.m.

She sat up, forcing a fuller state of wakefulness. Her heart racing, she tried to calm herself as she went to the closet for her bathrobe and slippers. Thinking that the noise had resembled thunder, she proceeded to the window. But all she saw was a clear, star-filled sky. She wondered where Jacques was, walked out to the hallway calling his name, and began descending the stairs.

"Jacques," she called one last time from the foot of the stairway, acutely aware of the anxiety in her voice.

Still nothing.

She turned and saw a light emanating from a crack in the door to his study. Nervously, she pushed the door open.

Her first reaction to what she saw was a gasp. Then, a scream.

Her husband lay with his head on the desk, a river of blood

flowing from his mouth. She approached the desk and saw the revolver beside his right hand, with his left hand closed into a fist. In front of him lay a piece of white paper, partly covered with blood, bearing two words: *I'm sorry.*

Crying his name, she frantically shook him. Quickly realizing the futility of her efforts, the shaking turned into pounding, the hope into rage.

He had done this to himself, *to her*, and at that moment, she hated him for it.

Agent Richard Schwartz was awakened by the telephone. The FBI field agent on duty reported that a 911 call had been made from the Benoît residence regarding a suicide.

"*What?*" Schwartz hollered.

"That's what we heard, sir."

"Who made the call?"

"The wife."

Schwartz pounded his fist on his knee. "Shit! Stay put, don't do anything. I'll get right over there."

By the time Schwartz had arrived at the scene, there were four police cars and a coroner's wagon in the mansion's large circular driveway. Schwartz parked his car and proceeded to the front door, where he was stopped by a uniformed cop.

"Can I help you?" the uniform asked.

Schwartz flashed his badge and the uniform stepped aside with a curious stare.

Schwartz entered the house and noticed the eyes of five other uniformed cops on him. Again, he showed his badge and walked through the procession toward the room in the back from which he heard voices and a woman weeping. He stepped into the study and saw three detectives and a medical examiner. The medical examiner was taking pictures of the corpse, two male detectives were checking out the room, while a female detective was sitting with the widow.

No one even acknowledged Schwartz' presence until he approached the widow.

"Mrs. Benoît," he said before any of the others could stop him, "I'm Special Agent Richard Schwartz of the FBI." He held his badge in clear view for the others to see. "I'm here because we picked up a transmission on the police radio scanner about this situation. With something like this, involving an international figure like your husband, the bureau feels it ought to get involved."

The female detective was a looker, Schwartz noted. Young, black, shapely, dreadlocks, and a serious mien on an otherwise pleasant face. Schwartz acknowledged her as he spoke to the widow, noting the what-kind-of-bullshit-is-this expression she wore when he explained his presence. He knew he would have to do better with her and her colleagues afterward, and was grateful for their smarts not to press the matter just yet.

Suddenly, one of the male detectives asked, "What do we have here?"

The others turned in his direction as he pried something from Benoît's left hand. He held up a piece of jewelry for all to see. Schwartz walked over and examined it.

"It's a brooch," Schwartz said. He held the ornament up as he looked at the widow. "Mrs. Benoît, do you know why your husband had this in his hand when he died?"

"Let me see," she said as she got up and walked over to Schwartz. She examined the brooch with interest, particularly the inscription. "I don't know. I have never seen this piece before." She looked at it more closely. "It's an antique, quite beautiful." She translated the inscription for the benefit of the others, and then muttered, "I don't know anyone named Leila or Philip," as if she were talking to herself.

"Might be some kind of family heirloom," Schwartz said.

Martha Benoît put the brooch on the desk and stared off into space. Schwartz picked it up and slipped it to the medical examiner, who then bagged it as evidence. He figured the widow was still too much in shock to think deeply about it. In time, it would come back to her and she would wonder. But for now, the explanation he had offered was as good as any.

Schwartz then checked out the body. Trails of blood flowed

from both the mouth and the back of the head. Benoît had apparently eaten the gun and fired. Schwartz turned and saw the bullet lodged in the wall behind the desk.

He swallowed hard. It was an ugly scene, regardless of who the victim was. There was no rejoicing, no victory to be had in an ending like this. It wasn't that he felt sorry for Benoît; it was more that he felt sorry for the world. He had seen too much in his time, he had lost too much, and had been in this miserable business far too long. This was it for him, as close to a last hurrah as he would get. And, paradoxically, he somehow found it fitting.

DAN GIFFORD OPENED THE FRONT door, stepped out, and reached for the newspaper on the stoop. He looked at his surroundings and took a deep breath. His old neighborhood, his own home, sleeping with his wife in their bed, his son in the next room. It was all he had ever wanted, yet there was a time, not too long ago, when he had just about destroyed it. He had to remember that. He couldn't allow himself to forget for even a second; his memories were his strongest deterrent against slipping back to that destructive place.

He stepped back into the house and smelled the coffee brewing in the kitchen. Stephanie smiled at him as he entered the kitchen, and handed him a cup of black, just the way he liked it.

They sat down together at the round oak table, as they used to every morning before he took the job heading up the major crimes unit; before the late nights, the breakdown in communication, the arguments, the weeks of not seeing each other; before the drinking had taken over. He looked at her – she always looked great in the morning – and simply smiled back. He felt good for the first time in a long time and he was determined not to let any of it change.

He unfolded the paper and was jolted by a picture of Jacques Benoît on the front page beneath the headline: *Billionaire Dies In Apparent Suicide*.

"Everything okay?" Stephanie asked.

"Yeah, sure," he said, containing his reaction. "Just this story here about this guy who killed himself."

She leaned over and glanced at the article. "I've heard of him." She examined the picture and added, "So that's what he looks like."

"Yes, that's what he looks like," Gifford muttered.

Stephanie didn't seem to catch on, or if she did, she knew better than to ask. It was a small concession to allow him to shield her from certain aspects of his work. And in the end, she trusted his judgment; if she needed to know something, he would tell her.

Gifford proceeded to read the story, which cited Benoît's business achievements, the names of surviving family members, a few accolades from associates, and even the billionaire's "record" as a freedom fighter for his native France during World War II. Gifford imagined how many people were reading this article and actually believed its contents, a thought which nauseated him.

As he read on, everything seemed to fall into place. First, he kicked himself for not recognizing the billionaire in Rosen's waiting room. Despite the number of times their paths had crossed, and Gifford's gnawing sense of Benoît's familiarity, he simply hadn't made the connection. And, though he knew that Benoît's face had always been scant in the media, and his own preoccupations were enough to make any man slip, he still wasn't inclined to let himself off easy.

After berating himself, however, it occurred to Gifford that this suicide was an awfully convenient solution to Martin Rosen's conundrum. Convenient, and somehow just. Gifford felt jealous, thinking of the countless times he'd fantasized similar misfortunes befalling some of the people he'd faced off with. Pondering this, he lifted his eyes from the paper.

Convenient, and somehow just.

chapter 52

ASHOK REDDY LIFTED THE RECEIVER, began dialing Martin Rosen's number, then put it down without completing the call. He was concerned about the news of Benoît's suicide, not only because he had referred Benoît to Martin, but because Martin was his friend, and it was undoubtedly a professional crisis for any psychologist when a patient committed suicide.

He looked at the phone once more, contemplating whether he should make the call, and decided against it. The thought that Benoît might very well have been the mystery patient he and Martin had been discussing entered his mind, as did his promise to Martin never to speak of the matter again. It would explain why Benoît had attempted suicide the first time, and why Martin had been so reticent to supply any details about the mystery patient.

Reddy had concluded some time ago that Martin had been discussing someone they both knew. Now, with Benoît finally doing himself in, he found himself even more intrigued.

Whatever the truth, Reddy understood that his grasp of things would forever remain in the realm of speculation. He expected

Martin to afford Benoît the same confidentiality in death that the man had been entitled to in life.

Ashok Reddy leaned back in his chair and stared into space. Tomorrow was his weekly golf game with Martin. He knew that Martin would be there despite the suicide, and for more reasons than simply the love of the game. Yet, whatever might pass between them, Reddy was certain that any discussion of the mystery patient would be pointedly absent. And it really didn't matter. As far as Reddy was concerned, the mystery patient no longer existed.

MARTIN ROSEN WAS FINISHING HIS notes on the patients he had seen that day when he heard someone enter the waiting room. It was late at night and his last session had ended over an hour ago. The door to his inner office was open and he could discern that the footsteps were light, like those of a woman. For a moment, he thought it might be Galit, until the figure stepped into his office.

"Mrs. Benoît," he said, trying to camouflage his surprise.

"Good evening, doctor, I hope I'm not intruding."

"No, not at all. Please, come in." Martin gestured to one of the seats facing his desk.

Martha Benoît sat down in the chair. From this proximity, Martin could see that her appearance had taken a beating. He wondered for a moment just what she knew but was fairly certain it wasn't much.

"I am sorry about your husband," Martin said.

Martha nodded. "Yes," she said, "I'm sure you are."

They looked at each other. Martin's instinctive reaction was to ask her what he could do for her, but it seemed a silly question under the circumstances.

"My husband," she said, her voice halting, "I know he had secrets."

Martin nodded slightly, not indicating agreement, but rather acknowledging her statement. It's what shrinks do when they don't know what to say.

"I suppose you can't help me with this," she added.

Martin thought about that. It was likely that she now represented Benoît's estate and, as such, she might attempt to lay claim to his records. Doing so would not only satisfy her curiosity, it would also help if she were planning a malpractice suit, which many families would do in the wake of a suicide. Only, Martin hadn't yet completed Benoît's records and still wasn't sure of when or how he was going to.

He looked at her and doubted she intended any of that. "Do you really want me to?" he asked.

She thought for a moment. "No, I suppose not."

Martin was both relieved and saddened by her response. He watched her wordlessly.

"I don't know why I came here," she said.

"That's okay. Some of my patients don't know why they come either."

"Was Jacques among those?"

"Perhaps there were times when he wanted us to think he was, but in the end…"

"Yes. In the end, it was not as it seemed to be."

Martin nodded.

"You know," she said, "he was a good man." Her eyes began to tear and she reached into her bag for a tissue. "Whatever he may have been hiding, he *was* a good man."

Martin's expression remained neutral.

She rose from the chair. "I'm sorry I burst in on you this way."

"Hardly a burst."

"You're very kind. I've always thought that about you."

Martin appeared to accept the compliment.

She seemed to be on her way out, when she stopped and looked at him once more. "By the way," she said, "the police found something clenched in Jacques' hand, a pink and gold brooch. It had an inscription on the back, in French. I don't recall the names – I was in shock at the time – but I knew that they weren't familiar. I suppose that if Jacques was holding it when he died, it might have some significance." She stopped herself as if she didn't want to go on with this, but then the words came: "Do you know anything about it?"

Before he could answer, she added, "That's okay. I don't want to put you on the spot. I prefer to remember Jacques the way he wanted me to, the way I knew him."

Martin offered a tender smile, reflecting his admiration for her discipline and wisdom. He was relieved not to have to answer the question. There was no need to inflict any more pain upon this woman, nothing to gain by revealing the truth. It may well come out by other means, but *he* didn't want to be the source of more suffering.

"You don't need to say anything," she continued. "I just want to thank you for your time, and for how you tried to help my husband."

Without waiting for a response, she turned and departed. Martin sat staring at the spot where she had stood, wondering if he had done the right thing with her and, moreover, wondering if he had done the right thing with her husband. These were questions to which he would never have answers, he mused, and that was precisely what made them so difficult to live with. But live with them he would, and also with the sense that through all this he had discovered something within himself that he would never have imagined.

chapter 54

MARTIN ROSEN SIGNALED TO THE bartender for another. It was late, the bar was empty, he knew he should be home, and he also knew that he was about to exceed his limit. Steve looked at him and wondered, but poured the drink nonetheless.

"Rough day?" Steve asked.

"I'd say that's a fair assessment," Martin responded as he lifted the glass and sipped. He noticed Steve's eyes shift toward the door. "See something interesting?"

"Some*one* interesting."

"Oh," Martin said obliviously, not even bothering to turn around.

"Catch you later, Doc," Steve said as he backed off, still looking over Martin's shoulder.

Suddenly, Martin felt a presence at his side. He turned, and there she was.

"Hello, Marty," Galit said. She looked at the empty stool beside him.

"Anybody sitting here?"

"Suit yourself," he responded.

Steve reappeared with a glass of red wine. "Merlot, I believe."

"Thank you," she said.

Martin seemed to pay attention only to his drink.

Steve quickly departed, and the two of them sat in an awkward silence.

"Look, Marty," she said. "We have to talk."

"Talk? Us? What could *we* possibly have to talk about?"

"You're drunk?"

"Not yet, but I'm working on it."

She took a large sip of her wine, as if she needed it. "I'm leaving for Israel tomorrow."

"Have a nice trip."

"Damn it, Marty, there are things we need to say to each other!"

"I've already said all I have to say."

"And that's it for you? You just want to let me go like that?"

"I don't see that I have any choice."

"You do have a choice, Marty. Ask me to stay and I will."

"I can't ask you that."

"You mean you *won't* ask me that."

"It all boils down to the same thing."

She stood and set her glass down hard on the bar. "You know what, Marty? To hell with you! If you want to sit there like a pathetic little victim and drown yourself, then forgive me for interfering. I must have thought you were someone else."

He turned and stared at her angrily. "You have some nerve to come in here and talk to me like that after what you've done."

"*What I've done*? That's ironic, coming from you."

He looked at her, wondering what she was talking about.

"What I've done, Marty, is my job. What I've done is follow my convictions, my morality, everything inside me that tells me what is right and what is wrong. I'm sorry – and you can't imagine how sorry – that you got caught in the middle, that *we* got caught in the middle. I never intended to fall in love with you, or for you to fall in love with me. It just happened."

"You *did* intend to use me."

"Yes, and I'm not sorry for that. Sometimes, it is what I have to do. Our choices are not always pleasant ones. *You*, of all people, should understand that."

"*I* should understand? Why is that?"

"Because of what happened to Benoît."

"I don't know what you're talking about."

"Yes you do. You might pretend to others, but you can't with me. Whatever went on between you and Benoît, you somehow manipulated him into killing himself. You know it and I know it, so let's stop the act. You saw what he did and you wanted him to be punished for it, so you used all your shrink know-how and figured out just what to say to make him go home and stick that gun in his mouth. All the things you've always professed, your so-called professional ethics, none of that mattered. You as much as pulled that trigger yourself, and you did it because you believed it was the *right* thing to do. Think about that the next time you feel like condemning me."

"Benoît made his choice, he killed himself."

"Yeah, right," she said sarcastically.

He stared at her silently.

"You figured that suicide was fitting for Benoît because it gave him a way out of being exposed and humiliated publicly. You took into account his so-called benevolence these past few years, and meted out the perfect merciful punishment. You played judge, jury and executioner, Marty. Only, you won't admit it. And that's the sole difference between you and me."

"If you have such a high opinion of me, why are you here?"

"Because I *do* have a high opinion of you, and I know that you believe in what you did. The only reason you won't tell me is because you're angry and you don't trust me. And you have no idea how much I wish that wasn't the case."

"What about you? You mean to tell me that you're not angry that you didn't get your man?"

"Angry? I don't think so. More like disappointed. I suppose if I wasn't directing all my anger at you for being so stubborn, I might have some left for not getting Benoît. But in the end, Benoît is gone and we are still here. I can be content leaving Benoît's fate in God's hands. But *our* fate still belongs to us."

Martin looked at her, surrender painted on his face. He wasn't surprised a bit that she had figured it all out. He had even expected as much. The only surprise he had was with himself – how, in his mind and soul, he was at peace with what he did. It was a side of himself with which he had previously been unacquainted but would now have to get used to.

She noticed his face soften. "By the way," she said, "we found a solid piece of evidence supporting our case against Benoît. It was a brooch that was in his hand when he died. One of our eyewitnesses, a man named Henry Saifer, has identified it as having belonged to his mother. Benoît, or Lemieux as he was known then, confiscated it from Henry and his sister when he caught them trying to flee during the roundups in Lyon. Henry's mother and father had given the children a suitcase full of jewelry to help them buy passage to a safe place, only Benoît had other plans for them."

Martin swallowed hard.

"I wonder why Benoît had it with him when he shot himself?" she asked.

"Good question," Martin said under his breath.

"Still don't trust me," she said.

"It's sometimes best to let sleeping dogs lie."

"I hate American clichés. Most of them are pretty stupid, you know."

"We live our lives by them."

"I suppose you do."

They looked at each other.

"You're going back to chasing Nazis?" he asked.

"I doubt it. I don't even think there are many left, and the few that are, well, people are tired of this. Even my own government is tired of it."

"Then what will you do?"

"Anything else, maybe even a desk job."

"Doesn't sound like much fun."

"It is what it is."

She stared at him, waiting for him to say something to make her stay.

"Well," she said, "I should be on my way. I have a debriefing at the Israeli Mission in the morning, and my flight is right afterwards."

"They going to give you a hard time?"

"I'll handle it."

"Well, good luck," he said.

"Yes, Marty. Good luck to you too, and to Elizabeth. I hope she grows up to know what a brave man her father is… what a good man he is." She reached out and touched his cheek. "Goodbye, Marty."

He held himself back from grabbing her, and sat stoically as she walked away, muttering under his breath, "Goodbye, Galit."

chapter 55

GALIT STEIN STOOD PATIENTLY ON line at the El Al check-in counter, her ticket and passport in hand, her bags on the floor, Arik and Kovi beside her. It was Mossad policy for agents to fly as regular travelers – unarmed, no preferential or diplomatic privileges, nothing that might help a terrorist identify them. Aside from the obvious benefits of having well-trained people incognito on board, it was also for their own safety. The Mossad was the archenemy of virtually every terrorist organization in the world, and an identified agent would be an immediate target for execution during a hijacking.

She had been silent since the three of them left the consulate, and she knew that Arik and Kovi understood why. They had been together long enough to read one another without words. In fact, aside from the five-hour grilling from Jacob Lipton, the financier and PR mogul, and a few higher-ups at the consulate, there hadn't been much said among them about the case.

She knew that Arik, in particular, was disappointed with the way things had turned out, especially concerning her feelings for

Martin Rosen, but she also realized that he was glad it was over. In her heart, there was no doubt that she loved Arik. He had been her guardian, her source of strength through so much. But she was also certain that she could never be with him. He represented her past, and she needed to find a new future.

Jacob Lipton, on the other hand, was irate and appeared as if he would never get past it. He had financed this operation with the intention of a successful trial and international publicity. Galit, who for years had been his wonder girl, was now and forevermore on his shit list. In her world, that was not a good place to be.

Notwithstanding all this, the most prominent thing on her mind was Martin Rosen. She knew there would be more grilling in Israel, and she had already done as well as she could explaining how the Benoît suicide had nothing to do with her actions. Whether anyone bought it was of no consequence. She wanted out anyway; she wanted a different life. Only, she was suffering from a very clear sense that she'd lost her best chance for it.

This was what was running through her mind when she was jolted by a hand on her shoulder. As she turned and saw who the hand belonged to, she wondered for a moment if she was dreaming.

"Marty," she said, puzzled.

"Hi." He was panting and it was obvious he'd been running. "I thought I might not get here in time."

"In time for what?"

"In time to say what I have to say."

She turned to Arik and Kovi and looked at them. They ignored Martin, but listened as she muttered a few words in Hebrew. Martin guessed that she said something akin to *I'll be right back*, as she led him away.

"Your comrades in arms?" Martin said.

"You could call them that."

When they were out of earshot, she said, "What are you doing here?"

"I couldn't let you go, not with the way we left things last night."

She looked at him, thinking, *But you still can let me go.*

"I don't want this to be it, not forever," he said.

"Why not?" she responded, also wondering what he meant by *forever*.

He swallowed hard. "Because I see now that I was wrong, wrong about you, wrong about myself, wrong about a lot of things."

Hearing this, and seeing how difficult it was for him, she softened. She took his hand.

"I guess what I came here to say is that I need some time."

"I know," she responded tenderly. "I need time too."

With their eyes, they shared an understanding that they couldn't be together until they were both completely sure about it.

"Last night, you said some things," he said. "They were all true. But there is more." He stopped to gather his thoughts. "When I met you, I was a wreck. For two years, since Katherine and Ethan died, I hadn't lived. Sure, I went through the motions, but inside, except when I was with Elizabeth, I was dead too."

He saw tears on her cheeks and wiped them with his fingers. "I'm telling you this because I have to."

"I know."

"With you, everything changed."

She squeezed his hand tighter.

"The moment I learned the truth about you, I felt dead again. I was convinced I had fallen in love with an illusion, and that the feelings you had professed weren't real. Last night, when you came to see me, I realized that all that was wrong. I know now that it's *you* I love, not an illusion, and I believe that you love me too. If anything, I had my doubts about Cheryl Manning, reservations all along that there was something not quite right with her. I don't have that sense with Galit Stein."

"What sense do you have?"

"That we're alike. We're both very strong-willed, and each of us will do whatever we have to if we believe in our cause."

"But I *did* deceive you."

"And I didn't give you what you needed." He hesitated. "I knew about the brooch. He had given it to me out of some need to repent, and I gave it back to him."

She looked at him as if she wasn't surprised. "Are you saying that we're even?"

"I'm saying what you said last night, that we each did what we believed was right and neither of us could have done anything else."

"You believe that what you did was right?"

"I guess I'll have to let God be the judge of that."

She looked at him inquisitively. "God?"

"I told you I realized I've been wrong about *a lot* of things."

She smiled. "Through all this you found God?"

"Through all this I have been forced to find myself. I have been worshiping some false gods for a very long time. They weren't able to help me here, so I had to look inside for something else, something I'd lost a long time ago."

"You're a complicated man."

"Life's complicated."

She hesitated. "So, where do we go from here?" she asked softly.

He shrugged his shoulders.

They looked at each other awkwardly.

"Part of me wants to grab your bags and take you home with me," he said. "The other part tells me it's smarter to wait and sort it all out. I'm not alone in this world. I have a daughter."

Through her sadness, she managed to brighten up. "It's been quite a whirlwind," she said.

"That's putting it mildly."

"You're probably right," she agreed. "The dust does need to settle before we make any lifetime commitments."

He nodded.

She heard her name called, turned, and saw Arik waving her over. "Looks like I have to go check my bags."

He took out a pen and piece of paper. "Where can I reach you?"

She smiled as she grabbed the pen and jotted down her particulars.

"Have a safe flight."

They shared a tender hug, each knowing that anything more would only intensify the pain of parting.

"I guess… I'll hear from you," she said.

"You will."

epilogue

MARTIN ROSEN LOOKED AT THE house across the street, then looked down at his daughter standing by his side. It had been more than two years since he'd last stood in this spot, and he wondered if this time he would once again lose his nerve. He had promised Elizabeth that it would be a special day, that he was going to take her to meet the grandparents she'd never known. She was so excited about the prospect, she had insisted on wearing her nicest dress. And now he didn't know if he was going to disappoint her.

Earlier that morning, he had considered calling his sister to discuss the idea, then decided against it, though he wasn't completely sure why. Maybe he feared she might deter him, or maybe he just didn't want to put her in a position where she might feel torn between her loyalty to him and a sense of obligation to inform their parents of his plans. In either case, he was glad that he hadn't made the call, especially now that he wasn't certain if he was going to go ahead with it.

"Daddy, is that the house?" Elizabeth asked, pointing directly across the street.

The eagerness in her tone made him realize that he was indeed stuck with his promise. *Just as well*, he thought. Although he had some vague sense of how the events of the last few weeks had brought him to this moment, he was at a loss as to how this was all going to play out in the end. In any event, it was time for him to face his past, and it was time for Elizabeth to learn about hers.

"Yes," he muttered.

"You grew up there?"

"Yes."

"It looks like a nice house."

"I'm glad you think so," he said, turning once again to gaze at the Brooklyn brownstone. It was a simple edifice, similar to every other house on this Borough Park street, probably at least ninety years old, perfectly square, and possessing little distinction or charm. But he was flattered that she liked it and he understood why: because it had once been his home.

"Daddy, the people around here dress funny. The girls all look like Aunt Esther and cousin Michali and Devorah."

It was a Sunday morning and the street was crowded with pedestrians walking to and from the main shopping strip, which was only one block away. Most of the men had beards and virtually all were similarly garbed in black suits and black fedoras. The women, too, dressed in a like fashion, with ankle-length dresses and either hats or kerchiefs covering their heads.

Martin wondered if Elizabeth had actually seen many Orthodox Jews, aside from her aunt and cousins. It was something he hadn't thought about before. In any case, he was certain that this was the first time she'd seen so many in one place. "They dress that way because they're Orthodox Jews," he said.

"And why do Orthodox Jews have to dress so funny?"

"That's a long story."

"Do Grandma and Grandpa dress like that?"

"Yes, they do."

There was a brief moment of silence in which Martin considered whether any of the pedestrians noticed them. Elizabeth could pass in her dress, but surely he, in his tweed blazer and khakis, looked out of place. Suddenly, he began to feel uncomfortable. He reached into his breast pocket, took out the Yarmulke he had brought, and placed it on his head.

Elizabeth looked at him inquisitively. Before she could ask, he explained, "When a man goes into the home of an Orthodox Jew, it is polite for him to cover his head."

"What about a girl?"

"That's another long story, princess."

"Will you tell it to me?"

"Maybe, but I think your grandfather would be able to explain it to you better."

"Is that because he's a rabbi?"

"Yes, it is."

"Can I ask him to tell me today?"

He thought for a moment, weighing his response. Part of him wanted to tell her to leave that particular topic for another time, but he also didn't want to inhibit her. "Sure," he said, "why not?"

They looked at each other and shared smiles.

Martin took a deep breath and asked, "Are you ready?"

She nodded enthusiastically.

"Then let's do it," he said, reaching for her hand.

"Yeah, let's do it," she repeated as she grabbed hold of him.

Martin felt a sharp pang of anxiety as he glanced once more at the house. He turned to Elizabeth, smiled again, and together they stepped forward into the rest of their lives.

author's note

THIS IS A WORK OF fiction. The main characters, their names and the incidents in which they are involved, are strictly products of the author's imagination. Klaus Barbie, Boleslavs Maikovskis, Valerian Trifa, and John Demjanjuk are true historical figures, and, in alluding to them, the author has tried to remain as factual as research allows. The facts surrounding the cases of Maikovskis and Trifa were as described in this book. Barbie was the Gestapo Chief in Lyon during the period in which some of the events of this story take place, and he did lead a raid on a children's home in the small town of Izieu, in the hills a few miles east of Lyon, on April 6, 1944. The fates of those children and their caretakers were as described in this book.

John Demjanjuk, whose conviction of crimes against humanity was overturned by the Israeli Supreme Court in 1993 as a result of new evidence pointing to another Ukrainian as the infamous "Ivan the Terrible," was eventually deported from the U.S. in 2009 to Germany and tried in Munich on charges of participating in the killing of thousands of Jews at the Sobibor extermination camp in Poland in 1943. He was convicted, sentenced to five years in prison, and was appealing his guilty verdict while residing in a nursing home in Germany when he died at the age of 91 from natural causes.

Between the years of 1940-1944, the Vichy government collaborated with the Nazis in the organized deportation of some 76,000 Jews to German concentration camps. It should be mentioned that a segment of the French population objected to this policy, and allied themselves with the Resistance to fight against the German occupation and the persecution of the Jews. History has recorded numerous examples of French citizens risking their lives for this purpose. To learn more about these events, the author recommends the following volumes:

Finkielkraut, Alain. Remembering in Vain: The Klaus Barbie Trial and Crimes Against Humanity. Trans. Roxanne Lapidus with Sima Godfrey. New York, Columbia University Press, 1992.

Marrus, Michael R. and Paxton, Robert O. Vichy France and the Jews. New York, Basic Books, 1981.

Morgan, Ted. An Uncertain Hour: The French, the Germans, the Jews, the Barbie Trial, and the City of Lyon, 1940-1945. New York, William Morrow and Co., 1990.

Paris, Erna. Unhealed Wounds. New York, Grove Press, 1985.